Waking Beauty

Also by Elyse Friedman

Then Again
Know Your Monkey

Waking Beauty

A Novel

Elyse Friedman

THREE RIVERS PRESS
NEW YORK

The author gratefully acknowledges the support of the Canada Council for the Arts.

 Canada Council Conseil des Arts
for the Arts du Canada

Published by Three Rivers Press, New York, New York.
Member of the Crown Publishing Group, a division of Random House, Inc.
www.crownpublishing.com

THREE RIVERS PRESS and the tugboat design are registered trademarks of Random House, Inc.

Printed in the United States of America

DESIGN BY KAREN MINSTER

Library of Congress Cataloging-in-Publication Data
Friedman, Elyse, 1963–
    Waking beauty : a novel / Elyse Friedman.—1st ed.
    1. Young women—Fiction. 2. Metamorphosis—Fiction. 3. Beauty, Personal—Fiction. I. Title.
PR9199.4.F74W35   2004
813'.6—dc 22

                                                        2003024713

ISBN 1-4000-5106-1

10 9 8 7 6 5 4 3 2

First Edition

This one's for Robyn

Waking Beauty

God, I'm beautiful. I can scarcely believe how beautiful I am. I take my breath away. I still have to pinch my golden, unblemished flesh every once in a while to convince myself of it.

Do I sound conceited? Insufferably narcissistic? Well, okay. If anyone deserves a bit of wallow and gloat, it is I. I who have spent the first twenty-two and a quarter years of my life loathing every aspect of my aspect, despising every quark of every atom of every sicko cell in my squat body. Now I can't take my eyes off myself. And what exquisite eyes they are—large and blue and expressive, wide set, of course, with delicately fanned lashes. My mouth is adorable. So puffy. So kissable. Even my fingernails are attractive. My feet, too. I didn't know that toes could be so elegant, so Hyannis Port beachcomby. I'm not even going to get into my breasts, except to say that they're perfect. An absolute joy.

Confused? Well, take a number. *Confused* is putting it mildly. I was confounded, jolted; my entire worldview was summarily (and merrily) smashed. I went to sleep a troll. I awoke a goddess. Quasimodo hit the hay, and

Grace Kelly's better-looking cousin emerged lovely from the bedclothes. I have no idea what kind of science or magic occurred in my dank cocoon of a futon, but I can tell you this: It scared the hell out of me. At first I was so alarmed I actually passed out. And I never pass out. I am neither flighty nor light-headed. I don't even believe in this sort of thing. Or I didn't until a few months ago.

Wondrous, happy Saturday; what was it about that morning? I keep harkening back to the twenty-four hours before the Big Change, trying to figure out if anything extraordinary occurred on the preceding Friday. Did I inadvertently murmur an incantation, ingest a potent potion, or perform an act so noble and good that the gods had no choice but to bless and redress? No. I've gone over it again and again and I'm quite sure there wasn't anything unique about that day. Perhaps it was a bit on the warm side for May, but other than that it was depressingly typical. . . .

Before

1

At 7:45 A.M. I awoke to the gaudy ululations of my roommate, Virginie, getting vaginally plumbed by her latest conquest. This one was called Fraser, and as usual he was good-looking, albeit in a deliberately grungy, vaguely artsy, I-may-be-harboring-pubic-lice kind of way. He was dimmer than most of Virginie's cerebrally challenged boy toys, but cuter, too, bigger—and I liked the way he smelled. He exuded a strong but healthy sweat smell that was likely loaded with pheromones. My ex-roommate, Elda, once told me that man-smell falls into one of two categories: cat urine or Campbell's tomato soup. She was joking, but she wasn't far off. Fraser existed somewhere in the tomato soup camp. He tried to camouflage it with cologne, but it came through anyway, and I found the effect of the two comingling quite devastating. Sometimes, after he showered, I'd nip into the bathroom, scoop a wet towel from the floor, and sniff it before depositing it in the hamper. On a couple of occasions I almost wanked to his image, but I stopped myself, realizing that that's exactly what Virginie figured was going on in my sad-sack room. Fat, ugly Allison probing her sweaty flesh folds, drooling and dreaming about the handsome hunks who paraded half-dressed around the apartment, who were allowed to strut muscled through the kitchen in tiny towels, or lounge lanky in the living room in their threadbare Calvins because clearly pathetic Allison represented no threat whatsoever. So I stopped myself. And one night after overhearing Fraser regale Virginie with an insipid regurgitation of some fresh-faced faux-journalist's view on the cultural significance of reality-based television shows, the urge, mercifully, diminished.

"Listen," I said on that particular occasion, trying in vain to enliven, or perhaps, I'm mortified to admit, momentarily enter their conversation, "*we* are *God's* reality-based entertainment. That's why there are earthquakes and tornadoes and tsunamis. God isn't dead; God is bored. The Mesozoic Era seemed like a good idea at the time, sure, but the dinosaurs turned out to be dull stuff—God's juvenilia. Like the people on that show *Big Brother,* the dinos were okay to gawk at for a while, but they didn't really do much—eat, sleep, fight, fuck—so God turned on the deep freeze or coin-tossed a two-hundred-mile-wide asteroid at our blue ball and started over with a marginally more interesting cast."

They didn't say anything, they just stared at me like chickens with their heads cocked to one side. I continued, not believing a syllable I was slurring, but vaguely amused by the concept anyway.

"I'm not saying Darwin was wrong. We do evolve and adapt. It's just that God is watching the process as a form of entertainment, you know? So anyway," I went on, "this new cast of characters was more engaging, because they could invent things, like Silly String or stuffed-crust pizza or hair plugs. They made pyramids and giant sporting arenas with retractable domes—that was sort of nifty. And the Chrysler Building. They filled the sky with hot-air balloons and helicopters and rocket ships. They had a field day with the water—everything from breezy galleons to sneaky submarines. Under the ground they put subways. On top, they put baby-blue 1959 Cadillacs. I mean, this cast would erect entire cities and then flatten them with a Little Boy and a Fat Man. They came up with stuff like 'Ode to Joy' and *Pride and Prejudice* and 'I Got a Gal in Kalamazoo.' It was better than the dinosaur show. There were plenty of big-time baddies: Stalin, Adolf, Papa Doc—and lots of little heroes, too. Plus, this show had Shakespeare and Chopin and Harry Houdini. . . . But I guess there aren't enough of those types in the cast—too many extras, not enough stars. Or maybe everything gets tired after a while. Who knows? All I know is that if you want to save the world from another tidal wave or ice age, you'd better do something unusual. Do something that will amuse God."

They seemed surprised that I had spoken more than six words in their presence. I usually didn't. But on that night, I was absurdly hammered (I remember because it was my twenty-second birthday and I had spent the evening in my room with my Discman, a Chet Baker box set, and a jumbo bottle of Baileys Irish Cream).

Fraser lit a cigarette and blew the smoke out of his mouth with a long "whew."

"What's she on about?" said Virginie, as if I wasn't even in the room. And then I wasn't. I was in the bathroom, emptying my creamy Baileys guts into the toilet.

Funnily enough, Fraser was a gaffer. This dimmest of bulbs made his living by plugging in lights on film sets—low-budget film sets, I might add, but he swaggered cocky like some super-sized Scorsese coming off a Palme d'Or victory. Likewise Virginie. She was assistant wardrobe person on one of those *Little Hose-Bag on the Prairie*—type TV series. Fraser got her the job. He introduced her to a production manager who liked her French Canadian accent and thought she was cute. She *was* cute. She tried very hard to be cute. She never sat in a chair, she *curled up* in it. She wore pigtails and little girlie clothes: knee socks and Mary Janes and tiny plaid skirts that forced you to see her underpants every five seconds—she was a terrible exhibitionist—and big, loose-knit sweaters that slipped off her bare shoulders or let her perky tits poke through, and she offset the whole Junior Miss Slut look with a chunky pair of Buddy Holly glasses. Uch. So anyway, the pedophilic production guy thought she was cute and, bingo, she went from making eight bucks an hour as a hostess at the Pasta Garden, to eighteen bucks an hour as assistant wardrobe thingy, and even though she spent her days steaming the creases out of period frocks or blocking saggy bonnets, the I'm-in-the-biz attitude she exuded was titanic. Between the two of them you'd have expected Brad and Jennifer to be dropping by for cocktails every evening; you'd have expected Wolfgang Puck over every morning to rustle up their breakfast.

Alas, it was I who usually prepared the morning coffee, after Dumpster-diving in the sink to locate the filthy Bodum. My aim was always to brew up a pot and get it to my room before the bloodhounds sniffed it and came panting, but on the morning in question they caught me. I had just set the water on to boil and was spooning out the coffee when they emerged, scantily clad, from their love lair. Fraser was wearing one of Virginie's shorty kimonos. He had a cigarette hanging macho in his mouth. Virginie was wearing a pink pop-top and Fraser's cotton boxer shorts. Cute. Her hair was mussed and her face was all red and scratched from sex with Fraser and his two-day growth of Marlboro Man beard. She curled up on a kitchen chair and said, "Mmm, coffee."

Fraser opened the fridge and surveyed the contents. "You want eggs?"

She stretched languorously and sniffed her left armpit. "Yummy," she said.

I concentrated on the kettle, willing it to boil. I surreptitiously tugged at the front of my sweatshirt, pulling it away from my gut so it wouldn't cling and reveal. I thought about bringing up the smoking thing again—there was supposed to be no smoking in the common areas, since I'm allergic to it, and it makes my eyes water and my nose clog up. "I thought you weren't going to smoke in here," I said with a little quaver in my voice. That fucking quaver fucked me up.

"Ahh," said Virginie, throwing her arms in the air. "I haven't even had coffee and she's starting with this business!"

I decided to let it go. I turned back to the stove.

Fraser plonked the egg carton onto the counter. He

cupped his private parts in his hand as he squatted to look in the lower cupboard for the frying pan. He gazed, as if mesmerized, at the soup pots and mousetraps therein. His face was blank. An ash fell from his cigarette to the floor. I thought perhaps he had frozen into position, but then a synapsis succeeded in firing and he straightened abruptly and blinked at the sink.

"Shit," he said helplessly. "The pan's dirty."

The handle was sticking up and out of the mad tangle of dishes. It reminded me of Picasso's *Guernica.*

"Maybe Allison would like some eggs," said Virginie with a smirk.

"No, thanks." There was no way in hell I was going to scour out their refried-bean remnants again.

"You should eat breakfast," she said coolly, lighting a cigarette, miffed that I'd refused to do her bidding. "It gets the metabolism going."

The kettle started to scream. I switched off the burner and poured the water.

"We'll go out after coffee," said Fraser.

"Goody," said Virginie. "I'm ravishing!"

Fraser laughed. "You mean you're *ravaged,* dum-dum." He kissed the top of her head and dropped his cig into a beer bottle on the table. She grabbed him by the kimono belt, pulled him close, and nuzzled her face into his belly. Then she tilted her face upward and presented him with a big mock pout. He leaned in and they started to neck.

"*Ravenous,*" said my mouth as I pressed down on the Bodum plunger.

"*Quoi?*" said Virginie, peeking around from behind Fraser. She took a puff of her cigarette and blew the smoke toward me.

"Nothing." I poured my coffee and retreated to my room. As I closed the door, a burst of suppressed laughter erupted in the kitchen.

I got back into bed, drank java, and waited for the lovebirds to clear out. For the zillionth time, I fantasized about kicking Virginie's ass out of the apartment—opting for the highly illegal, immensely satisfying change-the-locks-and-toss-the-heap-of-belongings-on-the-front-yard method. Better yet, I would move myself into an airy one-bedroom apartment with hardwood floors, a wood-burning fireplace, a claw-foot tub, and a private perennial garden. Yeah, right. I couldn't begin to afford the former scenario and the latter was absurdly pie-in-the-sky.

I stared at the peeling ceiling paint and cursed my lack of judgment for allowing her to move in in the first place. But then, as I always did when I ran through this particular loop in my mind, I remembered that I had no choice. My first roommate, Elda, had lit out with virtually no notice to shack up with her new boyfriend. "My first real boyfriend," she told me with tears in her eyes as she stuffed her bedding into garbage bags. I was happy for her—Elda was a fat girl, too, much fatter than I—but I was pissed that she was leaving me in the lurch. Still, I understood. The boyfriend had lost a roommate and wanted her to hustle in right away. She wasn't going to risk love for friendship. Who would? And besides, we weren't really friends. We had cohabitated peacefully for several years, maintaining a chummy facade, but we never really connected. Elda was a ditz. A hairstylist. A club chick. She drank raspberry coolers and listened to A.M. radio. She read *Cosmo* and *Fitness* and *Shape* magazines. She shopped incessantly and was always on an outlandish diet—low-fat, or no carbs, or nothing but bananas and yarn. She was constantly tweezing her eyebrows or waxing her gams, painting her toenails or fiddling with her hair—cutting, perming, dyeing it different colors (including blue). In the early days, when she was still in hairdressing school, I allowed her to experiment on my lank locks. She sharpened her two-hundred-dollar scissors and went to work. With a snip-snip here and a snip-snip there and a snip-snip through the cartilage of my left ear. *Just an inch off the top, thanks.* Four hours in emergency and eleven hideous stitches to sew the thing back in place. But the most gruesome element was the haircut. For six months I looked like Moe Howard from *The Three Stooges*.

In truth, the only things Elda and I had in common were excess flab and vigorous PMS cravings. Once in a blue moon we would slip into the same menstrual cycle and be PMSed Up at the same time. Then we'd rent *Terms of Endearment* or some other cathartic tear-yanker, and hunker down on the sofa in our elastic-waist pants with a party-sized pizza, a couple bags of rosemary and olive oil potato chips, some M&Ms and Doritos, and several single-serving liters of Ben & Jerry's Chunky Monkey. We'd get a good salty-sweet-salty-sweet rhythm going. Elda had an enormous shelf of a chest, and by the end of the evening a sprinkling of chip crumbs and assorted food remnants would have fallen from her mouth and collected there. She'd call it "dessert," and would make a show of cleaning it off when all the other munchies were gone. One time she took a straw and vacuumed it directly into her gape. It was sort of amusing.

Unfortunately, as soon as Elda started bleeding, she'd be back on some draconian diet, sticking pictures of *Sports Illustrated* swimsuit models on the fridge door, ordering toilet-seat-like fat-free grilling devices from the Shopping Network, and toting around tomes with exclamatory titles such as *Eat, Cheat, and Melt the Fat Away!* But Elda could never remain in the Zone for very long. Binge, Purge, and Flush the Flab Away! was more like it.

Personally, I had sloughed that bilge a long time ago. No more juice fasts or Thighmasters or diet pills for me. I ate what I wanted when I wanted. But Elda persisted. Elda persisted because Elda was pretty. She had glossy hair and smooth skin and a fabulous smile with big Chiclet teeth. Yes, Elda was one of those fat girls with a pretty face. The kind who could proudly model plus-sized lingerie on daytime TV talk shows. The kind of whom it is said or thought every time someone clamps eyes on her: *Such a pretty face. If only she could lose sixty pounds.* Nobody thought that of me. If I'd lost sixty pounds, I would have been a hideously ugly thin person. My dead-mouse hair would still have laid limp, my golf ball skin would have continued to ooze boils, my pellet eyes and potato nose would have remained, as would my broad back, hunched shoulders, and flat ass. My teeth would still have sat snaggled and mossy in my thin-lipped mouth, my legs would have remained too short for my torso, and my beige-nipple tits would have gone on dangling, lopsided and slack. That brown birthmark would still have sprawled like an obscene diarrhea stain over my left shin, and those three black hairs would have continued to sprout from the mole above my upper lip. I was one of those rare individuals who possessed nary a good feature. I didn't have nice eyes or a winning smile or a creamy complexion. There was no single feature in which I could take comfort. I was a physical disaster. I always had been (since the age of two, anyway). No wonder that Elda had allowed me to move in with her—in contrast, she looked like a supermodel. And no wonder that nobody wanted to take her place when she bugged out. At least half a dozen prospective roommates had trooped through the freshly scrubbed, centrally located, and reasonably priced flat, but there were no takers. They had all found my presence too disturbing. Too depressing. I could tell. I have a sixth sense, a radarlike detection device that can pick up the faintest frequency of compassion. Ultimately, only Virginie jumped at the chance to shack up with the ghoul next door (at a slightly reduced rent—she had a sixth sense for weakness and desperation).

I heard the front door slam. Virginie and Fraser had finally gone for breakfast. I went to the kitchen to see if there was any coffee left. There wasn't. Not in the pot. There were two barely sipped mugs sitting, cold and greasy, on the kitchen table. I thought about brewing up a fresh batch, but decided to shower and skedaddle before the sweethearts returned. I didn't even blow-dry my hair. I just pinned it into a bun, dressed quickly, and left.

The day was lovely. Yellow and shiny and warm. Bees were back in the city. Grass, too, all moist and fresh. And everywhere outside, people dizzy with spring and hungry for sun were taking it in: Mrs. Silva planting annuals around her cement shrine to the Virgin Mary, Nuno Benitah lovingly soaping up the spoiler on his red Camaro, Debbie and Sergio Big-Wheeling down the sidewalk, and as usual, as always, my neighbor and coworker Isadora on her front stoop, hosing down her paved front lawn. Twice each day in spring/summer/fall Isadora would carefully unravel a perfectly coiled garden hose and proceed to blast the interlocking patio stones with about a thousand pounds of water pressure—as if it were a rioting crowd that needed to be controlled, as if the Ebola virus had flopped down in her yard and shouted: *Hi, honey, I'm home.* Needless to say, not even the most roguish dandelion seed would be bold or crazy enough to settle upon this pristine surface. Yet there she was, every morning and every afternoon, washing away the phantom dirt. Not only would I cheerfully eat a meal off of the DeSouzas' front lawn, I would confidently stretch out and undergo major surgery without fear of bacterial infection.

Isadora waved as I passed by. "Off to your mom's?" she said, smiling sympathetically.

"Yup." I knew better than to stop and chat while she was purifying pavement. "Talk to you later."

"Later."

I was surprised when I discovered that Isadora was only a few years older than I. She was just twenty-five, but there was something patently middle-aged about her, something low to the ground and matronly. Maybe it was the childbearing that did it—she already had two rug rats. Maybe it was the facial hair—she sported a bit of a Fu Manchu mustache. She was always smiling sympathetically. "How was your weekend?"

she'd ask, smiling sympathetically. "My cousin Paulo is getting married," she'd say, smiling sympathetically. When I first moved onto the street, the sympathy smile annoyed me. I got it every time I walked by her. But soon she started throwing in a "Hot enough for you?" or "Have a nice evening," and then one afternoon she was at my door with a plastic bag fat with zucchinis from her family's vegetable garden. Nice. The following day, I countered with a bouquet of snapdragons scrounged from a neglected planter at the side of the 7-Eleven. The day after that, Isadora responded with an armload of dazzling, homegrown tomatoes. I lobbed back a bundle of fresh rosemary, purchased, then passed off as something I'd cultivated and had more than enough of. Isadora one-upped me with a plate of sardines that had been barbecued in a brick structure at the back of her yard. A day later, as I scanned my apartment for some sort of reciprocal goody, I had a disquieting vision of neighborly escalation, and saw myself in a week's time dragging my sofa or television set down to the DeSouzas'.

A friendship of sorts had begun. One that was given shape and purpose when Virginie, on her way to the subway, casually flicked a cigarette butt onto the damp, freshly sanitized DeSouza lawn as Isadora stood watching/rewinding her hose. Thereafter, Isadora was hungry for stories of my roommate's treachery, and I was happy to oblige. *The enemies of my enemies are my friends.* Suddenly we had something to talk about. One thing in common.

Isadora wasn't very bright, but she was extremely cordial. She lived with her extended family in a semi-detached house at the end of the street next to the alley. Back in Lisbon, Isadora's father was a well-paid hydro technician. Here he was a janitor. Even though he spoke nothing but Portuguese, he managed to secure a contract to clean a small office building downtown. Every weekday at six-thirty, the DeSouza clan piled into a van and headed to 505 Richmond Street to fight grime and restore order. And for ten months I went with them—after Isadora's sister got laid up with multiple sclerosis. The DeSouzas needed an extra body, and since my unemployment insurance was about to run out, I needed some semblance of an income. It would take at least twelve years before Isadora's children were of broom-wielding age, so Mr. DeSouza reluctantly agreed to hire a non-relation (after concerted campaigning by Isadora on my behalf). I was grateful for the job and I did my best to keep up, but the DeSouzas were the most energetic and thoroughly clean family I had ever encountered. What the Wallendas were to flying, the DeSouzas were to scouring. And while I found them inspiring on a certain level, it was often difficult to marshal adequate enthusiasm for my eight-dollar-an-hour scrub gig. Mind you, I found it difficult to get up for just about anything back then.

By the time I got to the subway, I was sticky with sweat. After a leisurely seven-minute waddle to the corner, my freshly laundered blouse was damp and clinging, and my crotch was broiling in my blue jeans. It was a relief to go underground and get into an air-conditioned car. I fanned myself with both hands and tried not to gawk at all the people in their summer clothes—tank tops, shorts, tiny sundresses with spaghetti straps. This was the part of spring that I detested: the doffing of the duds. The Annual Molt. All that exposed flesh, all those beautiful bodies on display. How I envied women who could wear sleeveless tops. How impossibly breezy and fine would it feel to be out in public, wearing a top without sleeves? I just couldn't imagine it. With my arms, even T-shirts were out of the question. So I went with long-sleeved blouses rolled to the elbow, and either full-length jeans—the shit smear on my shin precluding the cooler Capri pant option—or a skirt that went down to the ankles. Spring was tolerable. Summer was a five-alarm hellfire.

Okay, here's a question: When did teenage girls start dressing like whores? I must have spotted at least a dozen kinder-whores as I made my way to my mom's that morning. They were everywhere, in halter tops and miniskirts, or skintight blue jeans cut just above the pudendum with the thong underwear sticking out, teetering high on Franken-stein platform shoes or strappy stiletto sandals, with their toenails screaming in lacquered Technicolor. I thought: Even if I could get away with it, I wouldn't dress like that. No way. Not in a million years. Little did I know.

So I got to my mom's house, the house in which I grew up, and realized that I was starving. Bad news, because even if she had any food around—unlikely, since I'd be taking her gro-cery shopping—she wouldn't offer me any. It made her uncomfortable to see me eat. I thought about backtracking to the corner and grabbing something but decided to tough it out. I wanted to get the mission over with as quickly as possible.

She was on the cordless phone, lighting a Salem Menthol, when she answered the door. "But I'm already a subscriber," she said. "I just want to pay via credit card." No smile, just a nod and a small step back to gesture me in. "Uh-huh," she said, ". . . uh-huh," as she turned and padded barefoot up the hardwood stairs. I heard her bedroom door close.

I bypassed the just-for-show living room with its pristine sofa and love seat, its perpetually empty candy dishes, and white baby-grand piano (that as far as I could recall had never been played). I moved through to the kitchen and sneaked a peek in the fridge. Mayonnaise, mustard, a urine sample, one Medusa-like potato, and some rag doll celery sprawling limp over the edge of a wire shelf. I listened for her approach, then quickly checked the cupboard: an unopened jar of cocktail olives, a jumbo bottle of Worcestershire sauce, some crusty old Tabasco, and a jug of Coco Lopez Cream of Coconut Mixer—vestiges of happier days. I closed the door quietly, marveling at her ability to finish to the crumb every item of food we had purchased the previous Friday. Then I spotted one remnant, a box of All-Bran on the counter beside the stove. I listened for sounds of imminent mother, and then went for the box. I struggled with the resealable cardboard flip tabs, unrolled the wax paper liner, and dug my fist into the dusty gerbil pellets disguised as breakfast cereal. I almost scraped open knuckle flesh in the process of excavating a handful, which I was cramming into my mouth when my mother walked in. The look on her face . . . a brilliantly subtle cross between disgust, disappointment, and disdain. As if she had found me with my pants around my ankles, taking a dump in her Crock-Pot.

"Haben't eaden today," I said, trying to speed-masticate the gravel into a swallowable sludge.

She looked away, her lips curling slightly, and I could tell she was thinking, Yeah, right. She plonked her giant purse on the kitchen table and began fishing through it.

"Ready to roll?" she said, digging deeper in the purse.

"Whenever you are." I sealed the box and placed it back in its spot.

"Where the fuck?" More brisk digging, followed by frantic rummaging, followed by an exasperated yelp and the upending of the purse onto the table. "Christ!"

"What are you looking for?"

She swooned a little and slumped into a chair. "The Holy Grail," she said. "Jimmy frickin' Hoffa." She closed her eyes and pressed a hand to her forehead. One of her dizzy spells. From the medication.

"If you're looking for your keys, they're right there." I pointed to the key ring, which was caught in the folds of the wallet under the cell phone in the pile of makeup, matchbooks, gum wrappers, prescription bottles, Bic lighters, Wet-Naps, hair clips, pens, and pocket combs snagged with peroxide tresses.

She opened her eyes and plucked the keys from the pile. Then she stood up and started sweeping everything back into the purse. She smiled and spoke condescendingly: "I wasn't looking for my keys, Allison. My keys are right here. What I was looking for are my . . . my sunglasses."

I should probably mention that she's not my real mother.

"Well," she said, snapping the purse shut, "do you want to help me find them or do you want to just stand there?"

"They're on your head."

She reached up and felt them there. "Oh," she said. "Let's go."

For the seventeenth Friday in a row, I backed the yellow Audi slowly out of the driveway. For the seventeenth Friday in a row, she said, "Careful," while I was doing it. And for the seventeenth Friday in a row, I thought: Careful? Don't tell me to be careful. I'm not the one who got stinko, backed up over a schnoodle, and had my license suspended.

"Where to?"

She unfolded and scanned her list of errands. "Um, I guess we should head north first. I have to pick up something at Eloquio."

"What?" I asked, in a misguided attempt to make conversation. She's not big on conversation.

"A lawn mower," she sniped. Boutique Eloquio was the clothing store where she spent all her money (after she had ceased spending it at the liquor store and various upscale bars).

She flipped down the passenger-side sun shield and surveyed herself in the tiny mirror. Satisfied, she flipped it back up. Then she reached into her purse and pulled out her cigarettes.

"Do you mind not smoking in here?" I said (for the seventeenth Friday in a row). "We'll be there in a few minutes."

"I'll open the window," she said, lighting up. She cracked the passenger window three inches.

I pushed the button to open mine.

"Allison," she yelped, "my *hair*." She held it against her head as if it was going to come loose and escape out of the car.

I closed my window. We drove in smoky silence for about a minute. She checked her reflection again. Still satisfactory. My eyes began to water. I had a sneezing fit. Another minute of silence.

"So," she said, as if the strain of mouthing the words was immense. "What's new?"

"Um . . . nothing really. What's new with you?"

"Not much. Same old thing." Relieved to have that over with, she turned on the radio. And, miracle of miracles, one of my favorite songs just happened to be playing. And it had just started.

Okay, I'm now going to share a secret with you. There is one good thing about me, one small gift that very few people know about. I can sing. I have a good voice. Better than good, actually. It's quite a lovely voice. Not particularly powerful, but sweet, mellifluous, and multi-octave-spanning. A little like Tori Amos minus the histrionics. And when my mother turned on the radio and one of my favorite songs was playing, I had the urge to let loose with a perfect harmony and impress the hell out of her. But a nanosecond later she changed the station and settled on Rod Stewart croaking "Da Ya Think I'm Sexy?" Apparently, she thought he was. I noticed, with mild alarm, that she was gyrating rhythmically in her bucket seat.

When we got to Eloquio there were, as usual, no available parking spots in the vicinity. And, as usual, my mother insisted that I let her out in front and go find one.

"If you don't get something nearby, just keep circling," she said, stepping out of the car.

"How long are you going to be?" I asked.

"How should I know?" She flung the door shut with a flourish.

Okay, you're probably wondering why, why did I put up with the abuse? Why did I go every Friday for seventeen weeks to chauffeur her around and help her do her lousy errands? Especially since she wasn't even my blood mother. Good question. Well, there were several reasons. The first is that I felt sorry for her. She was an alky, a real piss tank, a total lush. She'd been on and off the wagon for as long as I could remember. Mostly off. And it had damaged the thing she prized above all else: her looks. Once upon a time, she was quite a beauty. She even won a pageant. Miss Beef and Barley. Small-town, agricultural-fair-type thing. There was a framed photo of her on the living-room étagère, perched straight-backed on a throne of hay bales, crowned, sashed, and sceptered, waving to her adoring farming public. The waist-length flaxen braids and the milkmaid complexion were long gone. She was still attractive, but she had the puffy, haggard look of the drunkard. The baggage under the eyes, the marbled nose, and the trailer park belly—the lower belly that protruded and hung on an otherwise slender body.

Not that I was all busted up about her not being drop-dead gorgeous anymore. I mean, boo fucking hoo. Cry me a highball. No, it was the weakness and shame mixed up in the boozing that got to me. The way she'd painstakingly hide the empty liquor bottles in the bottom of the recycling bin, or take her morning cocktail in a coffee mug, as if that could fool anyone with a sense of smell. The way she'd chalk up her hangover heaving to "a trace of the stomach flu," or her detox shakes to it being "chilly in here." I found the denial oddly touching. Maybe she was trying to deceive only herself, but I liked to think that the charade was at least partially for my benefit. As long as I was worthy of her deception, she was worthy of my pity. And the last year had been particularly pity-inducing. She felt very bad about the schnoodle incident. She lost all of her friends over it. FYI: A schnoodle is a cross between a schnauzer and a poodle. It's a very cute breed. I know because there were pictures in *The Toronto Sun* when it happened, a picture of Bijou the schnoodle (before she got backed up over, snagged and dragged under the yellow Audi for close to a hundred meters) curled up in her sleeping basket with a little doggy-sized beret angled jauntily on her fluffy head. There was a photo of the owner as well, a wide-angle shot of the frail and elderly Mrs. McNaughton posed in front of her tiny bungalow, looking bereft and mopey, holding Bijou's favorite squeaky toy in her arthritically twisted hand.

A vast torrent of grief and rage followed the accident. Thousands of dollars in unsolicited donations were mailed to Mrs. McNaughton. Scads of furious letters were sent to the newspaper, demanding justice, revenge, life imprisonment, blood. I found it astonishing. I mean, how many articles about ethnic cleansing and suicide bombing and famine and earthquake and death squad and disease, and not a peep from the public? But a fourteen-year-old schnoodle gets flattened and out comes the mob with their pens, wallets, and torches waving. Why do we humanize animals and do the opposite with humans?

Anyway, my mother was fined heavily and had her license suspended. She was ordered off the booze, into treatment, and onto ReVia—a pill that helped curb her alcohol cravings but gave her headaches and the occasional dizzy spell. So that's one reason I drove her around every Friday. I felt sorry for her.

The second (and truly delusional) reason was that I still entertained the faint hope of making some kind of connection with her. Even after enduring a lifetime of neglect verging on malice, I couldn't quite rid myself of this desire. I thought maybe now that she was isolated, abandoned by friends and former drinking buddies, she might let me in a little. Soften. I would be the only one to stick by her in a trying time, and I would be rewarded with a semblance of warmth and openness. Perhaps now she would finally show me the side of her that was so appealing to her numerous preschnoodle/going-on-the-wagon cronies.

The third reason was gratitude, because she pretty much raised me on her own. My parents adopted me when I was an infant, only three weeks old. Hard to believe, but apparently

I was a very cute baby. The one and only photograph of me on display at my mom's place is of me at the age of two, still cute, sitting on the love seat between my mother and father—the still sober and, if anything, more mature and beautiful Miss Beef and Barley, and the still present and dashingly handsome Mr. Big Shot Designer. What a lovely picture we made. But not long after that things started to get ugly. Very ugly. Daddio moved out—a trial separation that lasted and culminated in a sordid divorce and custody battle. Mom hit the bottle and eventually Pops went long distance, moving to Los Angeles when I was around seven.

I didn't realize it at the time, but it was pretty much downhill for me after the age of two, although it wasn't until kindergarten that I truly became aware of my status in the world. I'm not going to get into all the boo-hoo details. Suffice it to say that I was clued in by the usual drill—when I wasn't being excluded or ignored, I was being taunted and tormented. And whenever we had to play or "work" in partners, I was inexorably paired with the hateful Janice Dirk, a scrawny, mildly retarded girl who ate staples and pencil erasers and her own snot, and was given to bitter, entirely unaccountable fits of rage.

For years I endeavored to compensate for my appearance. I tried to be helpful and friendly and nice. Gosh darn it, I was the most generous little girl you ever did see. *Who would like to eat the delicious portions of my lunch today? On whom can I press my allowance? Can you borrow my Barbie Camper? Why, that'd be swell, take it for as long as you please, the entire summer if you wish! Yes, of course you may copy the answers to the test, sit right here next to me. Will I go to the corner and bring back Popsicles for everyone? I'll go just as fast as I can so they won't be all melty. Of course I'll buy! You lost my bicycle? Oh, well, don't you worry your pretty little head about it. I'll tell my mom that I lost it. What's that, you want me to steal some nail polish from the drugstore? I'll give it a shot. No, don't sweat it, I didn't tell when I got caught. Yeah, sure, I'll try again next week. Oh, wow, I can't believe it, you all wanna come over to my house and go swimming in the enticing new aboveground pool! That's swell, how about this afternoon?*

Oh, you wanna come on the weekend, when I'm away. Hmm, I don't know about that, you nasty little bitches.

Helpful and generous was a bust. I changed tack. I figured if I couldn't be the easiest to look at or the sweetest, perhaps I could be the smartest and the funniest (they're not laughing *at* you, etc., etc.). Up until grade nine, I managed to maintain a straight-A average while simultaneously laying claim to the title of class clown/shit disturber. *Look, there's Allison firing her peas across the cafeteria. Ho ho, what a funny fart noise Allison made during the vice principal's important safety speech. Wasn't that just hysterical when Allison pretended to vomit up her tuna casserole in home ec?*

The self-deprecating, let-me-be-your-John-Belushi shtick deflected far more hostility than the sweet 'n' nice combo, but it made me feel smarmy, like an organ-grinder's trained and chained monkey, or like a member of the Buchenwald orchestra. Eventually I became so disgusted with myself and the powerful morons all around me that I gave it up and grew silent. Amazingly, pride won out over personal safety. I say "amazingly" because at the time, I detested almost everything about myself. The fact that I was able to muster an iota of self-respect still impresses me. Thinking back on it, I can conclude only that even though I was consumed with a fervent self-loathing, I must have hated everyone else just a teensy bit more.

Boutique Eloquio. It could have been designed by my father—all blond wood, chrome, mirrors, and clean lines. The clothing was displayed like works of art. And for the size and airiness of the store, there seemed to be hardly any clothes in there at all—three or four skirts, five or six blouses, a few dresses, an evening gown, one silk scarf. Of course, everything was absurdly expensive and the sizes ranged from zero to eight. Eight was as big as you could get at Eloquio.

I was relieved to see that the usual snobby salesgirl wasn't there. A different snobby salesgirl, another tall job, another supermodel wanna-be had either replaced her or was covering her shift. When I walked in she glanced up with an expectant smile, instantly appraised my appearance, then went back to what she was doing: adjusting, with long, pale fingers, the lacquered chopsticks that held her elegantly tousled hair in place.

"How are we doing?" she said to the freestanding full-length mirror outside of the fitting room.

"Be right out," came my mother's muffled reply.

I touched a white shawl, displayed with virtuosity on a blond wood pedestal that had been lathed into a seductive Henry Moore—ish shape. The Tall Job looked my way, protective of the shawl's pristine whiteness. She was waiting for me to eyeball the price and hightail it out of there. I turned the tag over: $750. *100% Pashmina,* it said on the tag. Pashmina. What a creamy, decadent-sounding word. Here's what it didn't say: 100% beard fluff of a smelly Tibetan goat. I considered draping the shawl over my hunched shoulders to torment the salesgirl, but just then my mother emerged from the dressing room, decked out in a ridiculous frock.

"Oh, it's perfect," said Tall Job.

"You think?" said my mother, mincing in front of the mirror, obviously delighted with the effect. "Of course, I'll have my hair curled and scooped up."

"And you have to get big hoop earrings to go with it," said Tall Job.

Yeah, I thought, if you really want to look like an extra in the tavern scene in *Carmen,* better get those big hoop earrings to go with it. And maybe a jug of wine instead of a handbag. I sidled over to get a better look. The dress was red with black polka dots—some kind of "Gypsies, Tramps and Thieves" affair—the sleeves were pulled down to sit off the shoulders, a built-in bustier pushed the breasts up and out. It sucked in tight at the waist, then puffed out to mid-thigh in the front and trailed down to the ankles in the back—like a mullet.

"What do you think?" my mother asked, prematurely basking in my approval.

That episode of *I Love Lucy,* the one where she crushes the grapes with her feet, came to mind. "Um . . . where are you going to wear it?"

"To the Brazilian Ball, of course."

"Oh." Of course, the Brazilian Ball.

"Am I too old?" said my mother, twirling around. "Is it too young for me?"

Yes, I thought. Mutton dressed up as Lambada.

"Don't be silly," said Tall Job. "You have a dynamite body. I'd kill for that cleavage. Wouldn't you kill for that cleavage?" she asked me.

"Don't be silly," said my mom. "I'd kill to have a long, willowy figure like yours."

"Oh, no," said Tall Job.

I suddenly felt like killing them both. Not for cleavage, just for fun. Instead, I made for the door. "I'm going to go get the car," I said.

Mercifully, by the time I hoofed it a quarter mile to the Audi and wheeled it back around in front of Eloquio, my mother was outside, smoking, with her boxed frock clutched tightly under one arm.

Next up was the shoe department at Holt Renfrew, then to Creeds to pick up her dry cleaning, then to the MotoPhoto to have new passport pictures taken. She had the attendant snap them three times before she was happy with the result. Throughout this time, she uttered maybe ten words to me. When I asked why she was getting her passport renewed, she said: "Because it's time." When I asked her if she was thinking of going on vacation, she said: "Maybe." When I asked her how her addiction treatment was going, she said: "Fine, thanks." I think that was about it. No, wait . . . when a Miata lurched in front of me from the right-hand lane, causing me to brake abruptly, she said, "Allison!" as if I were the one who had failed to signal and veered crazily through traffic.

Finally we got to the last leg of the errand journey. The supermarket. It was almost one-thirty. As we entered the vast grocery emporium, we had to pass through a faux-street-market area where prepared foods were sold under quaint umbrellas: muffins, sandwiches, pasta salad, pizza, fresh-squeezed juices, and smoothies. By this point I was famished, and the aroma of fresh baking convinced me that I had to eat something, no matter how distressing it was to my mother.

"I'm just going to grab a muffin," I said. "Do you want anything?"

"No," she said, glancing sternly at her watch, as if my muffin purchase was going to put a big dent in her day.

They had blueberry muffins and carrot muffins, neither of which I like. I opted instead for a slice of pizza. Since I didn't want to hold up the expedition, I put the pizza on its paper plate in the front part of the cart. I would eat it while I shopped, as I had seen many people doing on previous Fridays. Mindful of not disturbing my mother, I consumed the pizza in small, delicate bites, dabbing a napkin to my lips after each swallow. I pushed the cart while she consulted her list and filled it with selected items (mostly processed and prepared foods, mostly frozen).

I was well aware of the fact that a fat person in a grocery store is inherently comical to some people. Whenever I went shopping, there were at least one or two individuals who smiled smug at the bag of chips or container of ice cream in my basket. I've even had people, ostensibly concerned about my health and welfare, comment on my purchases, as if it were any of their goddamn business. So I knew the drill. Still, I was surprised by the sheer number of indignant, amused, and disgusted looks I received as I rolled the cart down the aisles while simultaneously nibbling the pizza slice. I felt conspicuous and acutely aware, like I had ESP, like I could actually hear the *ha-ha* or *tsk-tsk* thoughts of the passing shoppers: The cute twenty-something guy with the border shorts and the goatee: *Just couldn't wait to get the grub home, Jumbo?* A CEO's overaerobicized and direly tanned trophy bride: *Maybe if you ditched the pizza and picked up an apple once in a while you wouldn't be in such*

a state. The sad-eyed old man in the porkpie hat: *Such a shame.*
That poor girl will never get a husband. The bulimic teenage whore-
girl with *Perfect 10* emblazoned across her pop-top chest: *Oh,*
gross, I think I'm gonna, like, hurl.

It was a relief to get out of there, and get my mother home.

"Keys," she said when we had finished hauling in the groceries.

I handed them over. The car would now be a piece of
driveway sculpture until the following Friday. Still, it never
occurred to her to offer the use of it to me. Or probably it
had and she had decided against it. Either way, I was too meek
to inquire. She was obviously feeling prickly—lips clenched,
shoulders tight—and I didn't want to incur her fury or end
the outing with a blast of wrath. Maybe next week, if she was
feeling calmer, I would ask her.

Maybe next week things would be different.

2

For the seventeenth Friday in a row, I took the subway
home from my mom's place, feeling disconsolate and burn-
ingly alone. For the seventeenth Friday in a row, I fantasized
about hooking up with my birth mother. It was Fantasy #9,
one of the more ludicrous but popular in my roster of about
a dozen. In this one, it comes to light that I, and not Kilau-
ren Gibb, am the long-lost love child of Joni Mitchell. It
doesn't matter that the dates and details don't line up, not to
mention the cheekbones. In the fantasy they line up. I am
tracked down by a private detective, hired by Ms. Mitchell,
who is determined to find the baby she reluctantly handed off
when she was a twenty-year-old art school student. As I said,
the particulars line up, but the clincher, the way the detective—a rumpled Colombo type—really knows that I'm the
one, is when he hears me sing. "That's the ticket," he says,

with a rumpled Colombo smile, his eyes moist, betraying emotion. The next day I fly to California. A poignant reunion ensues. Laughter. Tears. More laughter. We have so much to talk about. We can't stop clutching each other. The blood tie is mysteriously powerful. We bond instantly. We discover that both of us love jazz, ice skating, liver and onions. Joni is stunned to learn that "Little Green" has always been one of my favorite songs.

Before she can apologize for giving me away, I tell her that I understand completely. She was poor, practically a child herself, and just beginning to forge a career. It was a time when single motherhood carried a terrible stigma. She was doing only what she thought was best for me. Joni appreciates my empathy. She tells me what a joy and relief it is to have found me. I tell her what a relief it is to have found myself, to have found out who I am. She understands. She writes a song about it for her next album. I sing backup vocals. The voices blend beautifully. . . . Fantasy #9.

Ludicrous. Absurd.

In reality, it probably wouldn't have been very difficult to locate my birth mother. My mom had the original documents and had let me know that she would be happy to hand them over. I just never could muster the guts to go through with it. I figured if my real mother didn't want me around when I was a cute little tyke, she wouldn't have much use for me in my current state. Perhaps if I had accomplished something grand I might have been bolder. If I were a team leader mapping the human genome, a gold medal Olympian, an astronaut returning with data from a distant planet. Violin virtuoso. Pulitzer playwright. Filthy-rich Midas-touch-type entrepreneur. But I was none of those things. I was Allison Penny, high-school dropout—just before graduating from grade twelve, a particularly nasty year for social ostracism. I was a cleaning lady. A cleaning lady who spent most of her time alone in a peeling ceiling room. Destitute, depressed, and almost universally derided. *Hi ya, Ma. Long time no see!* No.

Clearly, if my birth mother had any desire to contact me, she would have already done so. More rejection was definitely not something I required, and so, for the seventeenth Friday in a row, I shut it out of my mind.

The post-fantasy portion of the commute was odious. I cursed myself for neglecting to bring my Discman along. Rush hour started preternaturally early on Fridays, and the subway was already too packed with humans for my liking. Every chatty couple, every shapely exposed limb, every tightly packed blue-jeaned butt seemed like a personal attack on my psyche. I felt hostile, grimy, and unkempt. Also tremendously hungry.

I stopped at Aida's on my way home and got four falafels to go—two for dinner, two for later when I would take my break. I bought a couple Snickers bars and some Twizzlers for dessert. I was really, really hoping that Virginie wouldn't be home when I got there. I just needed a couple hours to decompress before I had to go to work.

Here's what I heard when I opened the front door of the flat: Serge Gainsbourg singing "Je T'aime, Moi Non Plus." Loud. Here's what I saw when I passed through the vestibule and glanced to my left into the living room: Virginie, buck naked except for Buddy Holly glasses, high-heeled shoes, and a flashing light embedded in her navel—I'm not kidding, it looked like a tiny bicycle light—sprawled on the sofa with her legs in the air. Fraser was holding her labia open with two fingers, and quick-flicking his tongue on her clitoris. Her vagina had been shaved bare except for a tiny Mohawk strip down the middle.

Gross anatomy.

Life imitating porn.

Thankfully, I was neither heard nor noticed. I went to my room and ate my falafels—*feel-awfuls*—with the image of Virginie's splayed crotch and the music crowding in on me.

I took a long shower, thought about opening up a vein, and pictured the blood swirling down the drain. Then I toweled off, combed out my hair, and blow-dried it. I stayed in there until I heard an insistent rattling of the locked door-knob—someone wanted in, which meant it was safe to come out. The sexcapade was over. Both urge and Serge had been silenced

"Are you in there?" said Virginie.

No, I'm out there, dumb-ass. I'm cartwheeling down the hallway.

"Almost done."

"Well, hurry up. I have to pee!"

Virginie kept several coffee cans full of makeup in the bathroom—a myriad of mysterious powders and paints, for lips, cheek, lash, and brow. There was a container reserved exclusively for the face artist's numerous brushes, everything from a big puffy one for dusting on beige "light-diffusing crystals" to a miniature brush for taming unruly eyebrow hairs. I fished out one of her newer lipsticks and examined it: #043, Pretty in Pink. It smelled good and the color was fresh and summery. It occurred to me to try some on, you know, just for laughs, but I was wary. There was something vaguely herpetic about Virginie, and the last thing I needed was an STD without the benefit of ever having experienced the S. I wiped the tip of the lipstick. Then I poured half a bottle of rubbing alcohol over it, swabbed the tip again, and dabbed a little on my mouth.

"Are you still in there?!" said Virginie, pounding on the door.

"Sorry," I said. "Just a sec." I surveyed the results in the mirror. Portly in Pink.

I wet some toilet paper and wiped the smile off my face.

3

"So how's your mom?" asked Isadora, smiling sympa-thetically.

"Not bad, thanks."

"She still off the . . . ?" Isadora tipped her hand to her mouth as if she were drinking.

"Yeah," I said.

"Good. Good for her. And the *Porco,* what's up with that?" Porco—pig in Portuguese—was Isadora's name for Virginie.

"I've got a good one," I said, knowing that Isadora would be equally titillated and disgusted by Virginie's living-room sex antics, "but I'll tell you when we get there." I gestured to her parents, indicating that it was too lurid to discuss in front of them.

I was seated with the DeSouza offspring on a homemade bench that had been bolted through carpeting to the metal floor in the back of the industrial van. It was pretty much the same drill every weekday: We'd exchange greetings and climb on in. Isadora would ask me about the Porco, and I would fill her in on Virginie's latest transgression. Apart from that, the ride to work was largely silent, punctuated by the occasional *"Bandido"* or *"Idiota!"* from Mr. DeSouza as he navigated through traffic. Aside from hello and good-bye, Isadora was the only DeSouza who talked to me. The parents didn't speak English, but Paulo, Mina, Alvaro, and Abril did. I noticed that Paulo, Isadora's handsome young cousin, wouldn't even look at me; that is, he would never meet my eye. He wore dark sunglasses, even in the van, and listened to a Discman. Mina, typically, would wile away the journey, inspecting and picking at her cuticles or chipped fingernail polish. Mrs. DeSouza would lock her fierce gaze on the road—keeping the van on track with mind control. And the twins, Alvaro and Abril, would fiddle with their matching Game Boy devices, occa-sionally comparing scores. I would chat with Isadora and sneak peeks at Paulo until we arrived at our destination, at which point the DeSouza scouring squad would spring from the van and launch into a flurry of action.

My duties were relatively light. I would pick up the keys and my cart—essentially a giant garbage bag on wheels—and forge ahead on my route, moving from office to office, emptying trash cans. That's all I had to do. The DeSouzas would come up the rear, sweeping, vacuuming, dusting, wiping—taking care of the tough stuff, entrusted to family members only. For me it was easy. A paid form of exercise, I guess. And if I had to empty office garbage cans for a meager living, 505 Richmond was a comparatively pleasant place to do it. In fact, 505 Richmond was a thing of beauty—an old warehouse that had been thoughtfully transformed into a funky, four-story office building. Many of the original features remained: tastefully worn pine plank flooring, huge casement windows that actually opened, sandblasted brick walls, twelve-foot-high ceilings with exposed rafters, and snaking ductwork that had been painted in rich Farrow & Ball colors.

It was an impressive building that attracted well-heeled, artsy tenants. There were all kinds of design firms—industrial, fashion, furniture, graphic. There was an animation company, an ad agency, several entertainment lawyers and PR firms. There were photographers, film producers, and loads of multimedia types. *WUT Up* magazine was headquartered here. As was IZ Talent Management, one of the country's most prestigious modeling agencies. On the main floor there was a groovy little café (just closing for the day by the time we got there) and a progressive day-care center (that looked like Keith Haring had a happy hand in the design). The whole joint just reeked of young, edgy success. And the fact that it was located in the middle of the club district—most of the surrounding warehouse buildings had been turned into ultra-groovy nightspots—further enhanced its hip factor.

One of my favorite features of the building was its abundant plant life. On every floor, between the large industrial service elevator and the passenger lift, the owner had installed a growing station. Long shelves of African violets, cyclamens, gloxinia, star jasmine, creeping fig, golden pothos, grape ivy, and emerald ripple glowing happy and healthy under fluorescent tube lights. There was also a lovely display of rock, cacti, and other succulents on the main floor by the front doors. And then there was the crowning glory, a rooftop patio, brimming with tangled vines and bursting with flowers, where people could go to eat their lunch or take a smoke break.

I should point out that the only reason I know the names of all those plants is because Nathan taught them to me. Nathan had a part-time job taking care of them. On Mondays, Wednesdays, and Fridays, when he was done with his day shift at the video store, Nathan would come down to water, feed, and prune the plants. He was good with them, but he wasn't into them. Nathan was into movies. Big time. I'd never met anyone so obsessed with cinema. Virginie and Fraser put on airs, but they didn't know what they were talking about. They just adopted and parroted popular opinion (i.e., Indie film: good, Hollywood film: bad; Jean Seberg: good, Doris Day: bad). Nathan formed his own opinions, and really knew what was what. Plus he wasn't snobby about it. It wasn't like he saw only foreign art films featuring endless close-ups of sad-looking actresses with adorable overbites. He saw *everything*. He seemed to have seen every film ever made, from every country on the globe. His typical evening viewing might include a South African documentary, a Hong Kong action pic, and Julia Roberts's latest romantic comedy. He was shocked that I had never seen or even heard of the original version of *The In-Laws*, one of his fave comedies. And he laughed his ass off when I said Antonioni sounded like something Chef Boyardee would make. Antonioni-os.

Nathan gave me lists of "must-see" movies, most of which I'd never even heard of, all of which I enjoyed when I was able to hunt them down and view them (the truly obscure titles he would occasionally lend me from his personal collection). He laid the titles on me in groupings that had a logic known only to him. This was one list: *Charade, Carnal Knowledge, Crumb, Cat Ballou,* and *The Conversation.* Semi-alphabetical, right? All C titles. But the list before the C list was not a B list, it was a Y list: *You Can't Take It with You, Young Frankenstein, Yojimbo,* and *You Can Count on Me.* The list before that was evidently name-based: *Harold and Maude, Zelig,* and *All About Eve.* And the one prior to that seemed to be a simple rhythmic pairing: *A Taste of Cherry* and *A Touch of Class.*

I once asked Nathan what his favorite film was. He responded with a tortured groan and the look of a parent who had been asked to select his favorite child. "No," he said, shaking his oddly shaped head from side to side, "no, it's not possible." The next time I saw him, he presented me with a list of one hundred of his favorite films—not, I repeat, *not* ranked in order of preference—which, he told me, he agonized over and altered regularly.

In a dilapidated khaki knapsack, Nathan toted around a giant paperback called *Video Hound*—a guide to every film that had been released on video or DVD. It was his bible. He would invite you to flip to any page and select a movie title at random. He would then tell you who wrote, directed, and starred in it, provide you with a synopsis, tell you how many bones it rated in the guide, and then give it his own cogent review and rating. We would often play this *Video Hound* game when I took my twenty-minute break at ten o'clock. I enjoyed it. I looked forward to it, actually. Not so much the game, just being in the presence of Nathan. He was the one person in the world with whom I felt simpatico, not comfortable—he made me nervous, actually—but temperamentally . . . correct. I think the New Age notion of humans giving off vibrations is true. It seemed to me that Nathan and I were like adjacent strings on the same instrument. We vibrated at slightly different frequencies, but in good harmony.

I was already looking forward to seeing him, as I rode the service elevator to the second floor to continue my rounds.

The first floor had gone smoothly enough. Apart from a lawyer trying to explain a contract to her mystified-looking client, I hadn't encountered anyone working late. 505 Richmond had the kind of energetic young tenants who regularly stuck around until the wee hours, but because it was the first summery night of the season, a lot of people had lit out at closing time, slipped out to sip Mojitos in trendy outdoor cafés, or gone home to their loft-style condominiums to rearrange the placement of their Eames chairs. Good. The fewer bodies around, the better. Even though most of the late workers completely ignored my presence—I now know what it feels like to be an apparition, a trash-can-emptying ghost—I found it depressing to be carting away the garbage of people roughly my own age while they were sitting there in front of me, toiling at their glamorous, challenging, and well-remunerated jobs. Still, there were only two offices in the building that I truly disliked going into. One was the *WUT Up* magazine office, the other was IZ Talent Management. *WUT Up* was on the second floor, and as I rolled my cart off the elevator, I could already hear the boisterous shouts of the managing editor reverberating beyond the imposing *WUT Up* doorway. I shuddered and rolled on by. I decided to do the rest of the floor first. Maybe by the time I was done . . . Alas, no such luck.

"Hazel, my friend, how's it going?"

As usual, the *WUT Up* office was still populated with a bevy of young, attractive hipsters, including the youngest, most attractive hipster of them all, Andrew McKay, the founder/managing editor, reclining in his oh-so-ironic 1970s stereo chair. He was smoking a Nat Sherman cigarillo and drinking a beer, with his long legs and his giant Italian shoes stretched out in front of him.

I gave him enough of a fake smile to protect my employment status, then went about my business, emptying the bulging trash cans of the filthiest office in the building.

"Hazel," he shouted, standing up and moving to his desk. "C'mere, I have something for you."

A small titter emitted from a trio of idiot hipsters lounging on a faded velvet sofa.

"It's a present!" said Andrew, laughing, showing off his adorable dimples.

"She doesn't understand, dufus," mumbled an anorexic-looking sofa-dweller, clad in a polyester leisure suit that either cost two dollars at the Salvation Army or two thousand dollars in a retro boutique.

Somehow, Andrew McKay had gotten it into his head that I was Portuguese and didn't speak English. So I went with it, taking a small measure of comfort and amusement in playing dumb. The funny thing was, Andrew knew me, or he should have known me. We went to the same high school. Out in the suburbs. We actually had quite a few classes together. Of course, I remembered him. Six foot two, curly blond hair, big blue eyes, and those dimples. He was very good-looking and wildly popular: Mr. Yearbook Committee, Mr. Football/Hockey Hero, Mr. Everybody Adores Me (until the incident that almost got him expelled). Yup, it was pretty hard not to notice and remember Andrew McKay. But I guess I never registered on the radar. Either that or he didn't recognize me. Either way I was glad.

"She may not understand me, but she knows her name," said Andrew. "Hazel," he shouted. "Yo, Hazel!"

I finally looked up. I had to. He smiled and gestured me over, his long arms beckoning as if I were a toddler taking my first steps. I moved toward him.

"No, bring your cart," he said, miming the activity. "Your cart," he shouted, as if I were deaf.

I had a flash of mowing him down with the rolling garbage can, and stepping on his larynx until all sound and breath had stopped.

Instead, I rolled my cart docilely to his desk.

"Here you go," he said, taping a photo of a smiling Shirley Booth as Hazel Burke onto the cart. "Isn't that nice?" Another titter from the sofa hipsters. Then Andrew made a big show of emptying his own trash can into the garbage bag. Mr. Magnanimous.

I smiled and moved on, thinking about how I would tell it to Nathan on my break. Nathan was the one who clued me in about the Hazel business. I couldn't figure out why Andrew kept calling me Hazel. Then Nathan told me that Hazel was a maid on a TV sitcom in the early sixties, and that it was probably another lame attempt on Andrew's part to be amusingly ironic.

Nathan despised *WUT Up* magazine. He hated the hipperthan-thou attitude, the vomitous fluorescent color scheme, the headache-inducing practice of rendering text unreadable by torturing it into groovy swirls of graphic cacophony (not that there was much text, mind you; *WUT Up* was primarily images). Most of all, Nathan detested the film reviews, which he found muddled, witless, and phlegmatic. He also took umbrage with the quarter-page glamour pic of *WUT Up*'s regular film columnist—a cute twenty-something blonde who called herself Shelly D. The glossy photo showed her seated naked in a red velvet theater chair, her private parts obscured by a giant pink-and-white-striped box of popcorn, a comehither expression on her face.

"Jeez, why didn't *The New Yorker* think of that?" he said during one of our rant sessions on Andrew and *WUT Up*. "They could have ditched Pauline Kael and hired Pamela Anderson. You know, a nice shot of her with thirty-five-millimeter film frames over her nipples like pasties. Hell, it's not too late, they could fire David Denby and hire Ben Affleck or Antonio Sabato, Jr. I mean, who gives a damn about the review?"

Nathan deeply admired Pauline Kael. He told me that she was the reason he'd decided to become a film critic (her and somebody named Jay Scott). I was surprised. I figured that Nathan, with all his movie blab, wanted to be a director or a writer or, at the very least, a producer. But no, apparently he didn't want to make movies, he simply wanted to review them—and, he hoped, scratch out a living at it. Unfortunately, he hadn't had much success. He did contribute reviews to a small bimonthly newspaper, but it was a low-circulation freebie, and he made only forty bucks a pop. He told me that, a while back, he almost got a gig reviewing film on cable TV, à la Roger Ebert. He had noticed an ad in several film mags and one of the daily papers soliciting three sample reviews from burgeoning cinephiles who wanted to try out for the plum position. Nathan sent off three fine ones in short order. He got a call from an enthusiastic associate producer asking for three more. He sent those off. Then he was summoned for an interview, which he felt he had handled with verve and panache, wowing the producers by doing an impromptu review of Woody Allen's *Small Time Crooks* (there was poster for it up on the wall), comparing it beat for beat to the film on which it was apparently based: the superior *Larceny, Inc.*, a 1942 production written by Laura and S. J. Perelman, starring Edward G. Robinson, Jane Wyman, Broderick Crawford, Jack Carson, and Anthony Quinn. *Go, Nathan, go.* Next, the producers asked him to do a videotaped audition. He felt no fear in front of the camera and was certain that he had aced it. Soon after, the producers called to inform him that an actor had been hired to host the show. According to Nathan: "Some pretty boy in a vintage motorcycle jacket who knew fuck all about film."

I was surprised. Nathan wasn't exactly a poster boy—put him in a tank top and the effect would be more Appalachian than Calvin Klein—but he was hardly a beast. He had a David-Letterman-meets-Howdy-Doody-on-the-way-to-Woody-Allen sort of look. Thin reddish hair receding from a curiously bulbous forehead, pale skin blanketed in barely noticeable freckles, intelligent brown eyes behind wire-rim glasses, and a goofy, gap-toothed smile. He was about five foot ten, of average weight. He wasn't pumped up, but he appeared moderately muscled. I thought he was rather adorable.

"It's their loss," I told him.

"Thanks," he said. "But when I hear about this clown getting free industry passes to every film fest in the country, it feels more like my loss." He laughed. "I think it's more accurately my loss."

As usual, I zipped through the third floor so I would have a few minutes to spare before I took my official break. I ducked into the ladies' washroom and ate my falafels and Snickers bar. It was an unpleasant place to dine, even right inside the entrance door facing away from the stalls, but I didn't want to be seen. Occasionally I would run into Nathan in the hallways while he was bringing water to the plants at the growing stations, and I didn't want him to catch me with cheeks full of pita and a chin dripping with tahini rivulets. Not that he would have said anything, but the idea of it made me uncomfortable. When thin people eat, it looks like humans taking nourishment. When fat people eat, it looks like gluttons self-destructing. I finished quickly, rinsed my mouth in the bathroom sink, and then proceeded to the fourth-floor roof garden.

Nathan wasn't there yet. I sat down to wait. Something about the place—the up-aboveness of it, the isolation, the leafy oasis quality—always made me feel slightly melancholy. It made me feel like singing.

I had been singing the first time I encountered Nathan. It was a few weeks after I had started with the DeSouzas, September of last year. I was out on the roof, taking my break. I had finished my food—there was no reason not to eat out there back then—and I had about five minutes to kill. I remember sitting there in the city dark, the not-quite dark, feeling a bit bummed out. The night was cool and there was a trace of wood smoke in the air. For the first time that year it smelled like autumn. I felt like singing, so I did. I remember the song, too. It was one that I had written, an embarrassingly mopey ballad called "One Man's Trash," a sort of Vic-Chesnutt-meets-Eleni-Mandel-type dirge. Anyway, when I came to the end of my scowl-howl, I heard clapping and nearly soiled my pants. I turned and saw Nathan, standing at the entrance to the patio, smiling, looking like a balding, bespectacled Alfred E. Neuman.

"That was beautiful," he said, "really beautiful."

I was too shocked to speak. And my heart was going about a million beats per minute.

Ten-fifteen and no Nathan. Just when I thought he wasn't going to show, just when I started to feel a sick constriction in my chest, he appeared on the patio, sweating and out of breath.

"Hey."

"Hey."

"What time is it?" he said, dropping his knapsack on the ground and wiping the sweat from his forehead.

I checked my watch as if I didn't know perfectly well.

"A quarter after ten."

"Shit," he said. "Can you believe I just got here?"

"Why? What happened?"

"I left my fucking knapsack on the subway. What a schmuck."

"Yikes. But you got it back, though."

"Yeah, three hours later, minus the cash in my wallet, my Criterion *Grey Gardens* DVD, and my *Video Hound.*"

"Oh, no."

"Oh, yes," said Nathan, sitting down beside me. "Oh, well, at least they returned my credit cards and ID. That would've been a nightmare. And it seems the thief had good taste. He took *Grey Gardens* but left a VHS copy of *The Mexican.*" Nathan laughed.

"He probably checked the *Video Hound.*"

"Yeah, really," said Nathan, smiling at the idea.

"Did you lose a lot of cash?"

"A whopping twenty-five bucks."

"Still . . ."

"Yeah, it's unfortunate. Oh, well. No great tragedy. How are you doing?"

I told him about my latest encounter with Andrew McKay.

"What a wanker," said Nathan. "God, I can't stand that jerk."

The words warmed me. Someone on my side. "Well, I guess I'd better get back at it," I said, checking my watch. It was five minutes past my allotted break time.

"Yeah, me, too," said Nathan. "Unless you want to sing me something first?"

He always asked me this. And I always refused. It was a little game. A friendly joke.

I went inside and retrieved my cart. "See you Monday," I said.

"See you," he said, moving in the opposite direction down the hallway.

Little did I know that Nathan would never see me again. Not that version of me, anyway.

4

As I cleaned my way through the fourth and final floor, I found myself thinking about Nathan. One thing I liked about him was that he never tried to feed me any bullshit line about quitting my scrub job to pursue a singing career. He knew I had a good voice, good enough and then some, but he also knew what was what in the modern-day music world, a world where the Visual had completely, astonishingly, overtaken the Audio. Okay, you're thinking: Big deal, so Nathan knew that the business of selling music had become absurdly shallow. So what? We all know that it's not about how you sound; it's about how you look in the video. Thanks to the miracle of audio technology, everybody and their grandma can sound good. But not everyone can look good. Not everyone can make a teenybopper swoon, or give a million guys a million hard-ons. Of course, there were always pretty people in the music biz, but I think there used to be more room for the less-than-gorgeous. There used to be room for Geddy Lee's schnoz and Joey Ramone's teeth. No one cared if the "Velvet Fog" was short and pudgy or if Janis Joplin had bags under her squinty eyes. The ratio was more sane. For every Jim Morrison, there was a Van Morrison. For every shimmying Tom Jones, there was a simian Tom Waits. For every perky Olivia Newton-John, there was a paunchy Dr. John or a pug-nosed Elton John. For every extraordinarily enhanced Janet Jackson, there was an average and ordinary Joe Jackson. Now it's *NSYNC and Shania Twain, Lil' Kim and Christina Aguilera. Now it's All Saints and Britney Spears and Destiny's Child and the Backstreet Boys. And it's not just MTV. Check out the CD covers of up-and-coming classical musicians. You'll find dewy-eyed young women with flowing backlit tresses and their tits bulging out of their satin gowns. You'll find "babes" who sing medieval songs. So what? So everyone knows this. Fine. I agree that it wasn't such a big deal that Nathan knew what was what. But most people would've played dumb and fed me a line. "Ooh, with a voice like that, you should be filling stadiums, not emptying trash cans, Allison. You should go try out for *American Idol.*" Nathan was too honest and respectful to feed me any ostensibly well-meaning horseshit. He never encouraged me to go be the token ugly girl who makes it almost all the way through *Popstars.*

Unfortunately, I had learned my lesson the pathetic way, trying out for every band imaginable when I dropped out of school. I remember regularly buying all the daily newspapers, as well as picking up the weekly alternative mags to check the "Musicians Wanted" classifieds. Vocalist Needed for Blues/Rock Group, Vocalist Wanted for Heavy Melodic Band, Retro 80s Electro Seeks Vocals, Female Singer for All-Original Progressive Moody, Voc. Required for Country-

Flavored Folk Band, Singer for Funk/Post-Pop, All Girl Metal Band Seeks Front Vocals, Carnival Cruise Line Now Auditioning Singers, Dancers, Performers. I contacted them all indiscriminately. If I sang over the phone or mailed my demo cassette (recorded a cappella in my bathroom), they always wanted to see me. Of course, once they saw me, I was finished. Suddenly my voice wasn't "quite right" and it was: *Thanks for coming, we'll keep you in mind, best of luck to you.*

The only singing gig I was able to score was as a KJ, a karaoke host, in the sleazy lounge at the Gladwell Hotel—a faded-glory, Victorian behemoth where rooms went for twenty-five dollars a night; sheets changed weekly. Aside from operating the karaoke equipment and announcing the ten-cent chicken wing specials, my job was to warm up the crowd by belting out a song or three early on in the evening while people lubricated themselves sufficiently with plastic-pitcher draught, or whenever there was a lull. There was rarely a lull. The Gladwell attracted a band of regulars who needed little prompting to emblazon the stage. Most of them were over the age of fifty, and hailed from the subsidized housing slum southwest of the Gladwell. All of them seemed beaten down and broken by life. Until they started singing. Then they were magic. Each of the hardcores had their own signature song. There was Doreen, a Shirley MacLaine look-alike, who pranced perky around the stage, in Stetson and fringed cowgirl outfit, trilling "Back in Baby's Arms." There was Little Kate, a six-footer on a motorized scooter, her withered legs held vertical by soiled white go-go boots, doing "To Sir, with Love." And my personal favorite: Edgar Whittle, a tattooed octogenarian with a nicotine-stained ducktail, and the biggest, most dazzling dentures I'd ever laid eyes on. He would move himself (and me) to tears every time he crooned "Stand by Your Man" in a voice that, at one time, must have rivaled Tammy Wynette's. It was beautiful. And tragic. I adored the whole scene.

Unfortunately, I had no choice but to turn in my mic. I just could not handle the smoke. There wasn't one Gladwell regular who didn't suck up a pack per night, and by last call, I was barely able to breathe, let alone send the folks off with a wheeze-free rendition of "Goodnight My Someone."

I tried not to think about singing or Nathan as I headed for the last stop on my cleaning journey: IZ Talent Management. A misnomer if you asked me. It wasn't talent that was being managed, but genetic fortuity. I unlocked the vast double doors and rolled on in. Usually I only had to contend with myriad photos of perfect-looking people, lining every wall, and myriad photos of slightly less-than-perfect people smiling up from the garbage cans where they had been unceremoniously stuffed. That was Monday to Thursday. On Friday nights, it was far more annoying. On Friday nights, the co-owner, Peter Igel, would hang around and hold late-night confabs in his lavish corner office. Peter Igel looked to be in his late forties or early fifties. He had lank blond hair and a ruddy, borderline rosacea, complexion. He was fit, trim, and expensively dressed—so well dressed that, initially, I assumed he was gay. I soon discovered otherwise. It was either my second or third Friday on the job when I rolled my cart past his glassed-in office and saw him clawing the clothes off of a Naomi Campbell look-alike. The Friday after that, I caught him in a lip lock with a bony brunette. A week later, I actually witnessed him being fellated by a Teutonic-looking blonde squatting muscularly on high heels. Either Igel was an exhibitionist or he considered me a nonentity. The blinds on his office were never drawn, and he rarely closed his door to shut in the sound.

At first I figured he was diddling his clients, making his way through the IZ Talent Management roster. But over time I discovered that Friday nights were when Peter Igel met with the models who didn't have a hope in hell of fitting the IZ

Talent Management bill. The ones who didn't have what it takes to make it in the big-time. In other words, the ones who would never be cash cows for Peter Igel, and were destined for Sears-Roebuck catalog pages. Powerless. Going nowhere. Ripe for a different kind of exploitation.

He was fiddling with one of them that night. I heard signs of it as soon as I entered the reception area—the faint jazz music emanating from the corner office, the far-off shriek-giggle of some beautiful, hungry creature laughing too hard at one of Peter Igel's jokes.

If she had known what I knew about Igel's dirty game, she would not be guffawing, that's for sure. Igel's method was to point out the girl's flaw and tell her why she absolutely shouldn't be on the high-class ID roster—perhaps she was a smidgen under five foot nine, or a little knock-kneed, maybe the torso was disproportionately long for the legs. He'd tell her that she should probably go downstairs to the Malcolm Anders Agency, a small shop on the first floor that dealt with C-level models. But then, just when the pretty eyes—perhaps a little too close set—were filling with tears, Igel would offer a whiff of hope, suggest that the girl in question just might be something special, the unusually stunning exception to the rule. "After all," I heard him say on at least five occasions, "Kate Moss is under five-eight." Yup. Peter Igel would dangle that carrot. Then he'd turn on the music, open the wine, and dangle something else in their hopeful, tear-streaked faces.

I once witnessed a lovely snaggle-toothed teen ask him if braces and cosmetic whitening were the way to make it into IZ Talent. He suggested that she have all her teeth knocked out and replaced with dentures. I have no doubt that she did it.

"The fact is, lips are still hot," I overheard him tell a gorgeous blonde with lips that didn't appear to have been punched repeatedly by George Foreman. I'm sure she ran out the next day to have them pumped full of ass fat. The following Friday, he told a gorgeous East Asian woman with a big poufy mouth: "Unfortunately, ethnic is out at the moment. Still, there's something about you. A certain quality . . ."

Essentially, he'd criticize and mislead them, screw them and dispose of them. When they came back, new and improved after alterations and enhancements, he wouldn't see them, speak to them, or even return their e-mails. I know all this because one Friday night, a postoperative redhead slipped past me through the door as I was letting myself in to clean. She charged down the hallway, into Peter Igel's office, and let him have it, right there in front of another redheaded wanna-be.

"Calm yourself," he kept saying as she screamed out the dollar values of her various surgical procedures. "Calm yourself."

"Fuck you! *You fucking pig!* You think you're gonna get away with this? Huh?! Well, you're not. You're not going to get away with this, you piece of shit!"

"Calm yourself," he said.

Of course he was going to get away with it. Peter Igel was too savvy to make any promises. Everything was voluntary. Everything was consensual.

"FUCK YOU!"

I heard something crash and shatter. I heard the other girl scream.

Another man in the same situation might have called the cops or tried to wrestle the rampaging redhead out of the office, but Peter Igel was too clever for that. He just sat there, telling her to calm herself, waiting for her to flame out and leave on her own accord. Eventually she stormed past me, her lovely face contorted with rage and covered in ugly pink blotches. Peter Igel followed a couple seconds later, presumably to make sure she had left the premises and to lock the doors behind her. He came upon me in the hallway, still tensed and listening. We locked eyes for a single sinister moment. It was as if he was waiting for, or challenging, me to say something. But I didn't say anything. I wasn't the say-something type.

"There's some broken glass in my office," he said softly with a nasty little smile. It was the first time he gave me that smile, but not the last. I caught it practically every Friday after that. Because Igel knew that I knew what he was up to.

On the night in question, I found Peter Igel seated behind his large desk when I rolled my cart up to his office. The jazz music was still playing, but the laughing girl was nowhere to be seen. I figured she had gone to the bathroom and it was safe to enter. But as I moved toward my target, avoiding eye contact, Igel suddenly lifted his small trash can and placed it on his desk. This was something new. What wasn't new was the stinking mess inside. Igel was the only one in the entire building who thought nothing of dumping unwrapped food into his unlined plastic receptacle (which meant I'd have to take it to the kitchen to wash it out). That night it was chili. I emptied it, took it to the kitchen to rinse, then returned and set it back down in the same spot on the desk. Peter Igel smiled. And something about the smile, and the way he had barely moved his torso when retrieving the trash can, made me suspect that the Evangelista wanna-be was down below, sucking on his noodle. Uch.

As I was leaving IZ Talent Management, the DeSouza twins were on their way in with brooms and dusters to finish the job. A barely perceptible nod from Abril as we passed each other in the reception area. Nothing from Alvaro. I proceeded downstairs to empty my cart and wait for a ride home plus my weekly cash payment of two hundred dollars.

It was a nice night, so I went outside to wait. My work was done and I was ready to go home and veg in front of the tube. I leaned against the van and stared across the street at Ochre, where the night was just beginning for a bevy of spruced-up teens and twenty-somethings lining up to get into the trendy club. An electro-pop dance beat spilled onto the street. Two grim-looking musclemen were guarding the massive brown leather entrance doors. Nobody seemed to be going in or out.

Ochre was one of my father's clubs. That is, he designed it and owned a fifty percent share. There had been an article about it in the Style section of the newspaper before the thing even opened. My roommate at the time, Elda, had read it and was eager to check it out. Elda was quite the club girl. She used to go dancing every Friday and Saturday night, sometimes Thursdays as well. When I told her that the man in the article was my father, she almost passed a brick.

"Oh, my God!" she said, jumping out of her chair and bouncing up and down on the spot. "That means we can get into the invitation-only opening night party!"

"No, it doesn't. I don't have an invite and, trust me, I'm not likely to receive one."

"Well, can't you just call him and ask for one?"

"I don't even have his number. He doesn't even live here."

"What do you mean, you don't have his number? He's your flippin' father."

I explained that I hadn't seen or even spoken to my adopted dad since I was five years old.

"Oh," said Miss Sensitive, mulling this over. "Well, can't you, like, get his number from your mom?"

"Are you kidding? She gets enraged if I even mention his existence."

"Well, couldn't you just call his office? I mean, if I found out the number, you could call, right?"

Right. I had tried it on three separate occasions over the years. Ages thirteen, fifteen, and sixteen. What I wanted, I suppose, was to get his side of the story and possibly reconnect in some way. I would let him know that I wasn't bitter about him leaving, and that I agreed that my mother was eminently leavable. I would tell him that I understood his anger over losing custody and remind him that I was old enough now to choose whom to be with. I would tell him that I wasn't upset about him not staying in contact while I was growing up, but that I would welcome the opportunity for us to get to know each other now, as adults. I called on three separate occasions over the years. Each time I got a secretary or assistant taking a message, followed by a three-week period of wondering if he ever received it.

"I could call," I said, "but why would I? I don't want to go."

"Oh, my God," said Elda. "How could you not want to go?!"

Easy. In the first place, I had no desire to attend a dance party. Second, if I was going to finally gain access to my father, I didn't want it to be in a nightclub teeming with trendies.

Nevertheless, after several days of unrelenting pestering, I finally agreed to try to wrangle an invitation for Elda, mostly to get her off my back but also because she was one of the few people in the world who treated me decently. Also, I hate to admit, it gave me an excuse to once again place a call to my father's office. It would have been too humiliating to phone again, out of the blue. This time I had a bona fide pretext to get in touch with him.

"He's out of town," said the secretary, "but he'll be calling in for messages. Is there someone else who can assist you?"

"Um . . . no, it's personal."

"Oh, I see," said the female on the other end, and I got the distinct impression that she was more interested than the situation warranted. "Can I take your name and number and have him get back to you?"

I gave her the info. He never called me back. I told Elda to forget about it, but she wouldn't let it go.

"You should call him again," she said. "He probably didn't get the message."

I had wondered about that. Something about the secretary's tone. "You're the one who's not getting the message," I said, knowing it was useless to call again.

Elda huffed off to her room, and I figured that was that. But on the night of the opening, she was all restless and agitated, more determined than ever to attend the party.

"Let's just go down there," she said. "I'm sure we'll be able to wheedle our way in."

"I wouldn't be so sure."

"Oh, come on, Al," said Elda with a pleady expression. "We'll take a cab. I'll pay. And if we can't get in, I'll take you out for Amato's pizza."

"It's just another stupid club," I said. "Why do you want to get in so badly?"

"Because it's *exclusive*. Because only the *coolest* people are going to be let in tonight. Because I might finally meet someone. . . ."

This was before fat but pretty Elda met her first real boyfriend and left me in a rental lurch.

"Please, Allison? C'mon. Don't you wanna see your dad? I'm sure he wants to see you. He'll probably let us into the VIP room! Come on. Pretty please with a cherry on top?"

"Fine," I said. "Whatever." I had a flash of my father taking us on a private tour of the club, pointing out the unique design elements that he had dreamed up.

Elda ran off to her room to get ready. Several minutes later, she dashed back into the kitchen, wearing a miniskirt and a giant silver lamé bra. She was applying a deodorant stick to her massive underarms, rubbing fast and ferocious. "Don't you want to get changed?" she said.

"Nah." I feigned indifference, but in truth I was already wearing my least lousy outfit. Black jeans, black blouse, black Reeboks.

"We'll tell the doorman you're Simon's daughter," she said confidently. "He's not going to fuck with the daughter of the owner, right?"

Wrong. The beefy doormen were unimpressed.

"Step out of the way, please," said the big black one, herding us out of the path of the invitation-wielding beautiful people who were streaming in. A giant spotlight machine was set up on the sidewalk. I watched the beams of light crisscross in the sky.

"Do you value your job?" said Elda, refusing to give up.

"You're not on the list," said the bouncer. "There's nothing I can do about it."

"Yes, there is," said Elda. "There's something you'd better do about it or her father is going to be very pissed off."

A mild smile from the bouncer, who seemed to be enjoying the confrontation.

"Fine," said Elda. "If you don't want to take five minutes to go tell Simon she's here, that's your prerogative. But tomorrow, when he wants to know why she didn't show up, she's going to tell him that you were personally responsible for his darling daughter not getting in, and you know what's going to happen then? He's going to fire your ass."

A shadow of uncertainty flitted across the amused eyes of the bouncer. He covered with a weary smirk and a big theatrical sigh. Then he stepped up to the entrance and murmured something to another doorman—a Lou Ferrigno look-alike.

"What did you say your name was?" said Bouncer Guy.

Elda elbowed me in the side.

"Allison Penny," I said.

The Incredible Hulk slipped into the club. Bouncer Guy took his place at the door.

"We're in," said Elda. "I can feel it." She fished in her tiny handbag for lip gloss and applied a thick, slick coating.

We waited. At least twenty minutes. It was degrading, standing barred on the sidelines while the worthy and smug slipped by. I felt an anvil of dread in the belly, wondering if my father might come out to see if I was really at the door. It hardly seemed like the time or place for a family reunion. Would he think I was just using him to get into the party? Would he be pissed off that I was interrupting him on his big night? Would he emerge, take one look at me in my scuffed Reeboks, and then disappear back into the club? Elda was oblivious to my discomfort. She spent the wait scoping out guys on their way in, remarking upon which ones were "bad" or "hot." Finally the Incredible Hulk reappeared. Bouncer Guy gave him a questioning look. Hulk simply shrugged. Bouncer Guy flashed us a satisfied smile and crossed his arms over his chest.

"Asshole," hissed Elda, clicking high-heeled down the street.

I'm fairly certain she was referring to the man at the door.

I wasn't all that tired when the DeSouzas dropped me off, but since Virginie and Fraser were in the living room watching *Blind Date,* I went straight to my room, got undressed, and crawled into bed. I read the newspaper until I couldn't take it anymore, then I turned out the light and just lay there.

The newspaper always deepened my depression. Still, I read it daily. I felt I should try to keep abreast of world matters, even if I was unable to take them in and remain impassive. All the tragic tales, all the strife and disaster—it was astonishing how much bad and sad news could be crammed into a fistful of daily pages. I couldn't help but feel doleful. It occurred to me that perhaps our hearts and minds hadn't evolved as fast as information technology and globalization, that maybe our Stone Age brains were designed to deal only with local levels of despair, and simply didn't have the capacity to take in worldwide quantities of gloom. Or possibly I was just too thin-skinned. News from the big hot spots always distressed me—the Congo, Colombia, Sierra Leone, Afghanistan, the Middle East—especially the Middle East, but even small local reports could plunge me into full-throttle dejection. I remember the story that got to me that night. It was about a pharmacist who had been diluting chemotherapy drugs and merrily dispensing improper dosages. Cancer patients weren't getting what they needed to make them well, but this guy's profit margin was growing faster than a tumor. How cold. How evil. How depressing.

I started to think about those cancer patients and their families, which led me to wonder about all the heartache that didn't make it into newsprint. I began to think about all the horribly sad things that were happening somewhere in the world at that specific moment in time, at the very moment that I was lying there, safe in my bed, pondering it (a little game that often sprang up in my somber imagination). Somewhere, someone was being mangled in a car wreck, someone was having her third miscarriage, someone was OD'ing on heroin, someone's lungs were filling with water in the bottom of a drowning river, someone was dying of heart failure, someone was being beaten to death, someone was getting gang-raped, someone was watching his house and young children go up in flames, someone was being bitten by a deadly mosquito. All of those things were definitely happening somewhere in the world at that very moment. No wonder I felt an undercurrent of sad all the time.

I tried not to think about it. I started to think about something else that I generally tried not to think too much about. Nathan. I wondered how obvious it was that I had a crush on him. Probably painfully obvious, even though I did my best to conceal it. Nathan was always very friendly, but also very careful not to lead me on or make me think that we could be more than patio buddies at work. I suspected that if he hadn't sensed the crush, he would've welcomed me into his life as a pal—someone to see a movie with now and again. I figured he was afraid of offering me hope, afraid of intensifying my feelings. He probably wanted to avoid that moment when he'd have to pluck out my heart and Cuisinart it. Ultimately, I believed, he was just being kind.

Nathan wasn't shallow. I had no doubt that he would date a plain woman, even a plain woman with bad teeth or pimply skin—fat but pretty Elda, for example, would make the grade—but I was pushing the envelope of ugly. I do believe that a modicum of physical attraction is necessary. It isn't shallow to require that.

Oddly enough, even though he wasn't holding out for a Lara Croft look-alike, Nathan had been single since I'd met him, and, apparently, for quite a spell before that. On several occasions he had referred to his ex-girlfriend, Muriel. I once asked him when they had split up. He looked embarrassed as he told me that it had been "about six years ago."

I was surprised. Nathan was too clever and nice to have been single for six years or any years. There was absolutely no reason for him not to have a girlfriend.

That's not true. I suppose there was a reason. The reason was that the priorities of most females shifted after they left school. In school, people were concerned mainly with attractiveness levels. Remember how people consistently paired off according to how appealing they were? The gorgeous prom queen and the studly football player, the pretty girl with the braces and the cute guy with the pimples, the nerdy frump girl and the greasy-haired guy in flood pants. It was as if people had an innate ability to measure their own level of goodlookingness and then find someone on precisely the same plane. Someone in his or her own league.

If life were like school, Nathan would have had a moderately attractive girlfriend. But out in the real world, people don't couple up with their appearance-equals. In the real world, ugly but powerful men can get cute women. If the ugly, powerful men happen to be wealthy, they can easily attract the beauties. (And bully for them. It doesn't work in reverse. A fat woman with a Porsche is just a fat woman with a Porsche.) And if the powerful, wealthy men are also handsome, they can use up the pretty starlets like Kleenex.

Unfortunately for moderately attractive Nathan, most women would want him only if he came with a snazzy job or a fat bank account—or at least great expectations for bank account girth. They weren't terribly interested in a thirty-two-year-old video clerk/plant waterer who had no money, little ambition or future earning potential, who dwelled in an atomic bachelor apartment in a horrible high-rise on the sorry side of town, and who possessed a strangely shaped head.

I was interested, but it was of no consequence. I remember thinking: If only Nathan were uglier, disfigured in some way—missing a limb or two, maybe afflicted with a harelip or a hideous full-body skin condition. Chronic eczema. Acute psoriasis! Like the Singing Detective (only not in pain and not hospitalized). Some rudely stamped combination that would sink him down into my league—not even the little leagues, more like twenty thousand leagues under the sea.

I reproached myself for mulling it over. *Quit it, idiot. Abandon hope. And for fuck's sake, stop feeling sorry for yourself. There are worse things than being alone. Are there not worse things than being alone? You have freedom. Food. Shelter. No tanks rumbling down your streets. No burqua. Think of how lucky, tucked safe in your bed as calamity rains down on the world, tragedy, torment, disease, famine, drought, war, terror . . .* My brain churned with the misery of the masses and mine. Shortly thereafter I drifted into my usual uneasy and fitful sleep.

How funny to reflect back on the thoughts that filled my head that night—typical lying-in-bed thoughts after a typical day in the life of Allison Penny. It was my last night as me, but I didn't know it.

If only I had known.

After

1

Something was amiss. I felt it even before surfacing into consciousness. Though my eyes remained shut, my body was slowly gaining awareness, like a lens bringing something gradually into focus. As I emerged from the muck of sleep, I sensed a peculiar lightness about myself. I sensed *length.* My hand moved instinctively to my belly, to cradle the warm swell of flab, but my hand found a vast absence instead, a taut flatness. One nanosecond of total incomprehension followed by a powerful blast of fear and adrenaline. I flung back the duvet and gawked at my body. *Not my body!* A new body. *Not mine!* A completely foreign form. I sprang from bed and stood on the alien legs. I clutched at the flesh. It was real. *Not a dream!* This body contained me. My disoriented brain wasn't able to process the nonsensical information. Catecholamines spewed from my nerves into my throbbing heart. I blacked out.

When I came to, I went through a similar though marginally less horrifying series of shocks, gawks, and realizations. This time I didn't faint. Instead, I rushed to my bedroom window. It was morning. The sky was blue (not crimson or green, or filled with spaceships). My next-door neighbor, Mrs. Silva, was in her backyard, calmly watering her recently planted vegetable garden. Her daughter, Debbie, was seated at the picnic table, playing with Barbie dolls. Everything seemed normal. Apparently, only I had changed.

My heart was still going like Buddy Rich on a mad timpani, but my breath was beginning to slow and even out a little. Tentatively, I tried the voice. "Hello," I said softly. *Not my voice!* A different voice. A powerful shiver fizzed through my body. *Not my body.* I sank down onto the edge of the futon and took several deep breaths—in through the nose, out through the mouth. After several frightening minutes, I regained a scrap of composure.

With slender, alien fingers I picked up and examined a lock of glossy blond hair that hung heavy and cascaded over my breasts. I pulled on the strand and felt a corresponding tug at my scalp. *Bizarre.* I touched my face with my hands. It felt small, smooth, and elegantly contoured, not like my face at all—a most peculiar sensation, a strange braille. I could feel prominent cheekbones sitting high under silky skin.

What I needed at once was a mirror. But there weren't any mirrors in my bedroom. I tried the window to no avail. The angle of the light outside prevented reflection; all I could get was a ghostly head shape with indiscernible features. I searched the room for reflective objects but couldn't find anything. Where were all the giant belt buckles, patent-leather shoes, or handbags when you needed them? My purse was canvas, all my non-running shoes were suede. I didn't own a belt. The face on the alarm clock was dull plastic, scratched to rat shit, and useless for my purpose. The furniture was black Ikea—matte finish, dead melamine. *Did I possess nothing that shined?* Afraid to leave my room, but desperate to get a glimpse of my face, I emptied a yogurt container of Laundromat quarters onto the dresser, pushed the coins together, and hovered over them. No good. The diffused image was hopelessly soft and, of course, broken by the spaces between the quarters. I could barely make out an eye. It seemed that I would have to go to the bathroom. In the bathroom there were plenty of mirrors—a narrow three-quarter-length one on the inside of the door, a big one on the front of the medicine cabinet, and a silver antique hand mirror that Virginie used to check the back of her hairdos.

I would risk it. I had to pee anyway.

I put on my robe—a strange feeling since it was now ridiculously short and about ten sizes too big for me. I cracked my bedroom door half an inch and listened. I knew that Virginie's TV show was on hiatus, and I was fairly certain that Fraser was between film gigs. Typically, they were early risers, but occasionally on the weekend they slept late. Had they gone out or were they still in Virginie's room? There were no signs or sounds to confirm either scenario. It was 9:40 A.M.

I stole to the bathroom and locked the door. With eyes downcast, I stepped back from the three-quarter-length mirror, loosened my robe, and let it slip to the floor. Then I lifted my head and looked.

Oh, my God.

I will never forget that moment, the moment that I saw me in my entirety for the first time. It was beyond magical. Beyond wondrous. It was the truest, most essential moment of my life. All panic had flown, replaced by a feeling of profound relief. An exquisite joy, a supernatural happiness flooded through my perfect body.

It wasn't merely because of the staggering beauty I saw reflected in the mirror. It was more than that. Ever since I was a child, I had sensed something powerful and mysterious swirling behind the flat screen of reality. As I grew older and more rational, I convinced myself that the source of that feeling was psychological, a juvenile projection born out of the need for love—all-encompassing, unconditional God/Mommy/Daddy love. Clearly, nothing of the sort existed. There was no God. The evidence was everywhere and easy to interpret. Think Hitler. Think Stalin. Just consider the number of innocents starved or slaughtered in the last century alone. Only a fool could believe that there was a benevolent deity keeping a grand eyeball on the human race.

Yes, that's what I told myself as I grew older and more rational. And I wanted to believe it. But in truth, I continued to sense that unknowable force, to feel a special connection to the mysterious miasma that seemed to lurk behind everything. Occasionally, I would feel, in the pit of my stomach, that I had caught a glimpse of that strange energy—in the frenetic movement of butterfly wings, in the similar movement of pinpoints of sunlight sparkling crazy on lake water. I thought I saw the shadow of it in a birch tree once—the way the wind and the light played on the leaves, the crown seemed to be shimmering and buzzing an electric otherworldly message. I thought I recognized it in art, in the splatter energy of Pollock patterns. And in music, in the architecture of certain compositions, and the way in which certain musicians performed. Like Glenn Gould at the piano, playing as if he were, in fact, the instrument, as if the unknowable thing was flowing through him. Not performing so much as *channeling*.

And so at that moment, as I gazed upon my miraculous transformation, my childish suspicion was finally, undeniably confirmed. There was something out there. I was not alone. God or some equivalent power existed in the universe. And I, Allison Penny, had been blessed!

A sharp rattling of the bathroom doorknob interrupted my religious reverie.

"You in there?" said Virginie.

Sort of is what leaped to mind. Hesitant to answer in the alien voice, I flushed the toilet in response. I heard Virginie groan and move off. I sat down to quickly empty my bladder. It was an odd sensation, a familiar pose, but an entirely new bearing. My thighs no longer met in the middle or bulged over the sides of the seat. My stomach was now totally flat, and for the first time in memory I could watch myself urinate. I'm not ashamed to say that it was a lovely sight. My vagina was a tight little cleft fringed with soft curls. I dried it tenderly and donned my robe. Then I pinched Virginie's antique hand mirror and was making a quick dash through the kitchen to my room, when I heard a voice behind me: "Hello?"

I had been spotted, but I didn't stop. I ducked into my room and closed the door, hoping that Virginie would just proceed to the damned bathroom and leave me the hell alone. But no, a second later she was tapping at my door with her fingernails. *Tap tap tap.*

"Just a minute . . ." I hid her mirror under the blanket, gathered my wits, and opened up. I stood in the doorway so she wouldn't come in. "Hi," I said, going on the offensive. "You must be Virginie."

"Who are you?" she said.

"Me? I'm a friend of Allison's."

She looked confused. Could Allison have a friend? Perhaps. But such a beautiful friend? Doubtful. "Where is Allison?" she asked, peering past me into the bedroom.

"Um, she's not here," I said, trying not to smirk. It felt strange to be talking about myself in the third person. "She had to go away for a few days. She said I could stay here while she's gone."

"Oh, really?"

"Is that a problem?"

"I don't know. This is the first I've heard of it."

"Well, she had to leave kind of suddenly. Early this morning. Her father's been having some medical trouble. Heart trouble. She had to fly to Los Angeles."

"Her father lives in Los Angeles?"

"Didn't you know that?" The stupid cow never listened to a word I said. Fine. It would be easier to fake her out.

"I can't remember. So you got here when?"

"Middle of the night, actually. My plane was delayed for six hours. What a nightmare. And then as soon as I get here, I find out that Allison has to leave. Oh, well, I guess I'll see her when she gets back. She's great, isn't she?" I couldn't resist tossing that one in there.

"Yeah. Um, how do you know her again?"

"We were best friends growing up. She must have mentioned that I was coming." It felt odd to be looking down on Virginie. She seemed stubby all of a sudden.

"I dunno. Maybe she did. I haven't had coffee yet." She rubbed her eyes and forehead. It was all too much for her.

"Anyway, I'm glad we didn't wake you with all our nocturnal arriving and departing."

"Mmm. Did she leave a number where she's going to be?"

"No. But she said she'd call as soon as she got settled." I had no idea how I was going to get around that one, but I just wanted her out of my face. It worked.

"I have to use the bathroom," she said, slinking off through the kitchen.

I closed the door.

For the next half hour, I used Virginie's hand mirror to familiarize myself with my astonishing features. If only I could show, rather than tell, you what I looked like. Mere language doesn't seem suited to the task. Beauty, true beauty, is difficult to convey accurately with words. If I say that a woman has brown hair, large eyes under heavy brows, pale skin, high cheekbones, and a sweet full-lipped smile, do you get the real picture? If I tell you that her neck is long and graceful and that she exudes charm, do you necessarily see the unique loveliness that is Audrey Hepburn? No. Thousands of women possess similar features and would match that description, and while all of those women may be pleasing to the eye, only one might emanate a true, transcendental beauty. It isn't the individual features; it's the magical way in which they all fit, or don't quite fit, together, true beauty being slightly unconventional. And so, while it is impossible to do it justice with words, I will attempt to describe what I saw that morning.

My height was approximately five-nine. My body was long, lithe, and graceful. There was an unmistakable refinement to my posture, owing in part to my slender neck, which had seemingly doubled in length overnight. It gave me a certain Paltrow-like poise, but at the same time I was quite voluptuous. Although my figure was slim, my breasts were large, perfectly symmetrical, and absurdly gravity defying. My ass was plump, round, and just slightly too prominent. The legs were well-shaped and long, as were the arms. The feet were narrow and high arched. The hands, soft with pleasingly tapered fingers. All of my flesh was delightfully firm and springy to the touch. The skin was blemish-free and had a healthy-looking tone—the kind that turns golden in the sun. My face was truly lovely. Heart-shaped with extraordinarily large eyes of a deep blue color, emphasized by a black ring encircling each iris, which gave them a catlike intensity. The nose was straight and fine, with haughty nostrils. The mouth was unusual, both broad and full. A Cupid's bow on the upper lip gave it a perpetual pout, but when I smiled, the corners stretched wide and curled up mischievously—like the Joker on the old *Batman* TV series, only attractive. The teeth were white and evenly spaced, the upper two front ones being just the tiniest bit buck. The tongue was pink and smooth. My hair, Nordic blond, hung heavy and straight and reached halfway down the back. I tucked it behind my tiny, perfect ears and tried a smile in the mirror.

God, I was beautiful! *But how long would it last?* With a jolt, it occurred to me that this might be some kind of Cinderella story, that I might turn back into pumpkin Allison at the stroke of midnight. I couldn't waste the gift hiding in my room. I had to get out there and enjoy it.

Through my closed door I heard Virginie and Fraser puttering in the kitchen. I could smell cigarette smoke, but no coffee. If they hadn't made coffee yet, it meant they were heading out soon. Good.

I pulled open my underwear drawer and fished through the grim garments—a limp pile of dead elastic and threadbare cotton in various shades of washed-to-oblivion black. I pulled on a pair of my so-called Jockey briefs. They were laughably large and plunged comically to the floor the instant I let go of them. Inspired, I decided to root through my blue-jean archives.

In the back of my closet, in a dusty cardboard box, there lived close to a decade's worth of favorite jeans that I had grown too big for. When I turned twenty, I had abandoned the sad practice, but beginning at the age of eleven and all through my teens, when a pair of pants became too gut-sucking for my steadily increasing girth, I would purchase a pair of "fat jeans" to wear temporarily while I dieted my way back into the "thin" pair. Of course, the new "fat jeans" inevitably became the old "thin" pair, and the stupidly hopeful blue-jean archive was born. I wrestled the box out of the closet and popped the top. The too-tight Lees and Levi's were folded and stacked in order of waist size, largest on top, smallest at the bottom. It was an interesting archaeology, the waistbands like tree rings charting my slow growth. At the very depths of the box, I found a musty pair of acid-washed straight-legs that I had last worn when I was around twelve years old. Size eight. They looked tiny to my eye, but when I tried them on, they were delightfully huge and hilariously short. The weird thing is, they actually looked good on me. If I'd owned a belt, I could have gone for the cutesy skinny-girl-in-the-ill-fitting-jeans look.

"Ready?" I heard Virginie call out to Fraser.

"Coming," he said. Clunky man-steps down the hall, followed by the front door closing hard. Silence. I was alone. Emboldened by my transformation, I decided to go where I had never gone before: into Virginie's lair to borrow some duds.

Though the window was propped wide open, the room smelled unfresh—a heavy mixture of jasmine oil, settled smoke, and sex. The frameless futon was unmade and there were piles of clothes everywhere. On the floor, millimeters from the twisted duvet cover, sat several pillar candles, a bunch of matchbooks, and a massive butt-filled ashtray that also contained two yellowing condoms full of sperm, one tied closed at the top, the other spilling seed into ash. Also on the floor was a small lamp with a vintage silk scarf draped over it—a dark brown circle on the top of the fabric showed where the lightbulb had scorched it. The place was a freakin' fire trap. Blobs of colored candle wax had dripped down and stained the hardwood floor. There were numerous cigarette burns on the sheets and pillowcases. Cripes, I thought, how many times has she nearly torched the joint? Could a roommate get any worse? I shuddered and made my way to her underwear drawer. I had to root through a tangled mound of thongs before I found something that hadn't been wedged firmly in Virginie's ass crack. I chose an ordinary pair of white bikini panties that looked clean and passed the sniff test. I was jamming them in my robe pocket when I heard the front door open. *Shit!* In a flash, my brain processed the fact that they would undoubtedly see me if I bolted into the hall, and there was no closet in which to hide. So I went out the window, sliding hands first into the cement laneway between houses. I landed at the feet of Mrs. Silva, who was cranking her garden hose back onto its holder.

"Hi," I said stupidly, getting up and brushing my palms on my robe. She frowned and made for her backyard, pulling the gate shut behind her.

I moved to the front of the house and peeked around. Fraser was waiting on the porch, staring dumbly at nothing, tugging on his goatee. A moment later, Virginie emerged from the house.

"Got 'em?" he said.

"Yeah, let's go."

They'd forgotten something. Cigarettes or sunglasses. I waited until they were halfway down the street, then tried the front door. Locked. I had to hoist myself back through the window to continue scavenging.

As I was rifling through Virginie's vast collection of bras—everything from frilly push-ups to sporty cotton contraptions—I came across a small stack of photographs. The top one was of Fraser in boxer shorts, stretched out on the futon. He was grinning goofily, and his eyes had been caught in mid-blink. He looked subnormal. The next one was of Virginie in her tartan jumper, sitting cross-legged on a kitchen chair with her panties showing and her head cocked to one side, trying to be cute. The camera flash had turned her eyes into fiery red dots, which made her look like some kind of demonic Scottish imp. I flipped quickly through a series of shots taken outside at a downtown sculpture garden—Virginie clambering and posing cute all over a herd of Joe Fafard's bronze cows. I stopped abruptly when I came across a photograph of me. There were two actually, both dark and slightly out of focus, taken without a flash, I suppose. I might not have even recognized myself if it hadn't been for the familiar clothing/furniture. The first one was a full-length shot of me on the living-room couch. I must have fallen asleep watching TV. I was on my side and my mouth was hanging open. My sweatshirt had ridden up, exposing part of my gut, which drooped down and pooled on the sofa cushion. It was horrible. Humiliating. Obviously, a great source of hilarity for Virginie and Fraser. I felt my face blaze hot with shame and anger as I surveyed the second shot and imagined them trying not to laugh as they tiptoed nearer to snap the fuzzy, close-up view of my belly.

I buried the photos back where I found them and thrust the drawer shut. I didn't *need* a bra anyway. Fuck it. I rummaged through the remaining drawers, selecting a plain white T-shirt and the smallest, most indistinctive blue jeans I could find—I didn't want the bitch to recognize the ensemble if I happened to pass her on the street. Finally, I snatched a pair of ancient Converse sneakers. My feet were much narrower than before, but also far longer, and I could see that there was no way in hell any of my shoes would fit me. Even Virginie's looked on the small side. I figured the worn-out canvas ones would have more give. I ducked into the bathroom and dressed quickly.

All of my bad feelings about the sofa photos vanished in an instant. God, I looked great! Jeans, T-shirt, a stinky old pair of basketball shoes, and I looked totally hot. Like a real sexpot, I'm not kidding. It was bizarre. Downright porno. I was actually making *myself* horny. I brushed my gorgeous hair, dabbed a little Pretty in Pink lipstick on my pouty mouth, and after striking a dozen or so cutesy *Playboy* poses, tore myself away from the mirror's magnetic pull. I fished out some cash and a credit card, then hid my purse deep in the closet. It was best not to be seen toting it around, since it was "Allison's" and she was in Los Angeles.

There were several things I noticed as I walked down my street. First, how swiftly and effortlessly I could move—again that feeling of lightness and length. Second, that Virginie's shoes were definitely too small for my new feet. And third, that everybody seemed to be gawking at me. Nuno Benitah actually smiled, nodded, and made a lewd sucking noise with his mouth.

I noticed something else, too. Not only did I look different, but I also saw differently. The extra six inches or so of height had skewed my perspective and made everything appear slightly unusual and fresh. Also, I used to catch a bit of my potato nose in my peripheral vision. No more. My line of sight was suddenly unobstructed. For the first time ever, I could see clearly.

2

Horns. Men were sounding their horns. No fewer than three appreciative and zesty honks from passing cars in the ten minutes it took me to reach the local Second Cup. Feeling festive and frivolous—never before had I been honked at—I skipped my usual black java and ordered a jumbo cappuccino. The teenage cashier, an albino version of Ichabod Crane, glanced furtively at my boobs, blushed flamingo pink, and fumbled my change all over the counter.

"Oops, sorry 'bout that, heh, heh, heh. . . ." Ichabod scooped up the misbehaving coins, smiled (bashfully!), and handed them over. He had never smiled at me before. A cold albino stare is what I usually got. Ichabod's comrade in coffee—a plump and dour-looking young woman—set my drink on the counter. "Chocolate?" asked Ichabod, brandishing the shaker.

"Yes, please."

With a brisk flourish, he caved in the left side of the foam dome with a generous helping of cocoa. "Cinnamon?" he asked, holding up the shaker like a happy housewife in a 1950s magazine ad.

"Sure."

"Have a great day," said Ichabod, proudly presenting my cappuccino to me.

"Thanks."

"Lids and napkins over there." He extended a bony arm in the direction of the coffee station.

So helpful was Ichabod, so very attentive all of a sudden.

I went to the patio and drank my coffee. It was deliciously warm and sweet in my mouth. The sun was shining all over me, and the caffeine was kicking in. I felt good. Good, good, good. Every few seconds, I'd peek at my reflection in the plate glass window of the café. My hair was gleaming yellow in the light, my body poised and feline. I looked like a Northern Italian starlet on a coffee break, or Bridget Bardot relaxing between shots. Casual-glam. Effortlessly gorgeous.

I pondered what to do with my happy Saturday. Usually, I'd be dragging my duds to the Laundromat, cleaning up the apartment, or going for a Discman walk in the cemetery. Or else I'd be buying dull provisions like toilet paper and margarine, or getting some books from the library, maybe renting a couple of movies. Movies. Yes. I could go check out Nathan in his natural habitat, behind the counter at Art & Trash, something I had long wanted to do, but really had no excuse for, since the video store was way the hell and gone in the West End, and there'd be no reason for me to be there unless it was to see him. I finished my java and set out.

It was too nice outside to descend immediately to the subway, so I decided to walk for a while. I wanted to enjoy the feeling of moving brisk and lively in the sun without getting heat-bogged and sweat-sodden. A mile was but a few springy steps. My energy was buzzing high, my spirits were glad-happy, like white sails snapping in a blue-sky breeze. I felt confident and fresh, like the dementedly cheerful young women in tampon commercials. I bought an ice-cream cone for breakfast—big pink in a waffle cone. No remonstrative glances as I strolled and slurped sloppy down the street, strawberry all over my mouth and chin and fingers. Just the opposite, actually—what I got were amused, isn't-that-adorable looks from almost everyone I passed. And when I reached an intersection and paused at a red light, a rotund construction worker, sitting astride a low steel girder, eating lunch, shouted, "Looks tasty, baby." And his sunburned coworker added, "Lucky ice cream." And still another coworker—a studly guy in a sleeveless sweatshirt and tight jeans—called out, "Can I have a lick?" I don't quite know what came over me; I knew I was supposed to scowl and move on, as I had seen other women do, but instead my mouth said, "Sure," then smiled up at Studly Guy, who had thick, hairy arms and was kind of hoodlum handsome.

Surprised laughter. Jovial goading. *Go get it, buddy! Can I have a lick, too?*

Studly Guy smiled smug, stood up tall and macho on the girder and said, "I wasn't talking about the ice cream, baby."

"Whew hoo!" said the sunburned coworker.

They waited for me to flip him the bird and move on, but after countless years of sexual deprivation, and the suspicion that my day of beauty might be just that, one precious day, I wasn't inclined to pass up an opportunity with such a hunky specimen. So I said, "I know." Then I dropped what was left of the cone into a garbage can and licked some strawberry off of my finger in what I suspected and hoped was a suggestive manner.

A chorus of shocked exclamations followed. Studly Guy

looked uncertain as to how to proceed. He remained planted on the girder, laughing, glancing at his buddies. I could see the bravado draining from his face and posture.

"Whattya waitin' for?" said Sunburn.

"Go for it," said Rotund, slapping him on the back. "You still got ten minutes."

"And that's all he'll need!" shouted Sunburn.

Studly Guy mustered a bit of bluster and climbed down to ground level. "What is this, *Candid Camera*?" he said, guffawing, but he looked a little stressed.

I found the entrance in the wooden hoarding and advanced toward him. I was feeling quite randy, and for the first time in my life, sexually bold. Still, I didn't quite know what to do when I reached him. I couldn't just start molesting the guy in front of everyone. I ended up poking him in the belly with my finger—don't ask me why. His stomach felt hard and muscular.

"Let's go in there," I said, gesturing to a makeshift office, essentially a plywood shack, in the far corner of the lot.

"You're kidding me, right?" said Studly.

"Come on, let's just go." I started moving toward the shack.

As Studly Guy followed, he called out over his shoulder to his buddies still laughing and watching from their steel perch: "If this is some kind of joke, you assholes are dead meat. Seriously."

An indiscernible reply from one of the other guys, as Studly and I stepped into the office and closed the rickety door.

"It's not a joke," I said.

"What are you, a working girl?"

"Me? No. I mean, I have a job, do you mean—"

" 'Cause I don't pay for it, you know. I got self-esteem."

I laughed. "Do I look like a hooker?"

"Nah. You look like one of them supermodels."

"You think?"

"Duh."

I moved closer. He had a good sweat smell (tomato soup camp). I kissed his left ear, his rough jaw. I went for his mouth, but it didn't kiss back.

"I could get canned for this," he said. "You're not even supposed to walk in here without a hard hat and boots. Plus, I have a wife."

"Do you have a condom?"

"Jesus, Miss. No. I don't have a condom. If you're so hot to trot, how come you don't have a condom?"

"Hey, you're the one who propositioned me. I was just walking along eating an ice cream, remember?"

"Yeah, well . . ."

"Isn't this what you wanted?"

"Sure," he said. But he didn't look sure. He opened the door a crack, peeked out, shut it again. "The thing is," he said, "I just got married, like, six months ago. And I just found out we're gonna have a baby."

"Congratulations," I said, peeling off my shirt.

A second later his mouth was on me. It felt amazing. And it looked fantastic. Totally porno. He was all hairy and grimy; I was all white and clean.

"Fuck, you're hot," he said.

He popped the button on his jeans and unzipped. I reached into his Stanfield's—threadbare/blue—and grabbed his boner. The second time I had held a penis in my hand. It was bigger than the other one. I squeezed it.

"I wanna fuck you," he said. "Can I? Are you on the Pill?"

"No," I said, wondering if my temporary body could get knocked up. It seemed unlikely. But the last thing I needed was to Revert back and have an unborn construction worker growing inside of me. "We'd better not."

He was breathing heavy and staring fierce under black eyebrows. "Let me fuck your tits," he said.

I wasn't entirely sure what he meant by that, but I had a feeling that it wasn't quite what I wanted, so I said, "No. Do what you said before."

"Fuck you?"

"No, the other thing. Remember? You asked if you could have a lick. . . ."

He undid my pants and yanked them down.

"Oh, baby," he said. He got down on his knees, and he did what I wanted. Down on his knees on the dirty plywood floor. He had one hand on my ass and the other hand on his cock. He made me come—my first non-masturbatory climax—and then two seconds later he jizzed on my left shoe. Virginie's shoe, actually.

As we were covering our parts and tidying up, he said, "Can I have your number? I wanna call you."

"I'm just in town for one day," I said, thinking about the new wife and zygote. "But that was very satisfying. Thank you."

"I'm not gonna forget this," he said.

"No, me neither."

Not likely that I'd forget my encounter with Studly Guy. Not a chance, really, since prior to the Big Change, my interactive sexual experiences had been countable on one hand. There was a kindergarten kiss from Nelson Rumack, who, fulfilling a recess dare, pushed me down onto hopscotch cement, stamped my cheek with a clamped mouth, then ran away squealing. There was my neighbor and baby-sitter Martin Standish, who watched over me when my mom went to the bar, and, under the guise of "tickling," used to grope and probe and hold me hard against his safely blue-jeaned boner (he usually waited until I had changed into my nightie before initiating the frantic, leg-kicking tickle sessions, and he always disappeared into the bathroom immediately after). I'm pretty sure I was in love with him. Just after his thirteenth birthday, Martin experienced an obscene growth spurt, which was accompanied by erratic facial hair, rampaging acne, and a sick sourdough odor. My mother hired a new baby-sitter. Her name was Melissa. She ignored me entirely and would spend the night simultaneously staring at the TV and talking on the phone. She and her boyfriend would blab or just listen to each other breathe while they watched *Married with Children* or *Full House* or *Cheers*. She didn't even hang up when she went to empty her bladder; she'd say, "Pee break," drop the receiver in the sofa cushions, and dash to the can. If I tried to speak to her, she'd give me a withering look and say, "I'm on the phone, Allison." Sometimes I'd go to my mom's room, pick up the extension and, with my hand clamped over the mouthpiece and the volume down low on the portable, watch what they were watching, and listen in on their conversation (a kind word for the blather that slunk back and forth along the phone lines). Melissa was obsessed with what her boyfriend thought of the various females on TV. A typical exchange:

"Do you think she's pretty?"

"Who, *her*?"

"No. God! The older one."

"Mallory?"

"Yeah. Justine Bateman."

"She's cute."

"Do you think she's hot?"

"I guess so."

"Hotter than Lisa Bonet?"

"I dunno."

"Well, which one would you rather go out with?"

"I dunno. Mallory, I guess. But they're both hot. The mom's pretty hot."

"Who, Elise?"

"Yeah."

"You think she's prettier than Mallory?"

"No."

"So Mallory's the prettiest?"

"I guess."

"Prettier than Christina Applegate?"

"No way. She's the hottest."

"Hotter than Blair on *Facts of Life*?"

"Ew, she's a pig."

"I thought you liked her?"

"No, I like that Alyssa chick on *Who's the Boss?*"

"You like her better than Christina Applegate?"

Blah, blah, blah. I don't know why I bothered eavesdropping. Something to pass the time, I guess. Still, I'm happy to say that I could never stand it for more than two half-hour sitcoms, and I was jubilant when Melissa got reprimanded and replaced after failing to notice that I had left the house while she was supposedly taking care of me. I had gone to the corner 7-Eleven to play video games, and had returned much later with a bag of Doritos and a jumbo Slurpee, to find the house dark, the doors locked, and my mother's car in the driveway. Home early. I rang the bell, but Mommy had obviously paid Melissa and fallen drunk into bed. Luckily, it was summertime and sticky hot outside. I semi-slept in the backyard and then rang again at daybreak. It took a lot of nonstop staccato on the bell before my mystified and hugely pissed-off mom flung the door open. I'm still not sure if she canned Melissa because I was out all night or because I woke her up in the middle of a hangover. Either way, I was hoping for the return of Martin the Tickler, but instead I got an endless stream of bitchy females. And zero sexual activity until I was fifteen.

Grade nine. It seemed as if almost every girl in school was getting some form of action. The beauties, of course, had as much or as little as they chose. Ditto the cute chicks and the sort-of-cute chicks. Even the orthodontisized, dog-faced girls with half-decent bodies were attracting their share of hormone-fueled attention when the nights had worn on and the lads had smoked enough pot, or dropped enough E, or consumed enough booze. It took all of these elements working in concert to convince Servan Carp that I was a temporarily acceptable canoodling partner. It occurred after a Friday-night Youth Center dance—a kind of sanitized faux-rave that was held weekly in the school cafeteria. Kids from grades seven, eight, and nine danced the night away—not to techno, mind you; it was mostly mainstream rap and disco remixes, but they waved their stupid glo-sticks around and sucked on their ridiculous pacifiers anyway. I didn't dance, wave, or suck. I gravitated toward the marginally cooler stoner kids who spent the greater part of those Friday nights in the ravine behind the school, getting drunk and high. At that point I was still managing to fit in with my class-clown shtick, and was allowed to orbit the group because I provided fat-girl comic relief, and almost always provided a reasonably full, forty-ouncer of booze, pinched from my mother's endless and carelessly monitored stash.

Servan Carp was new to the clique. A recent immigrant from Romania, Servan had been doing everything possible to instantly assimilate himself. Within days of arriving at Tom Thomson Junior High, he had shed his Soviet-looking sweaters and Zellers grandpa jeans and adopted the standard hip-hop costume—the bloated Nikes, the fat and fake gold necklaces, the Starter football jersey, the oversized, falling-down pants that made him look like a rodeo clown. Even in his hip-hop uniform, there was something inherently geeky and Romanian-villagey about Servan (he wouldn't have looked out of place with a few goats trailing behind him), and he was doing his best to overcome this by being a boisterous "party animal," consuming awe-inspiring quantities of alcohol and drugs in daring and dangerous combinations. Everyone called Servan by his last name, Carp, and he thrived on the endless jokes about him being "pissed to the gills" or "drinking like a fish."

There were initially six of us together in the woods that night. I remember that Servan had been demonstrating his hopelessly uncool, therefore amusing, therefore redeemably cool break-dancing moves precariously close to the edge of the steep and muddy embankment where we regularly assembled. There was much laughter and shouting, especially from Servan, who had taken E, smoked several joints, and swallowed most of the contents of a plastic soda bottle full of home-brewed Romanian hooch—palinka, I think he called it. The plan was to get sufficiently buzzed and then go inside for a while to check out the dance (i.e., stand on the sidelines and mock the dancers—my specialty), but when it became apparent that a couple swigs of the Carp family's combustible cocktail had rendered Rachel slack drunk and perhaps fully seducible, Leon dragged her off into the bushes. Thirty seconds later, Bonnie (Leon's ex) led Steve away to their own little woodland revenge session. That left Carp and me alone, awkward without an audience, uncomfortable in sudden silence. He tried to lighten the moment by signaling to the departed lovers, making loud jungle-animal noises: ooh-ooh-ah-ah monkey screech, lion roar, elephant blast.

"Shut the fuck up," came Leon's stern reply from deep in the woods.

Servan obeyed Leon. He laughed weakly. He made a barely audible monkey sound and took a long pull of palinka.

"Well, I guess we should go in," I said, noticing that Carp was looking pale and sweating heavy in the cool night.

"Yeah," he said. "I will just make a piss." He moved to the edge of the embankment, where minutes earlier he had been spinning acrobatically on his shoulder blades. I heard the zipper come down, I heard the arc of urine hitting soil, I heard Servan groan with relief. Then I heard twigs snapping, a strangulated cry, and a distant splash.

I moved quickly but cautiously to the edge—I was pretty tipsy myself—and, hanging on to a sapling, peered down into the blackness that had swallowed Carp.

"Hey," I said. "Are you—"

"I'm okay," he whispered, from deep in the darkness.

To be honest, that far-off and diminutive "I'm okay"

struck me as patently hilarious after the cartoonlike sound effects of his ill-fated pee 'n' plummet, but I realized that I was stoned, and unable to accurately judge the severity of the situation. I suppressed a powerful urge to laugh and listened for sounds of movement down below. There were none.

"Should I get help?" I said.

"No!" he hiss-whispered. "*Please.* I'm okay. Go away."

He was obviously embarrassed. And who wouldn't be after tumbling dick-first through one's own piss into a ravine? I listened for a few more seconds. Nothing. No sounds of getting up or dusting one's self off. This suggested seriousness. I decided to spare Servan the indignity of immediately calling on Leon or Steve for assistance. Instead, I sat my ass on the ground and inched/slid my way down the slope to the river—which was more like a stream actually, about three feet wide and maybe eight inches deep in the middle. Still, I figured even in his pre-plunge condition he could've easily passed out, and if he passed out facedown in the water . . . The headline CARP DROWNS flashed in my head.

"Hey, Carp, where are you?"

No response.

I saw his white Nikes first, sticking up like rocks in the river, the toxic water eddying around them. Luckily only his lower legs had gone in. He was stretched out diagonally on the damp bank. He had his arms folded over his chest like a corpse. As I got closer I could see that he had put his penis away and zipped up his muddy jeans. I could also see that his jersey—the one he wore to school almost every day—was irreparably torn, and that his face was scratched and bleeding.

"Carp," I said, kneeling beside him and nudging his shoulder.

He opened his eyes and smiled up at me. "I'm okay," he whispered. "I'll see you in there."

"Sit up. Come on . . ." I tried to help him, but he waved me off, then sat up abruptly.

"Yo," he said. "You want to smoke a fattie?" He patted his chest as if there were fattie-containing pockets there, but he had stripped off his jacket earlier in the evening. "Let's smoke a fattie."

"I don't think so. Get your feet out of there."

He looked at his feet as if he had just become aware of their existence. He pulled them out of the river and struggled to stand up. "Fuck," he said, staring at his sodden Nikes. "Fuck!" Though he had gone in only past the ankles, his voluminous pant legs had absorbed water to above the knee, and the weight of it was pulling his pants even farther down than usual, exposing most of his underwear. He stood there trickling. Skinny and pale. White Fruit Of The Looms glowing eerily in the moonlight.

"Are you all right?" I said.

He touched the scratch on his forehead and surveyed the warm blood in his palm. He examined his torn jersey. Then—with his shoes making squishy sucking sounds—he walked unsteadily to a large flat rock, hoisted up his jailin' trousers, and sat down. He covered his face with his hands and hunched over. I could see his shoulders begin to heave. At first I thought he was vomiting up the palinka, but he wasn't vomiting, he was crying. Silently. I sat next to him on the rock and put my hand on his back. The heaving increased. I rubbed softly in a circular motion on his upper back. Bony. Narrow. The heaving slowed and eventually subsided. He hadn't made a sound. Carp surreptitiously dried his eyes before lifting his head and looking at me sharply.

"I didn't cry," he said accusingly.

"I know." I looked him in the eye. "I never said you did."

He held my gaze for a few seconds, realized that I was going to be kind about it, and then sighed deeply. He sniffed a couple times and wiped his nose. He stared at the ground and said, "Don't tell, okay? Don't tell those guys."

"It's no big deal, you just slipped."

"Please," he said. "I beg of you."

Again I wanted to laugh. Never had Servan seemed more uncool or more likable. "I won't tell," I said solemnly. "Don't worry about it."

"Swear that you won't tell any person?"

"I swear that I won't tell." And I didn't. Until now.

"My parents are going to kill me," he said, tugging on his wrecked jersey.

"Just tell them you got in a fight. Tell them you were defending someone who was getting picked on."

"Yeah," he said. "I'll tell them I was defending a Romanian that was going under attack by a Hungarian gang."

"Um, I don't think there are a lot of marauding Hungarians around here. Maybe you should just tell them—"

"Yo, Steve, Carp! Where are ya?!"

In response to Leon's call from the top of the embankment, Carp clamped one hand on my forearm and motioned with the other for me to be quiet.

"His jacket's here," I heard Rachel say boozily.

"So is the hooch," said Leon. "They're around. They're probably just dicking with us. *Hey, Rachel, you wanna smoke a joint? I got a nice big joint here in Carp's jacket. And we can have it all to ourselves. Unless, of course, there's anyone out here who would like to join us. . . ?*"

Carp squeezed my forearm and then, perhaps to silence me more than anything else (did he think that I couldn't refuse a toke?), leaned in and attached his mouth to mine. He stuck his tongue in there and moved it around. Palinka fumes, stale marijuana, and a touch of fresh autumn mud. It didn't taste bad.

"They probably went in, but they're coming back out," said Rachel. "Let's just go find them. I have to go to the bathroom anyway."

"Jerk-offs," said Leon.

I heard them move off through the woods toward the schoolyard. I expected Servan to stop necking with me as soon as the voices trailed away and they were clearly out of earshot, but astonishingly, he persisted. I concluded that while it was my first real kiss and I didn't really know what I was doing, I must have been doing it right, or right enough anyway, because after a few minutes of mad mouth action, he reached into my jean jacket and started kneading my breasts. It felt okay, but I was dead nervous, afraid that Servan's hand would move a couple inches lower and discover my belly flab, the existence of which I took great pains to hide under loose layers of clothing. In a preemptive move, I lay back so that my bunched stomach would flatten out (Carp went with me, his mouth fixed on mine). The rock was cold and jagged and dug into the back of my head, but I didn't dare sit up, as Carp had taken my recline as an invitation to inch his hungry hand down into my pants. He wrestled with the button on my Levi's for an excruciating amount of time before successfully popping it. He got the zipper down, thrust his icy fingers into my undies, and wriggled around in there. I felt the scratch of a fingernail as he located my hole and plugged a digit inside. More wriggling. It didn't feel so great, to tell you the truth. And while I was relieved that he hadn't drawn his hand back in disgust, I pretty much just wanted him and his nails out of there. I endured another thirty seconds of frantic poking, because I wanted to be polite and also seem as if I was experienced and accustomed to that sort of thing, but then I suddenly had this memory flash of Servan, earlier on, touching his bloody face with his hands, and a hot wave of HIV fear wowed through me. I grabbed him hard by the wrist and yanked him out of my pants. He used the tense grip to swing my hand over to his own crotch. Following his lead, I popped the button and dug around in there until locating my target. I had seen guys miming masturbation, and I imitated this rapid up-and-down stroke, marveling at the fact that it didn't seem to hurt, and wondering if an object of this size could possibly fit inside me. Then, just as I was completing that thought—concluding that, no, it could not—a few mils of watery splooge squirted out of Carp's tool and, for the first time in twenty minutes, he withdrew his tongue from my mouth. I dried my hand on my pant leg and then brought it to my nose for a covert sniff. *Salt. And the tap water in the fishbowl after I added the Sea-Monkeys.*

Carp sat up, zipped up, and stood up. "I think I should go home," he said.

"Um, yeah, me, too," I said, shivering a little. Dejection descending. It wasn't like I was expecting a protracted cuddle session, avowals of undying love, or even a lousy walk home, but neither was I expecting Carp to suddenly stumble to the river, empty the contents of his stomach into the polluted water, then turn and scrabble up the side of the ravine without saying another word to me.

I took it as a bad sign.

Sure enough, when I next saw Servan—midday Monday in the Burger King down the street from our school—he acted as if nothing had occurred between us. Clearly, Carp wanted to eradicate his little bottom-feeding frenzy.

"Oh, man, I was hammer-headed," Carp said to the assemblage of Whopper-munching stoners. "I was so wiped out of my head, I can't remember anything after that second spliff. Don't even ask me how I got home, 'cause I don't even know how I got home!"

So: Nelson Rumack's kindergarten kiss, Martin the Tickler's prepubescent grope, and Servan Carp's watery white squirt—my entire sexual history up to the age of twenty-two and one quarter. With that abysmal record, it wasn't likely that I'd forget my sensational encounter with Studly Guy too soon. No. Sex was suddenly available to me. Sex with good-looking guys who wanted to call me again and have more sex. After years of loneliness and frustration, the opportunity to lose my loathed virginity had finally arrived.

As I walked away from the construction site, I remember feeling strangely liberated, oddly powerful. As long as this Beauty thing held out, I was laughing. I could pick and choose. I could have whomever I wanted.

I headed for Art & Trash.

3

On my way to the video store, I stopped briefly at Mister Loonie to pick up a cheap purse or knapsack. My plan was to buy condoms, and I didn't want to be toting them around in a not-quite-opaque drugstore bag. Oddly enough, Mister Loonie had a wide assortment of inexpensive purses as well as discounted condoms. Mister Loonie also stocked towels, gift wrap, boxed chocolates, underwear, electronics, plumbing supplies, canned goods, shampoo, cigarettes, greeting cards, West Indian foodstuffs, Kleenex (with Christmas-motif boxes), glassware, breath mints, socks, fishing tackle, potato chips, and out-of-print self-help books. It was vaguely upsetting that all of these items were available in the same store, but the price was right and I didn't have time to waste. I selected an inoffensive black bag and a six-pack of Sensi-Thin (with Ribs and Dots for Extra Pleasure). The cashier smiled and gave me a semi-flirty look when he rang up my purchases. He was a teenager of, what I guessed to be, West Indian extraction. He had glossy black hair (a tad Elvis-y), gentle bovine eyes, and fantastically white teeth. For a moment, I considered asking him if he'd like to have intercourse with me, but before I could seriously mull it over, he sneezed, rather wetly, and then wiped his nose with the back of his hand. That put me off. Plus, I didn't want to get a cold. Plus, the 1950s hair was a bit much.

It was just after two o'clock when I arrived at my destination. The back of Nathan's curiously shaped head was visible through the glass storefront, and it gave me a start when I saw it. I felt like a spy. Or a stalker. I paused for a moment and pretended to study the movie posters and box sets displayed in the window while I calmed myself. Obviously, I couldn't be more incognito. There was no way on earth that Nathan could recognize me. Still, I felt nervous. I had a terrifying, worst-case-scenario vision of Reverting back while I was in the store. Picture Nathan calmly cashing out a customer when he is suddenly pinged in the neck by a flying chunk of metal—the button from my blue jeans as I erupt out of my borrowed clothing like a cross between the Incredible Hulk and two hundred pounds of McCain's rising pizza dough. Not pretty.

I did go in, though. I proceeded directly to the back of the store, plucked a video cassette randomly from a shelf, and tried to appear suitably absorbed as fragments of box hype flitted nonsensically before my eyes: *revolutionary storytelling technique . . . penetrating exposé of the nature of power . . . brilliantly, savagely funny . . .* I put it back in its place and continued faux-browsing.

After a minute, I summoned the courage to sneak a peek at Nathan. He was chewing on a hangnail and staring at a ceiling-mounted TV monitor, watching a strange movie. I started to watch it, too. A naked young man, a real Adonis—all muscle and chin and puffy lips—was frolicking on a pristine beach with an elephant. An incongruous image. The elephant was lolling on its side in the surf, letting the foamy water surge over its slick hide, while the naked young man splashed and played, caressed and patted it. Then the young man draped himself innocently over the beast's wide side in a limp and childish gesture that said, *I helplessly and hopelessly adore you.* The elephant looked drunk happy. Smiling, it struggled to its feet, extended its loopy trunk, and seductively encircled the young man's torso, lifting him off the beach and sweeping him slowly, slowly into the sky, holding him high and happy in bright sunshine. It was possibly the most beautiful thing I had ever seen. Mesmerizing. Without being entirely aware of it, I had drifted toward the front of the store, closer to the monitor.

"What is this?" I asked.

Nathan looked at me and then looked quickly back at the TV. *"Chop Suey,"* he said. "A documentary by Bruce Weber."

"Oh . . . Um, what is it about?"

"Well, as near as I can tell, it's about the beautiful things

that Bruce Weber worships and possibly wishes he could be."
The reply was entirely Nathan-like, but the tone was imper-
sonal, borderline unfriendly. I wasn't used to that. His gaze
remained fixed on the monitor, and I got the feeling that he
was purposely not looking at me.

A customer intercepted our exchange then. He plonked a
stack of videos on the counter and handed his card to
Nathan, who immediately busied himself with entering the
necessary info into the computer. I watched his fingers tap-
tap on the keyboard. The nails were gnawed ragged, and one
particularly pulpy hangnail was caked in dried blood. The
customer, a handsome middle-aged man with a salt-and-
pepper buzz-cut, an earring, and a faded motorcycle jacket,
looked me up and down and smiled unctuously.

"Nice day, eh?"

"Yeah," I said, looking away, waiting for him to complete
his transaction and clear off. For the first time in my life, I
was deflecting the attentions of a man, and a good-looking
man at that. I had seen women do this on TV and in the
movies, so I sort of knew the drill. Still, it made me uncomfortable, a tad guilty, as if I owed him something.

"Ten thirty-one," said Nathan.

The customer handed over a twenty. Then he cocked his
head to one side, squinted his eyes, and with a wry expression,
studied my face. "I've seen you in something," he said,
pointing at me. "You're an actress, right?"

I saw Nathan's lip curl slightly as he made change and
handed it to the man.

"No," I said, smiling in spite of myself. "I'm not an
actress."

"You sure about that?" said the man, as if I was trying to
pull a fast one and he was on to me.

"I guess I'd know," I said.

" 'Cause you sure remind me of someone. An actress."

"Really?" I have to admit it made me curious.

Nathan placed the videos on the counter opposite, past the

anti-theft gate, and went back to watching the documentary. The man made no move to depart. He just kept standing there grinning stupidly in my direction. I also kept standing there grinning stupidly, but mostly in Nathan's direction.

"Yeah," he said, "that gal . . . the gal in that racing movie. You know, the one with Sly Stallone."

"Hmm, I'm not familiar with that one. Anyhow . . ." I started to back away, not entirely sure how to politely extricate myself from the conversation.

"You should check it out," he said. "*Driven!* Yeah, *Driven.* It's a good little flick."

I saw Nathan smirk. A silent scoff.

"You want me to find it for you?" said the guy, "Hey, buddy, you got *Driven* here?"

"Yes," said Nathan dryly. "It's almost always in."

I felt embarrassed then, talking to the man. I was there to put the moves on Nathan, and this guy was wrecking it. He was making me look like a dumb blonde. I am *not* a dumb blonde. "That's all right," I said, retreating further into the store. "I'm actually looking for an Antonioni film."

"Which one?" said Nathan, looking at me for the first time since I interrupted his viewing. "We only have a few."

Shit! I insta-scanned the hard drive of my brain, trying to conjure the name of any Antonioni title. Nathan had recently been talking about one. *What the hell was it?* Oh, yeah! "*Sex in the City,*" I blurted out.

Nathan stifled a laugh. "I think you mean *Love in the City.* We don't have it, unfortunately. It's hard to find." His attention went back to the Bruce Weber movie.

My face blushed hot with embarrassment. Perhaps I was an idiot. What I did next was certainly idiotic. "Right," I stammered. "*Love* in the City, ha-ha. Duh! What a twit." Then I bolted out of the store—not exactly running, no, not quite, but moving unnaturally fast, past the man in the motorcycle jacket, who said, "Hey, hold up a sec—"

I did not hold up. I walked as quickly as I could away from

Art & Trash, away from Nathan and the leering motorcycle man. I was thinking: *Love* in the City, yes, yes, yes, not *Sex* in the City. Love.

Two all-beef patties, special sauce, lettuce, cheese, pickles, onions on a sesame-seed bun. And a large fries. And a hot apple pie. Food was still a comfort. With every gobble of grease, I felt slightly less mortified, slightly more tranquil. My appetite hadn't diminished with the Change, but my capacity had. As I poked the last few fries down my throat—the stragglers, the ones that had spilled from box onto tray—I realized that I probably wouldn't be able to do the pie. My stomach had shrunk. As I sat back to take a breather, I noticed that I was being watched. A few tables away, an expensively attired middle-aged woman was staring at me. She looked somewhat familiar. She looked somewhat amused. What, did I have a pickle slice stuck to my cheek, some special sauce congealing in my eyebrow? I wiped my face and checked my shirt for spills. Oops . . . a trickle of ketchup on Virginie's white shirt. I dabbed at it with a Sprite-soaked napkin and glanced back at the woman. Still staring. Still amused. I was about to say something like "Take a picture, it lasts longer" or "Stare much?" when she leaned over and spoke.

"Excuse me," she said, in a husky voice. "Sorry to disturb you while you're eating—and by the way, I think it's *fabulous* that you're eating—I was just wondering who you're with?"

"Um . . ." The woman was obviously dotty. I glanced at the vacant seat opposite mine to indicate the obvious. "Just here on my own," I said.

"No," she laughed. "Who are you *with*, what agency?"

"Oh." *Huh?* "I'm not with any agency."

The woman swept up the numerous shopping bags at her feet and moved swiftly to my table, resting her purchases on the chair opposite. She was tall and burly, and reminded me of a man in drag. Prodigious feet bulging out of too-tight pumps. Thick bologna ankles. Bronko Nagurski shoulders.

"You *must* be a model," she said in a perfect cross between incredulity and menace.

I laughed. "No. Actually, I'm a cleaning lady."

"A cleaning lady!" she roared. (I know that people generally don't "roar," but there's really no other word for how she said it.) "You're kidding me, right?" She pressed a massive, bejeweled hand to her heart.

"I'm not kidding. I empty trash cans for a living."

"Well, thank you, Jesus, Buddha, and Mohammed," she muttered, digging into her buttery leather briefcase and fishing out a business-card holder—elegant, brushed steel. "Listen, I'm a modeling agent, and *you,* my dear, are a knockout. Really stunning. Exceptionally beautiful. How tall are— Oh, my God, you're blushing. Are you blushing?! You're new to the city, aren't you?"

"I sort of just got here."

"Of course you did. And how tall are you, sweetie?"

"Um . . . I'm not sure." I have to admit, the "sweetie" warmed me a bit.

"You must be at least five-nine. Oh, you're wonderful. Perfect. And I have no doubt I can get you work right away if you want it. Would you like that?"

"Modeling work?" I laughed.

"Well, it beats cleaning up other people's messes, I'll tell you that much. And the money can be very good." I must have appeared skeptical because she said, "This is on the level, dear. The agency will pay for your photos." She fished out a card and handed it to me. "Of course, you'll probably leave me as soon as you hit, but what the hell, it'd be worth it to be the one who discovered— What's your name, sweetie?"

"Um . . ." I tried to instantly conjure a pseudonym, but the only name that leaped to mind was Mayor McCheese. "Allison Penny," I said.

"Allison Penny . . ." She rolled it around in her mouth, memorized it. "I'm Fiona."

I read the card. Fiona Ferguson. Malcolm Anders Agency—

the B-grade talent agency on the first floor of 505 Richmond. That's why she looked familiar. I must have seen her in the office at least once, probably emptied her garbage can a couple hundred times.

"You know, Allison, I hardly ever eat at McDonald's, but today I had one of those stupidly strong Big Mac cravings. Happens every six months and I'm powerless in the face of it. Resistance is futile!" She laughed loud. I saw mercury fillings. "Well, I'm glad I gave in. It must be fate."

"Must be," I said, shaking the giant, knuckly hand that was offered to me.

With Fiona's card tucked in my new purse, I headed to the park across the street for a little digestion session. It was just warm enough to stretch out on the grass and absorb some sun. The park—a narrow strip of city green between two squat buildings—had attracted a bevy of vitamin D–starved individuals. I gave my less-than-hot apple pie to a scabby man on a bench and then wove my way around bike couriers and pasty shop-clerk types until I found an unpopulated smidgen of earth on which to settle down. I was sleepy, a bit headachy, and more than a little overwhelmed by the events of the day. Also, my encounter with Fiona Ferguson had left me feeling unsettled. She seemed nice enough and, to be honest, I sort of took to her right away. Despite her heft there was something warm and mother-henish about her, like John Lithgow in drag in *The World According to Garp.* Nevertheless, I found it absurd and irksome that I could go have a burger at McDonald's and come out with an offer of gainful employment, and the prospect of earning good money almost immediately. As the old Allison Penny, I had spent years attempting to land a half-decent job, with virtually no success. The new Allison Penny had achieved it—without even trying, mind you—in a little less than seven hours.

I suppose my abysmal career history had a lot to do with not staying in school to pursue a vocation. Still, I never expected my inevitable foray into the menial job market to prove so inauspicious. Offices didn't want me greeting their visitors or filing their files. The food service industry didn't want me mixing their drinks or serving their grub. Retailers, in particular, didn't want me anywhere near prospective customers. Eventually, I had to settle for a series of odious telemarketing assignments, obtained through a temp agency that specialized in that most mind-dulling and low-paying of fields. I can't tell you how many times I was (justifiably) bawled out by indignant, exhausted, or irate individuals who just wanted to enjoy an evening at home unmolested. "Rot in hell!" someone once screamed at me. "Fuck off and die," was something I heard more than once. I was grateful to those who simply and huffily hung up on me. Almost worse than calling people who didn't want to speak to you was calling people who desperately needed to talk. Old coots, shut-ins, perverts, maniacs . . . I'm trying to tell them about a 75-percent-off-the-newsstand-price subscription deal to *Pet World Magazine,* and they're trying to tell me about their wayward children, bladder infections, foreign policy views, or sexual proclivities. It was unpleasant. It gave me headaches. I found no relief in my coworkers, who were boring and braindead and all too willing to embrace the farcical strategies designed, no doubt, by a team of social psychologists to increase sales. Empty strategies, devoid of genuine incentive, that included placing a bell on top of the upholstered dividers between cubicles, and demanding that workers leap up, bellow "Five and alive!" and ring said bell each time we racked up five subscription sales. The idea was that we would take such immense pleasure and pride in ringing the bell that we would phone that much faster and try that much harder to convince Joe Dipshit that he needed what we were hawking. The tragic thing is, it worked. Not on me. I refused to touch the bell, but my coworkers gleefully seized the opportunity to jump up, ring, and make rubes of themselves. It pleased the supervisors, who were working on commission—an odious bunch of bitter failures who had been granted the tiniest quark of authority and felt the need to exercise it whenever possible (i.e., laying down the law when it came to unscheduled bathroom breaks, gum chewing, or dress-code infractions). Typically, I would put in as many weeks as necessary to qualify for the dole and then skedaddle.

I lay in the park, feeling sorry for my old self and—just before dozing off warm in the sun—fantasizing about Fiona as a kind of Henrietta Higgins, balancing leather-bound first editions on my head and tilting my chin up just a touch as she taught me how to walk like a model in the book-lined study of her large but comfortable home. I have no idea how long I was out—thirty seconds, an hour? But I remember waking with a violent shiver to find a hideous woman hovering over me, blocking the light as she stared down at my face. I rolled to the left and scrambled to my feet, my heart adrenalinized and pounding. The woman looked crazed—she had straggly brown hair streaked with gray, and huge, lemurlike eyes lined with kohl. On each cheek was a greasepaint flower. She wore a faded denim jumper with yellow stars hand-painted on the skirt, burgundy galoshes, and numerous sweaters too warm for the weather—layers of hot pink, apricot, and Tidy Bowl–blue polyester. I grabbed my purse and lurched away.

Time to head home and regroup.

On the way, I stopped into Le Château. I thought it unwise to be sporting Virginie's duds when I walked into the house, especially since there was now dried semen on her shoe, ketchup on her shirt, and a stain that smelled like semi-composted dog shit on her jeans (I had rolled through something in the grass). The idea was to quickly snap up the cheapest outfit I could find, but once I got in there and started browsing through all the mod knockoffs of designer clothing, all the cutesy little clothes that I hadn't had a hope in hell of fitting into until that very day, I got carried away and started trying on everything in the store. And you know what? Everything looked good. Every damn thing looked good. Every tiny tank top, every strappy sandal, every micro-mini and slinky slut dress looked like a million flaming bucks. The fitting room no longer represented a chamber of horrors, the place where the last shred of self-esteem went to die. God, how many tears had I shed in those cruel cubicles with their overhead fluorescent lighting and malevolent mirrors? How many times had I *not* tried something on because there was no mirror in the fitting room, which meant I'd have had to waddle into a public area to view myself?

That afternoon, for the first time, I was actually enjoying the act of clothes shopping. I was bopping happy to the electro-pop blare, strutting right out into the open to the three-way mirror in the center of the store, putting on my own little fashion show. It was like that scene from *Pretty Woman,* except instead of doffing the whore clothes for modest attire, I was trading in modest attire for whore clothes (unfortunately, Richard Gere wasn't there to rescue my credit card from untenable abuse). As I spun jauntily around to check out my bum-cleavage in a pair of low-riding pleather stretch pants, I noticed a doleful face at the corner of the mirror. I turned and spotted a frumpy teen stealing a resentful glance in my direction. I recognized that expression. I had worn it a thousand times. I thought: I know exactly what you're thinking right now, and I am totally with you. I can't stand lucky bitches like me. I smiled in commiseration, but she must have taken it the wrong way, because when I looked back at the corner of the mirror, all I saw was a chubby hand flipping me the bird.

A rare and wondrous sight when I arrived home: Virginie up to her elbows in dishwater. Presumably, she figured that, just this once, it was futile to employ the wait-for-Allison-to-break-down-and-do-them plan, since I was ostensibly in Los Angeles with no fixed date of return.

"Howdy," I said, dropping my keys on the table, which had been tidied and wiped. The floor, I noticed with astonishment, had been swept and *scrubbed*. What could it mean?

"Oh, hi," she said. "How's it going?"

"It's going well." I proceeded through to my room, dropped purse and purchases on the bed, making sure that Virginie's rolled-up clothes were hidden, then went back to the kitchen to find out what was going on. The pipes in the bathroom made a familiar squeak as the shower was turned off, no doubt, by Fraser. I opened the fridge, reached past the gallon jug of Sunny Delight, and pulled out a small carton of orange juice. Virginie's orange juice. The good stuff, not from concentrate. The kind I could never afford. "Mind if I take a splash?" I was feeling bold.

"Go ahead," she said, glancing at the carton, then turning back to her task. I think I saw her butt cheeks contract. She was a real cheapskate when it came to anyone but herself.

"You guys went shopping, eh?" The fridge was crammed with new food and beer. There was a bag of tiger shrimp thawing in a bowl, and a cake box (from Desserts by Phipps, no less).

"We're having a friend over for dinner." She said it sharply, as if I was about to raccoon into her food supply as well.

"I'll have to get some groceries tomorrow," I said, grabbing a freshly washed glass, still warm, from the dish rack. I poured it full of juice, drank it down, and then poured some more, wondering which one of the tightwad's motley chums had been deemed shrimp- and Phipps-worthy. I put the nearly empty carton back into the fridge, drained the glass, and carried it to the sink. "Want me to wash it?" I asked innocently. It was lined with pulp.

"It's okay," she said tight-lipped.

I dropped the glass into the dishwater. A satisfying *glug glug* as it sank between her sudsy forearms. "Thanks." I took a seat at the table and eyed the pile of newspapers in front of me. I subscribed to all three papers on Saturday. A thick mound of weekend misery.

Fraser came out of the bathroom then, a towel wrapped around his hips, a steamy soap smell emanating from his damp body. He looked startled when he caught sight of me. "Hi," he said, furrowing his eyebrows, trying to look serious even as he was blushing. "I'm Fraser."

"I'm Allison."

"Jesus, put some clothes on," said Virginie in a jocular way, though it sounded a tad strained. I noted that she had never before exhorted Fraser to "put some clothes on" in my presence. Then again, he wasn't truly in my presence; he was in the presence of New Allison. He was standing half-naked and dripping in front of New Allison, stealing peeks at her/my cleavage. Fraser smiled sheepishly and padded off down the hallway. Virginie drained the dishwater, then dried her hands on a towel. "So," she said, curling up cute on a chair, sizing me up, "you're called Allison as well?"

"Yeah. That's initially what brought us together when we were kids in grade school. Two Allison Pennys in the same room. Weird, eh? I mean, what are the odds?"

"Yeah."

"As it turned out, we actually had a lot in common."

"Really?" Virginie looked skeptical.

"Actually, Allison and I are remarkably similar. Though you wouldn't know it to look at us." I smiled. This was fun. This being invisible yet present, this hiding in plain sight. A strong I-know-something-you-don't-know feeling came over me, and I realized that I could probably use this power.

"I like your dress," said Virginie, eyeing my new frock, a curiously sullen expression on her face. "Is that a Betsey Johnson?"

"It's a knockoff. I just bought it."

"Do you mind if I ask how much?"

"Twenty-four bucks."

"*No way!* Where'd you get it?!"

"Yes way! Le Château!" I said, mimicking her girlie gush, but she didn't catch on.

"It's really cute," said Virginie. And it was. A navy blue baby-doll dress with a pattern of little daisies on it. I had paired it with a cheap pair of navy sneakers and white anklet socks. I daresay I had out-cuted the reigning queen of cute.

Fraser came back into the kitchen. He went for the fridge and pulled out a six-pack of Sleeman Cream Ale. He had donned a white T-shirt and a pair of jeans that featured several provocative rips in the crotch and ass. His hairy feet were pale and bare. Vaguely Neanderthal. Sort of sexy.

"Who wants a beer?" he said, ripping the carton open.

"Shouldn't we wait?" said Virginie, frowning.

"Why? We got enough. And George'll bring something."

George. The mystery dinner guest. Who was he? And why was Virginie so tense about it? "I wouldn't mind a beer," I said, to enhance her anxiety; I didn't particularly want one. Fraser brought it over, twisted off the cap, and handed it to me.

"Thank you."

I smiled. He smiled.

"Guess I'll have one," said Virginie.

He got two more and carried them to the table. He plonked one in front of her, then sat down, spread his legs wide, held the bottle at penis height, and twisted the cap off. A little puff of carbon escaped from the top.

I sipped. He sipped.

"So," said Virginie, picking up her beer and making a big show of twisting the lid off with a passive-aggressive why-did-you-open-her-beer-and-not-my-beer snap of the wrist, "how long are you planning on staying, Allison?"

"That's a good question," I said. "It's possible that I may have to leave rather suddenly." *The stroke of midnight?* "On the other hand, I may be around for a while."

"You here for work? You a model or something?" said Fraser.

"God, no."

"Actress, right?"

"No." I laughed.

"I just figured, well, I heard you were from L.A., so I thought you were in the biz."

"Not everyone in L.A. is in the biz. Not every person does what *we* do," said Virginie, trying to emphasize the "we" of Virginie and Fraser, and also let me know that it was an alluring film-world "we."

Man, I was sick of that. "Well, actually," I said, "I recently had the chance to work on a friend's movie, but I decided to decline, even though Steve Buscemi was in it, and it might have been nifty to meet him."

Incredulous, Virginie said, "Why?"

"Well, I would have done it if it had been a *real* film job, but since I was completely unskilled, I was asked to be assistant wardrobe person. Essentially, they wanted me to keep track of some clothes, do ironing, and I figured, might as well get a job in the Laundromat, right? Not very glam. I mean, a trained chinchilla could do it."

Fraser shifted uncomfortably in his seat.

"And because it was low budget, they could only pay me twenty bucks an hour, so you know . . ." I snorted and guffawed at the ridiculous wage (over twice what I was earning at the time, two dollars more than Virginie was earning).

"Assistant wardrobe *is* a real job. Especially when you're on a period piece."

"That's what Virginie does," said Fraser.

"Oh, you're kidding? Gosh, what a complete idiot!" I said, looking directly at Virginie, meaning *You are the idiot,* but I don't think she got it. Then I leaned over—exposing a dangerous amount of cleavage—and squeezed her forearm in a reassuring manner. "I'm sure it's a really important job."

"Don't worry about it," she snipped.

There was a deliciously dense tension in the air, sexual and otherwise. Fraser tried to diffuse it with a familiar action—

pulling out a package of cigarettes. He removed one and placed it between his lips. He offered the pack to Virginie. She took one. "Cigarette?" he said, holding the pack toward me.

"No, thanks. I'm allergic to smoke," I said. "My bronchial tubes just close up."

"Oh," said Fraser, nodding, processing this information. Without glancing at Virginie, his hand went to the cigarette in his mouth. He removed it and carefully tucked it back into the pack. Yes, he did. Yes, he did.

An exasperated puff of air escaped from between Virginie's lips. "I guess we can smoke in my room for a day or two while you're here."

"S'that okay?" said Fraser.

"Of course. Thanks." A day or two? You think she was trying to tell me something?

Virginie huffed off down the hall, pausing at the door to her room. "Are you coming?" she said, hands on hips, a cig clamped angrily in her mouth.

"Um, yeah." He took a swig of beer and stood slowly, hitching up his cowboy jeans.

Galoot, is what I thought. He's a real galoot. I watched him lumber Neanderthal down the hall to Virginie's room. He paused briefly to glance back at me before entering. Two seconds later I heard the door slam.

Dinner that evening was oddly enjoyable. I had no idea that it was in me to vamp, but vamp I did. Old Allison watched in wonder and amazement as I embraced my inner coquette—a buried being that had been lying dormant forever—and brought it blazing to the surface for maximum pain and torture of Virginie. They say that revenge is a dish best served cold. In this case revenge was a dish served up hot and tasty in a Betsey Johnson knockoff.

I had resolved to try to secure an invitation to the meal

after discovering that the bathroom had been wholly and ferociously scoured. Two new hand towels hung fluffy on the rack, and the beige goo growing on the low ceiling had been bleached away. All the dimly embarrassing unctions—Compound W, Monistat, Virginie's prescription cortisone cream—had been stripped from the medicine cabinet.

Who the fuck was this George person anyway?

I took a long shower (soaping up and rinsing off my astonishing new bits until the fingertips started to raisin). On the way to my room I found Fraser in the kitchen, cooking up something fragrant and spicy.

"Mmm," I said, moving close, "what smells so good?"

"Curried coconut shrimp."

"My favorite," I lied, letting my robe slip open a little at the top.

"Plenty to go around," he said, taking a good gander. "If you want to join us, um, unless you have plans?"

"I have no plans." *Except, of course, to drive your evil girlfriend quietly bonkers by flirting with you incessantly.*

"Well, we'll probably chow down around eight, if you're into it."

"I'm into it," I said. "But maybe I should run it by Virginie, you know, just to be polite." *After all, she can hardly say no, and I'd like to see her face when I tell her you've included me.*

"Oh, she just went down to the corner. I forgot the coconut." He guffawed. "But I'm sure it's cool. I mean, there's a ton of food. So why would she mind?"

What a galoot.

Of course, there are a lot of men, even highly intelligent ones, who are thick to the tricks of women. They believe in the myth of "sisterhood," that fairy tale of female bonding and support, perpetrated by yeast infection medication commercials and movies like *Thelma & Louise, Boys on the Side,* and *Waiting to Exhale*—films in which women rescue one another from nasty, unfeeling men and then proceed to shore one another up ad nauseam, usually over white-wine spritzers in candle-lit rooms. What a crock. *Dangerous Liaisons* is more like it. *All About Eve* got it just about right.

So, dinner. Yes. I had my fun. At a quarter to eight I was already messing with Virginie's mind by digging in the dip every time she turned her back. I'd rake a piece of celery through it, she'd smooth it out with a knife. I'd dip again. She'd smooth again. Dip. Smooth. Dip. Smooth. A blue vein pulsing in her neck by the time the front doorbell rang.

"Hey, ya bastard."

"Hey," said Fraser, chuckling hearty. "C'mon in. How the hell are ya?"

"I'm well. Hey, what's that thing on your chin?"

"This? It's a goatee."

"Well, Ethan Hawke called. He wants it back."

A blast of mirth from Fraser/Virginie as the mystery guest breezed into the kitchen, all blond and lanky and smiling wide, and it was as if someone had pulled a curtain aside and let a little more light into the room, as if a zingy vibration had suddenly entered the atmosphere. And there was George. The only man I'd ever seen—outside of a biblical movie epic—who looked good (and heterosexual) in sandals. He greeted Virginie with a kiss on each cheek, French style, and slid a bottle of wine into her hands.

"Wow," she said, gaping at the label.

"Hi, I'm George."

"I'm Allison."

"Pleased to meet you," he said, and he did look pleased, the wide mouth smiling, the blue eyes shining. He reminded me of a young Peter O'Toole. Lithe. Good bone structure. He was dressed in fine clothing that hung loose on his lean frame, and he exuded an easy confidence. He didn't seem at all discomposed by Virginie and Fraser, who were darting around, pulling out chairs, mixing drinks, unwrapping appetizers, and apologizing for the state of the apartment and the wrong kind of highball glasses. George settled serenely onto the padded armchair at the head of the table, and I got the feeling that he was accustomed to being catered to and orbited. Perversely, I decided to deprive him of my attention for the remainder of the evening.

I proceeded to flirt with Fraser in a sneaky and subdued manner. Virginie responded by flirting outrageously with George—giggling giddy at his every joke, exposing boob or panties at every opportunity. George ignored her frequent flashings and flirted exclusively with me. It was like a Russian play, minus the intelligence. By the time the curried coconut shrimp had been cleared away, Virginie was seething and significantly sloshed, Fraser was all goo-goo-eyed and practically popping boners at the table, and George was offering to show me around town, in a new Aston Martin Vanquish, to be delivered on the morrow. George, I managed to glean from various snippets of conversation, was George Thomas, son of Nigel Thomas and nephew of Frank Thomas, the real-estate developers, the Thomases, one of the wealthier families in the city. George had taken a break from working with his father to try his hand at becoming an independent movie producer. That's how Fraser had met him. George had ponied up enough cash to be called an associate producer on the last feature Fraser had worked on. He bought himself the right to hang around the set and see what was what when it came to producing. I noticed how his eyes sparkled with excitement as Fraser recounted an anecdote about Mimi Rogers, who had had a part in their film.

"She was married to Tom Cruise," said Virginie.

George and Fraser nodded. They both knew this to be true. I noticed also how George's eyes lost their sparkle when Virginie and Fraser considered him warmed up enough to start their pitch. George wasn't stupid; I could see he was expecting it. He smiled tolerantly and listened respectfully while they went on about a documentary project they had dreamed up—something about the Déné Indians in northern Manitoba. Not that they had any connection to the Déné in northern Manitoba, it was just something they had dreamed up.

"Well, it sounds like a worthy project," said George politely. "But at this point, I'm primarily interested in funding narrative films, not documentaries."

"Yeah," said Fraser. "I told Virginie you wanted to make real movies."

"Not movies about real people?" I said.

George smiled. He asked if I was an actress. I told him no, I wasn't. He asked what it was that I did. I told him I was between jobs. He asked what I was doing in Toronto. I told him I was just visiting. He said he would be happy to show me around in the brand-new Aston Martin Vanquish. Fraser said that he would like to go for a spin in it and that maybe he could come along. And Virginie said, "Well, who's ready for dessert?" in a voice pinched with suppressed rage.

Throughout the evening I had kept a careful watch on the kitchen clock, having gotten it into my head that I might Revert back at midnight. At 11:40, I excused myself and headed to the bathroom. I wanted a moment alone with New Allison before she (possibly) disappeared forever. As I gazed at my reflection—made more alluring by the alcohol-induced flush to my cheeks—I bemoaned the fact that I hadn't slipped into a photo booth to document the Miracle. Then I remembered Fiona Ferguson's offer: "The agency will pay for your photos." The notion of Allison Penny as model seemed beyond outlandish, but the idea of having professional photos, a souvenir of my time of beauty, appealed to me, especially if someone else was proposing to pay for them.

When I returned, minutes later, to the kitchen, Virginie and Fraser were busy wrapping up food and clearing away dishes. I said good night and thank you, and a "Nice meeting you" to George, who followed me to my bedroom door and, whispering, asked if he could see me again. I said maybe and that I wasn't sure.

Which was true.

I undressed and slid naked between the sheets. I stared at the clock and listened to the dinner party wrapping up outside my door. I heard George say good night and take his leave. I watched the second hand tick slowly and ominously toward the twelve. I braced myself for the worst, but nothing happened. Midnight came and went and I did not Revert. I realized that Reversion would probably occur while I slept. I thought about getting dressed and going out somewhere, staying awake for as long as possible to make the most of it. But as I lay in bed, waiting for Virginie and Fraser to finish clearing and head to their room, I plummeted into a deep and dead slumber, as if I had been drugged.

When I opened my eyes it was noon on Sunday and I was still New Allison. Disoriented, unusually well rested, and still beautiful. I caressed my taut body under the covers. It had not been a dream.

I felt relieved, pleased, and immensely perplexed. Why had this happened to me? What was the purpose? Was my transformation part of a larger scheme? Did I have some sort of beauty duty to perform? And if so, what would it be? Posing naked for a PETA billboard? Administering blowjobs to ugly outcasts? I wondered if this sort of thing had happened to others. Was there a secret society of gorgeous people who had undergone the Change? I thought about supermodels like Elle MacPherson and Cindy Crawford. I seemed to recall hearing or reading interviews in which they had claimed to be wallflowers and beasts when they were growing up. Had it happened to them?

Almost everything I thought I knew about reality had been upended into uncertainty, if not entirely jettisoned. But instead of pondering the great mysteries of life and metamorphosis, I found my mind straying to commonplace, even trivial matters, like how I was going to spend my day, and about the dinner party with George on the previous night. I had never participated in anything like that before. The last time two men drooled over me was when I purchased a pencil from the retarded twins in the subway. And the closest I had come to partying with wealthy types was sneering at their festive faces on the society page of the weekend newspaper. It was strange to watch Virginie and Fraser fawning over George. Stranger still to watch George fawning over me. George was rich and connected and powerful, yes, but I felt as if I was the one with the power in the room that night.

Oddly enough, I was the one with the power.

4

The apartment was Sunday quiet. Virginie and Fraser had gone out. No surprise there. I suspected that for "the next couple of days" (i.e., until I was safely on my way back to from whence I came), Virginie would keep Fraser as far away from me as possible.

I made coffee and toasted a couple of waffles. I was eyeing the unread weekend newspapers stacked on top of the fridge when the phone rang. It was so rarely for me that I never picked up. I forked a chunk of freezer-burned Eggo into my gape as the answering machine kicked in: "Hey, this is George calling for Allison. So, listen, I know it's last minute, but I was wondering if I could maybe take you to dinner tonight? There's this restaurant called Tribe—it's, like, the new hot place—and I'm pretty sure I can get a table. Actually, I am sure, I already checked. The chef is sort of a buddy of mine. Anyhow, let me know. I was thinking eight o'clock for dinner, so I could grab you around seven-thirtyish if that's good for you. It's upscale casz. So if you get this message, give me a

call at 555–9171 or on my cell at 858–5623. Ciao for now."
Beep.

That was fast, I thought, chewing waffle. Clearly, when George saw something he wanted, he wasted no time in going after it. My contrarian instinct was to deprive him of his wish, to be the first hottie in history to say nay to eligible George. It wasn't that I disliked him; he was actually quite charming. But it annoyed me that I should have entrée to his world because of the way I suddenly looked. Would he be inviting Old Allison to dine with him? On the other hand, it intrigued me that I could go where no fat, ugly girl had gone before: into an exclusive restaurant, on the arm of George Thomas. I thought: Now that I have temporary access to a new realm, shouldn't I at least explore it? After years of solitary cave-dwelling in my peeling-ceiling room, should I not take the opportunity to experience something foreign and potentially pleasurable before Reverting? I had never been asked out on a date before, let alone to a fancy-pants restaurant. What would be the harm in having a look around? I could be like an anthropologist in a leaf-covered pith helmet taking a meal with an alien culture, or like a Method actor researching a part—in this case, the part of the quietly avaricious trophy girlfriend.

As long as I didn't disappear into the role, I would be fine, right?

Of course, an actor requires costumes and makeup, which settled what I was going to do with my day. I was going to do something countless young women do every sunny Sunday in spring. I was going to finish my breakfast, get myself dressed, and head to the mall.

Seven hours and just over five hundred dollars later, I was pacing the apartment, waiting for George to arrive. I ducked into the bathroom to check my hair (faux-tortoiseshell hair grabber: $18.95), makeup (blush, lipstick, eyeliner, mascara:

$63), and appropriately "upscale casz" outfit (white blouse, black palazzo pants, strappy high-heeled sandals: $285). Sundry purchases—undergarments, nail polish, etc.—had eaten up the balance of five hundred smackers and put a serious strain on my credit card. This being attractive was proving expensive.

Speaking of which, a disturbing thing happened at the mall that day, a thing that had nothing to do with the fact that every person there seemed to be staring at me, or that two teenage girls, all giggly and nerved out, approached me in a shoe store to ask for my autograph (I insisted I wasn't famous; they didn't seem to believe me). It was something else that happened that was alarming. How can I describe it? Well, put it this way: I'd always hated the mall. I hadn't been to the mall in more than three years. It wasn't as if it was a particularly obnoxious mall—there were no roller coasters or wave pools or mini-zoos with Lithium lions and Prozac penguins contained therein. It wasn't the dead Muzak, the ugliness of the architecture, the homogeneity of the chain stores, or the faux-ethnic food court cuisine that particularly bothered me. It was the sheer volume of merchandise. Store after store pushing pile upon pile of product, and superfluous product at that—foot baths, earmuffs, pen holders, egg square-ers—a half-mile of boutiques that specialized in everything from sunglasses to knives, bookended by giant department stores containing absurd amounts of the same wares. It seemed excessive and obscene, and even just trundling through it made me feel voracious and overfed, like a typical North American consumer. So I stayed away from the mall, and prided myself on being an anticonsumer, someone who pretty much stuck to the essentials. Sure, I spent every penny of my (meager) paycheck each week, but I spent it on food, rent, and justifiable cultural items such as books, CDs, and DVD rentals. In short, I sneered at materialistic types—anyone who owned more than four pairs of shoes—and considered myself, if not righteous, at least deep. So here's the disturbing thing: I discovered that it might not be true, that my anticonsumerism might have less to do with my principles/character, and more to do with the way I looked. Because suddenly all the products that Old Allison had deemed superfluous seemed not only desirable, but sometimes also necessary to New Allison. For example, as I loitered around the makeup counter area, it occurred to me that my bar of Ivory soap and jumbo jar of Nivea weren't going to cut it anymore. My flawless skin suddenly deserved, nay demanded, a comprehensive four-step system. I wanted the Splash Foaming Cleanser, the Clarifying Exfoliant Lotion, the Clean-Finish Purifying Toner, and the Oil-Free Moisture Surge. I felt it would be unwise not to include the Antigravity Firming Lotion and the Advanced Night Repair Recovery Complex. And that was just the skin on my face. What about the rest of the epidermis? What about cosmetics? Didn't my pretty new pout merit a lipstick or two? Certainly every shade I sampled looked appealing. Even brown. I wanted lipstick. I wanted many lipsticks. What about my hair? Were elastic bands and a box of bobby pins really adequate accoutrements for such lovely locks? Shouldn't I have hair clips and headbands and high-fashion fasteners? What about lingerie? Looking the way I did, was it not likely that I would be undressing in front of somebody in the near future? Could I really make do with a week's worth of serviceable cotton gotchies? As I wended my way through the lingerie boutique, I knew for a fact that I could not. I saw at least a half dozen items that I instantly required, and countless others that I merely wanted. Shoes, handbags, scarves, belts, jewelry, hats, hosiery, sunglasses . . . Everywhere I went in the mall that day, I saw things that I wanted and needed (including a metal contraption for curling eyelashes, and a box of temporary tattoos). It was completely out of character, and it made me wonder if the external Change might be causing some kind of internal shift. Could the inner be so determined by the outer? If anatomy is destiny, was I destined to become a vapid shopaholic supermodel?

"Hey, gorgeous," said George, greeting me with a kiss on the cheek. "Ready to roll?"

"Let me just grab my purse."

I was vaguely disappointed that Virginie and Fraser weren't around to see us off. They would definitely have come to the curb to eyeball George's new, illegally parked custom convertible. They would have oohed and ahhed over its sleek design, its Gatsby sportiness. The top was down and the leather seats smelled divine and looked plump and sumptuous. There was something brazen about it with the top down like that. It seemed too exposed, like a cracked nut with its soft meat showing.

"This is a very flash car, George."

"Why, thank you," he said, sounding proud, as if he had designed and assembled it himself. He swung the passenger door closed after I'd slid in, and it made an expensive, everything's-been-engineered-to-fit-perfectly sound—a lovely muffled *chnnk*.

As we traveled to our destination it occurred to me that we were an exceptionally handsome couple in an exceptionally handsome automobile. People were checking us out, drivers and passengers in other vehicles, as well as pedestrians when we stopped at intersections. A lot of people simply took a longer-than-average look, but there were quite a few admiring smiles directed my way, and some hostile glances as well. Some even felt compelled to comment. An old coot in an ancient Cadillac shouted, "Oh, yeah, baby!" And a teenage Goth girl in the back of a Mazda 323 stuck her pierced tongue out at me. George seemed to be enjoying the attention, which, I suppose, was the point of owning a car like his. I asked him if people always gawked in traffic. He said yes, but more so with me along for the ride.

I guess I was better than a leather-covered rollover bar or burr walnut trim. New Allison was the ultimate option for a baby-blue Aston Martin convertible.

We pulled into a back alley in the warehouse district. Garbage cans, delivery vans, and three dapper fellows standing in front of a heavy steel panel—a wide industrial door that appeared impermeable. No sign of a restaurant. One of the guys came trotting over.

"Valet parking," said George. He pressed a button on the dash and the car's top came up and slid smartly into place. The valet handed George a ticket, took his place in the driver's seat, and wheeled away.

"And that was the last he ever saw of it," I said.

George laughed. "Bite your tongue," he said, circling my waist with his arm. "Or better still, let me bite it," he whispered.

"Evening," said one of the dapper fellows, reaching for a handle at the left side of the steel panel. He slid it heavy to the right, revealing a miniature room. Two slip-covered chairs sat on opposite sides of a round table that held a squat vase crammed with white tulip tops.

George gestured for me to enter, and I thought: This is the new hot spot? You sit in a froufrou closet, stare at an alley, and try to keep your food down while the vermin scurry about your feet? But then I was inside, and so was George, and so was one of the dapper fellows, who pushed a button, which caused the room to lurch into motion, and I realized that we were in a decorated freight elevator.

"Hey," I said, "cute gimmick."

George smiled small, and I wondered if I had blown his I've-been-here-a-thousand-times-and-I'm-too-cool-to-be-impressed-by-this demeanor. But it *was* a gimmick, one that hipsters could comfortably embrace, even though they would undoubtedly sneer at restaurants such as the Noodle Factory with its equally gimmicky pasta machine—a Rube

Goldberg—like contraption that churned dough and squeezed cheese and stamped out fresh ravioli in front of the rapt faces of the suburban families that thronged there.

As the lift ascended to the fourth floor, I heard rising levels of crowd murmur and jazz piano. Then suddenly before us: a vista of impossibly high ceilings, bleached wood, billowing white fabric, and the bustle of waitstaff attending to the desires of the well-heeled clientele. Wow, I thought, if I wasn't beautiful, I would never even know this existed.

We approached a podium where a long blonde greeted George by name (Mr. Thomas) and told us that our table would soon be ready. "Would you care to have a drink at the bar?"

"Thank you."

I felt very much like an adult as we were led to the lounge area, a space that appeared to be illuminated primarily by the bar itself—a curve of glass that glowed from within and gave off a diffused turquoise light. It made the drinks set on top look like glittering otherworldly jewels, like space-age lamps. A black man played a white piano.

We took a seat at the bar. More tulips. Single ones with slender stems, hanging languid over the tops of narrow vases. They looked beautifully intoxicated. "White tulips," I said. "My favorite."

"Is that right?" said George, passing me a drink menu. "You have to try a martini. They make the best martinis."

I perused the dizzying array of concoctions—everything from the "Jackson" (a white chocolate martini) to the "Hemingway" (a questionable blend of absinthe and vodka). Each one of these chemistry experiments was priced at $14.95. More than I would typically spend on an entire meal.

"What can I get you?" asked a handsome bartender in a pec-hugging T-shirt. George ordered a Manhattan. I ordered the "Classic" martini. The thing was absurdly oversized—almost as big as my head, with three golf-ball-sized olives impaled on what must have been a shish kebab skewer.

There was a mirror behind the bar and I had to resist the impulse to keep glancing at New Allison's reflection as I sipped. I looked snazzy. I appeared to fit in. George was going on about his connection to la chef. Something about cottage proximity, about someone selling a boat to someone else, about learning that the lake neighbor was a food pro, about a fancy dinner becoming part of the boat deal. It wasn't uninteresting. I smiled and nodded at the appropriate moments, but with every gulp of gin, my surroundings and situation grew increasingly surreal. Who am I? How did I get here? The glowing bar, the billowing fabric, the babbling-brook ripple of the piano—it was all very dreamy and disorienting.

Before long our table was ready and we were escorted to a corner of the dining area, where another good-looking staff member materialized to take our drink orders and announce the specials of the day.

"Today's appetizer is pan-fried, cornmeal-crusted oysters, served with wilted greens in a smoked corn sauce with pepper relish. The main course tonight is a Nunivak caribou chop seared with juniper berry oil, Arctic cloudberry sauce, and Alsatian spatzle."

George ordered a bottle of water, and the waiter scurried off to retrieve it.

"Spaetzle," I said. "Isn't that what they use to repair ceilings?"

"That's spackle," said George, not realizing that I was joking. "Spaetzle is a kind of noodle, or more accurately, a pan-sautéed dumpling. German in origin."

"I see." I was disappointed by his humorlessness, but impressed by his spaetzle knowledge.

As George studied the wine list, I read the menu. Half the items I couldn't identify. I had no idea what a Périgord Confit was (endangered falcon?). Ditto the Foie Gras à Ma Façon (handful of grass in the face?) or the Soft Polenta (birth defect?). I played it safe and ordered mushroom soup and steak, or more accurately, Wild Morel Bisque ($16.95) and a

"12 oz USDA Prime Striploin in sauce Marchant de Vin accompanied by Rosti Potatoes" ($39.95). And dear God, the food was good. Exquisitely presented and shockingly tasty. I could have wept with the pleasure of having it in my mouth. I sampled George's appetizer: Baked Goat Cheese with Seared Anjou Pears ($15.95). And when his entrée arrived, I maneuvered my fork across the table to try that, too. "Wow," I said, swallowing a morsel of Roasted Squab with Fricassee of Seasonal Mushrooms, Quince Compote, and Lavender Honey Essence ($39.50). "I had no idea food could be this way. Ambrosia for the gods."

George laughed and said, "I'm glad you're enjoying it." But then he was smiling to himself, and silent for a few seconds. "So," he said eventually, "tell me about your family, Allison. What do your folks do?"

It occurred to me that my déclassé gushing over the grub had put George on alert about my background (i.e., just how blue collar was it?). I suppose I should have invented something middle-class and respectable, but the red wine on top of the Big Gulp martini had exacerbated my tendency toward recalcitrance.

"Well, I guess you could say they were farmers—they had a few pigs, a handful of chickens. . . ."

George nodded.

"But, actually," I said, "my parents are dead."

"Oh. I'm sorry." Sad face. Questioning face.

"Killed in a cougar attack."

"Oh, my God," he said, pausing squab consumption. "That's horrible."

"Yeah. They were disemboweling a hog at the time, and I guess the scent must have attracted it. There are a lot of mountain lions roaming that region."

"What region is that?"

"The hills of Kentucky."

"Ap—Appalachia?"

"Yes, that's right. Hooterville." I knew about Hooterville

because I had a photography book about a community of mountain people in Appalachia. It was a fascinating book, full of filthy, frightening families.

George took a sip of water. "I thought you were from Los Angeles."

"Um, yeah. After my folks . . . I was just a toddler at the time. I went to live with an aunt in California."

"Wow." George looked genuinely glum about my pawed-apart parents.

"I'm sorry," I said. "I shouldn't be talking about this. Especially while we're eating."

"It's okay." He reached across the table and squeezed my hand supportively.

I felt guilty after that and tried to lighten the conversation. I encouraged George to do the jawing. While we ate dessert—Homemade Sour Cream Ice Cream with Kahlúa Drizzle ($12.95)—he related several amusing anecdotes about his upscale upbringing: private schools, summers at the lake, learning to ski on Mt. Shirouma (the "Alps of Japan" apparently). He spoke fondly of his parents, "Liz and Nigel," whom I pictured as über-WASPS, tastefully taking their cocktails in the quiet drawing room of their immaculate Rosedale mansion.

To be honest, I couldn't really picture Appalachian Allison fitting into this scenario, and I found it surprising that George wasn't put off by my hillbilly heritage. It didn't seem to dim his interest in me at all. In fact, by the time dinner was over, he had asked me to come with him to a Cecilia Bartoli concert on Saturday, and hinted that a cottage invite would be imminent if I stayed in town for the summer.

I realized that, unlike brains, ability, or newfound wealth, beauty is the one thing that transcends class. It felt like a profound revelation at the time, but in retrospect I had known it all along, at least since I was old enough to read. After all, the Prince married Cinderella. He wasn't scouring the local villages for the wittiest gal, or the one who could play the meanest lute solo, or even the one of most noble birth. Snow White was well-born, yes, but I somehow doubt she would have fared so well with Prince Charming if she had been aptly named Porridge Gray or Eczema Red. And I suspect that somewhere out there in fairy-tale land, Sleeping Smarty-Pants is somnolently and vainly waiting for the tender kiss of a king's son.

After dinner, George let me drive the Vanquish. It was fun. Really powerful. I booted it down Cherry Street and did a couple doughnuts in the Docks parking lot.

"I'm not that tired," said George after he'd reclaimed the wheel. "Do you feel like doing something?"

"Like what?" The dashboard clock showed 11:03 P.M. Usually I'd be in bed with a book or the *Globe and Mail.*

"Well, I live pretty close," he said, idly stroking the stick shift. "I could make you my signature after-dinner beverage."

I took this to mean: *I could impress you with my* Architectural Digest *living quarters, then attempt to have sex with you.*

"Sounds good," I said.

5

When I arrived home on the following afternoon, I was surprised to see our blue plastic recycling box squatting fat on the edge of the sidewalk. Usually I was the one who had to haul it out there. But what really threw me was the sight of the four weekend papers stacked neatly at the top. Unruffled and unread. It was the first time in years I hadn't waded through the weekend woe.

"You're back," said Virginie when I walked in. She looked startled and displeased. Fraser seemed happier to see me. They were parked at the kitchen table, playing Kerplunk, of all things, and sucking on cigarettes. The air was choked with smoke.

"Why wouldn't I be?"

"No, I just—we thought you'd left."

"Because I didn't sleep here last night."

"And 'cause your suitcase and toothbrush were gone," said Fraser.

Of course, my suitcase and toothbrush had never arrived. Happily they hadn't noticed that I'd been using Old Allison's toothbrush.

"I guess that means the airline hasn't called about my luggage. The dolts lost my bag on the way here."

"Well," said Virginie, springing to her feet, "that explains it, then!" She charged into her room and returned moments later, red-faced, clutching the scrunched-up outfit I had pinched from her room—jeans, T-shirt, undies, sneakers.

Oops.

"I found these under Allison's bed!"

I had stashed the goods and promptly forgotten about them. "So?" I attempted to look mystified.

"So, these are my clothes! Clothes that were clean and now are filthy! *Pew!* Clothes that were *stolen* from my room!"

I took a breath. "You think I stole your clothes?" I said it with extraordinary aplomb considering how rattled I usually was in the face of confrontation.

"Maybe borrowed," said Fraser.

Virginie glared at him. "Well, I don't think they were running like little mouses across the floor!" Virginie's English tended to suffer when she was angry. "How else do they go from my room to under Allison's bed?"

I was reminded of several months earlier when she had accused me of stealing her dental floss. Apparently it had run out sooner than expected, and she concluded that I had been using it regularly. She was wrong. I never flossed back then. Old Allison felt that life was too brutish and short for flossing.

But because I had in fact once plucked off a ten-inch strand to dislodge a popcorn husk from between bicuspid and molar, I had allowed the paranoid cheapskate to rant and bully me for half an hour. I was in no mood for a replay. Maybe it was my new height advantage. I felt less inclined to cower.

"I have no idea why your clothes were under Allison's bed. Perhaps she borrowed them."

"Perhaps Allison borrowed my clothes?" she said, smiling.

"Maybe."

"ALLISON COULDN'T FIT ONE TOE INTO MY CLOTHES!"

I had an urge to silence her shriek with a fistful of Kerplunk marbles, but instead I just stood there, all cucumber cool. "Look, I told you I don't know anything about it. You'll have to take it up with Allison when she gets back."

"And when will that be?!"

"I have no idea. But as long as I'm her guest in this apartment, I'll ask you to kindly stay out of my private quarters."

Virginie gasped as I turned and sashayed—yes, sashayed—toward my room. Just before I shut the door with an indignant flourish, I heard her mutter quietly, but conceivably for my ears: "Right, like Allison could fit her blubber ass into any of my clothes."

It was at that moment that I resolved to break up Virginie and Fraser.

But what to do about work? At six-thirty, Old Allison would be expected at the DeSouzas' place. I couldn't just not show up. The last thing I wanted was to kindle any suspicions about Allison's absence. I wondered if I should head down there and feed them the line about the sick father in Los Angeles. Maybe offer to take my own place? Not that I particularly wanted to work, but I hated to leave Isadora, one of the few humans to show me kindness, in a janitorial lurch. Also, I was beyond broke and desperate for income. On the weekend of the Big Change I had flippantly frittered away more cash than I would typically spend in a month on rent and food. The DeSouzas paid me in hard currency, so I could collect at the end of the week. And maybe Fiona Ferguson would be working late at the Malcolm Anders Agency and I could talk to her about getting those free photos.

And maybe I could see Nathan.

I peeled off my constraining upscale-casz outfit, changed into jeans and an Old Allison sweatshirt, and returned to the kitchen. Virginie and Fraser had huffed off, leaving an unfinished Kerplunk game and a fog of cigarette smoke in their wake. I rummaged through the forlorn fridge and cupboards, but there was hardly any food that was mine in the house. A box of saltines. A jar of peanut butter. A blue tomato that resembled a ninety-year-old man with his dentures out. I took the crackers to the living room and crunched my way through half a row, thinking about the incredible meal at Tribe, and the incredibly strange hours that had followed. . . .

"This is it," said George as we stepped off an elevator that opened directly into his apartment.

"Jeez," I said, "what a dump!"

George laughed and tossed his keys into a decorative ceramic bowl.

His digs were snazzier than I'd expected. A corner penthouse loft in a converted brewery owned by his father's company. It was a vast open space, sparsely furnished with ultra-designed pieces—a severe chrome-and-leather contraption (more sculpture than sofa), two cantilevered chairs of metal tubing with cane seats, an absurdly long dining table with absurdly high-backed chairs. Real paintings hung on the walls—large, tasteful abstractions in muted cocoas, creams, and grays. It was all very handsome and austere.

"Make yourself comfortable," he said, getting busy with the hospitality. George used a remote control to turn on music—Norah Jones—and began preparing drinks. In the center of the room, against a thick cement support beam, George had a trolley stocked with liquor bottles and designer glasses and chrome cocktail shakers (one shaped like a rocket ship, another like a penguin). As he carried an ice bucket into the open-concept kitchen, I noticed that the freezer compartment of his stainless-steel refrigerator was located at the bottom.

"Hey," I said, "your freezer is at the bottom."

"Yeah," he said over the din of the automatic ice dispenser. "It's so much more convenient that way."

I wondered why that would be but neglected to pursue the matter. I sank onto the soft leather sofa and watched George prepare his "signature after-dinner beverage." He poured Tia Maria into one cocktail shaker, Baileys Irish Cream into another, Black Sambuca into another. He shook them all until chilled, then started layering thin stripes of each into liqueur glasses. It was easy to imagine him performing this fancy-pants act on every first date, and I noticed that his signature beverage perfectly matched the decor of his apartment.

"Here you are."

"Thanks. It's beautiful." I sipped. "And delicious." And it did its sticky trick. After two glasses I was horizontal on the sofa thingy with George scrabbling around on top of me.

"You know what I like about you?" he whispered, kneading my breasts.

"What?"

"You're so unaffected. I mean, you're incredibly gorgeous, but you seem so . . . real."

Real? I had never felt less real. The entire evening had seemed supremely surreal. "Ow," I said. "You're on my hair."

"Sorry." He shifted an elbow. "Do you want to go upstairs? I mean, we don't, we can just—"

"Let's go," I said.

We climbed a circular staircase to get to the bedroom, an open area that spanned half the length of the room below. There were skylights, floor-to-ceiling windows, and an unenclosed bathroom in the corner—glass shower stall, claw-foot tub, even a toilet right out in the open. George craps in his bedroom, I thought, then tried to banish the image by turning my attention to the bed, which was behemothic, both vertically and horizontally. It was covered in expensive linens and had at least a dozen cushions in tastefully coordinated pillowslips propped against the wooden headboard. It seemed like a grand enough bed in which to lose one's virginity.

Alas, it was not to be.

Being entirely snockered, I didn't wait for George to put the moves on; I simply started shedding clothes as quickly as possible. "Do you make your bed every day?" I said, taking off my blouse. "Or just when you think you'll be bringing someone home?" I hadn't made my bed in about ten years.

"Every day," said George, placing his watch on the night table.

I launched myself, naked, onto the duvet, and settled back to watch George undress. By the time he got down to his very nice silk boxers, I could see that he had a great body, all lithe and long, with well-defined muscles and excellent hair placement (nothing too furry or bare). He dimmed the lights slightly, stripped off his shorts, and joined me on the bed.

We began to kiss and grope each other. George whispered how beautiful I was while he caressed and licked my breasts and I squeezed and rubbed his penis. After a minute or two it became clear that we were both getting ready for action, but instead of reaching for a condom or asking if I was on the Pill, or even going down on me like Studly Guy had the previous day, George yanked my hand away and stood up on the bed. He straddled my body just below the knees and started stroking himself, all fast and furious. It was quite the sight, him towering above me like that with his knees slightly bent, thigh muscles bulging, taut balls jiggling as he pumped his member like a methamphetamine-fueled piston. It was pretty exciting, actually, but I felt a little left out until he said, "Spread those lips, baby. I want to see you touch yourself."

Um, okay, I thought. I mean, what did I know? I figured it was foreplay. So I did what I was told.

"Yeah," snarled George. "Let me see you stroke that clit." Ten and a half seconds later, he was braying and spraying all over me, jerking his cock around for maximum coverage, getting me on the belly, boobs, and a bit in my left eye (semen in the eye is not a good thing—it stings like hell, if you want to know). When he was done, George stood there for a few seconds with a sort of half sneer on his face. Then, as if he was finishing up at a urinal, he proceeded to shake and squeeze the last few droplets onto my thigh. He moved to the edge of the bed, jumped down, and padded to the bathroom area. He took a piss and returned with a box of Kleenex (enclosed in a handsome leather cover).

"God, I'm bagged," he said, lying down beside me. He took several tissues and started drying me off, tenderly, kissing the damp spots after he had mopped up. It was kind of sweet.

"Are you okay?" he said.

"Yeah. You?"

"I'm great. Just kind of tired."

Ah, too fatigued to fornicate.

George gathered up the Kleenex, used and otherwise, and took them to the bathroom. He washed his hands again and then started scouring his teeth with an electric toothbrush.

"Um, I guess I should get going?" I said, not really knowing what to do next.

George gestured for me to wait. He spat toothpaste into the sink and rinsed his mouth. "Don't be ridiculous," he said. "Stay. Sleep over."

"You sure? Maybe I'd better go. . . ." I had a vision of George waking up beside Old Allison.

"Please stay." He fished a boxed toothbrush out of a stainless-steel storage cabinet and held it toward me. "Here, you want to wash up?"

"Um . . . thanks." I hesitated for a nanosecond and then walked naked to the bathroom. I can't tell you how fantastic it felt, how liberating it was to strut confidently without clothing across a large room. Prior to the Change I was hardly ever naked. Once in a while I would sleep nude under blankets, but other than that it was only in the shower—drop the robe, step in, step out, wrap myself in a towel. I'm pretty sure I had never walked naked across a room. And I certainly hadn't been naked in front of another human (except my mom or a pediatrician when I was a toddler). In school it practically killed me every time I had to get changed for phys ed, and that was just stripping to my underwear in front of female classmates. I would always try to show up extremely early or stupidly late to avoid being eyeballed and taunted. I knew that my strategy was obvious, so much so that it had become tauntworthy itself, but it seemed the lesser of searing embarrassments.

Now here I was nude without shame, brushing my teeth, bending over to drink from the tap, even peeing in the wallless bathroom while George alternately watched and prepared for slumber. He methodically lowered the blinds on each window, removed the decorative cushions from the bed, and placed them inside a wooden blanket box for the night. Then he slipped under the duvet and waited for me to return before switching off the night-table lamp.

George pulled a black sleep mask out from under a milewide feather pillow. "Do you want one?" he asked. "I have extras."

"No, thanks. I'm fine."

"All right, then. Good night, Gorgeous."

"Good night." I lay there in the near dark staring at George as he drifted into unconsciousness. He seemed far away in the big bed. None of our parts were touching. Still it was lovely to sleep with someone, another first for me, though not the one I was expecting. With his mask on and his mouth falling open a little, George looked like an innocent superhero. Boy Wonder.

I felt like Allison in Wonderland.

For the third morning in a row, I awoke disoriented. I was starting to get used to my new body, but it alarmed me to be roused by the touch of another human. George had traversed the football-field mattress to press himself against me. I could feel his hard-on digging into the small of my back, his breath hot in my ear. I flipped to face him and we began to kiss. Less than a minute later, George flung back the covers, struggled to his feet, and straddled my body just below the knees.

"Show me the pink, baby. Come on . . . Show it to me!"

I showed it to him. And before you could click your heels ten times and say "I can't believe he'd rather do this again than have intercourse with me," George was padding to the bathroom to get the Kleenex.

"Actually," I said, eyeing the porcelain claw-foot tub, "I think I'll just take a bath, if you don't mind."

"Why would I mind?" said George, all peppy and cheerful. "I'll run it for you. And how about a coffee, shall I make some coffee?"

"That'd be great."

"Cappuccino, espresso, Americano, or latte?"

Twenty minutes later I was up to my neck in steaming fragrant water. George had prepared the bath with aromatic oils and sprinkled some fresh freesia petals into the mix. Sunshine streamed in and lit the room yellow and happy. Stephane Grapelli was fiddling sweet from surround-sound speakers. George placed a fat mug of cappuccino on a shelf that stretched across the width of the tub.

"Thank you."

"My pleasure."

He moved toward the shower pod and shed his robe. I watched him through the ripply glass, lathering up and rinsing off like the poster boy for Lever 2000. The scent of bath oil mingled with the aroma of strong coffee. I sat up for a sip of brew just as Grapelli started in on something slow and voluptuous.

Well, I thought, sinking back into the tub, I guess it doesn't get much better than this . . . .

The doorbell rang. I dusted the saltine crumbs off my face and chest and went to answer.

It was a handsome man in a handsome suit, holding a handsome white box with *Flowers by Marco* embossed in pink on the side.

"Allison Penny?"

"Yes."

He hoisted the heavy box into my arms.

"Wow! Thank you very much!"

"You're most welcome." He seemed to be enjoying my reaction. He bowed almost imperceptibly and then headed back to his shiny *Flowers by Marco* van.

I took the package to the kitchen and popped the top. An enclosed card said: *When can I see you again? George.* I parted the thick layers of pink tissue paper. Roses. Red ones. Three dozen of the long-stemmed variety, their preposterously plump heads beaded with cool moisture. I felt a tinge of disappointment. I've never cared for roses, particularly red ones. I find them gaudy and obvious, the streetwalkers of the flower world. Hot red mouths. Rude thorns. Still, it was thrilling to receive them. No one had sent me flowers before. The only thing I'd received via deliverymen was pizza.

I left a duly effusive thank-you message on George's answering machine and set about finding vessels to hold thirty-six Wilt the Stilt roses in our vase-less apartment. Pop bottles, Mason jars, wine bottles, even an empty milk carton was pressed into service. By the time I had wrestled the flowers into water and positioned them on windowsills, tables, countertops, and speakers, it was time to leave the mausoleum and go to work, or at least attempt to go to work.

Success. If you can call it that. Fifteen minutes later I was riding in the van, heading to 505 Richmond. I had told the DeSouzas the whole phony-baloney story, and after a protracted Portuguese huddle on the paved front lawn, Isadora signaled for me to climb aboard. She didn't seem too keen on the impromptu arrangement. When I first explained the situation, she'd made a number of brusque inquiries, and now regarded me with a vaguely hostile air. The rest of the DeSouzas, on the other hand, appeared eager to have me take Old Allison's place. Paulo, in particular, seemed pleased by the plan. For the first time ever he took the seat directly across from me. He didn't don shades or disappear into Discman; he asked questions, joked around, and offered to show me the ropes when we got to work. Alvaro and Abril kept their Game Boys switched off and ogled me the entire ride. Mina, who had never said boo before, wanted to know where I got my jeans, and what shade of nail polish I was wearing, and just generally treated me like a glamorous older sister whom she would like to emulate. Mrs. DeSouza, who usually kept her eyes fixed on the road, turned and checked me out a dozen times (risking life and limb by abandoning her mind-control traffic duties). Mr. DeSouza also scoped me repeatedly, in the rearview mirror, and kept uncharacteristically quiet. He didn't swear once at the *idiotas* who failed to signal before stopping to make a left. Bizarre. But it was Isadora's behavior that I found the most altered, and distressing. She sat as far away from me as possible and was barely civil, let alone her usual warm self. Not that I expected her to instantly treat New Allison like an old chum, but I did expect a certain level of openness and affability, at least the same level I'd encountered when she initially made friendly overtures to Old Allison. I had never seen Isadora so closed up. So clenched. In order to loosen the fist of her mood, I tried to engage her in chitchat, bringing up the one topic she invariably loved to jaw about: Virginie. I wanted to let her know that I, too, despised the "Porco," that I was a bona fide member of the Old Allison/Isadora Porco-hating club. I wanted to tell her about the clothes under the bed, how I had been cruelly accused, and how I had coolly stared down and frustrated the enemy. But I didn't get the chance to tell her, because every time I tried to kick-start conversation, she would shut it down with a curt retort. Had something horrid happened earlier in the day? Was Isadora in a rare foul temper that had nothing to do with me? Or, more likely, was she just treating me the way I would have treated me if I were in her place? Like a spoiled beautiful person, probably stupid, with whom I could have nothing in common, a person who was probably accustomed to getting whatever she wanted, more worthy of my scorn than my friendship. I noticed that Isadora had shifted her body position so she could stare out the rear window. Only once did she look over (to mutter "Down, boy" when cousin Paulo—engaged to be married to a nice Portuguese girl—got a little too flirty). I noticed something else, too. For the first time ever, I hadn't received one of Isadora's trademark sympathetic smiles. Not one. I had always suspected that the maudlin mug was reserved for Old Allison, and apparently I was right.

It didn't cheer me to conclude that Isadora had been something of a pity pal, and it cheered me less to realize that I would have welcomed her back in that capacity. It was galling to be felt sorry for and embraced, but worse to be resented and shut out.

Armed with keys and cart and the resolve not to take it to

heart, I rolled down the hallway with Paulo in tow. He had convinced the elder DeSouzas that he should accompany me through the first office to make sure I was doing things correctly. I told them I would be fine, but Paulo insisted. Oddly enough, now that he was all into me, I no longer found him appealing. Only days before I thought he was quite handsome in a silent, tough-guy way—the five o'clock shadow, the dark shades, the crucifix hugging the muscled, hirsute neck. Now he just seemed short (I was at least three inches taller). And I hadn't realized until he started chatting me up what a grating voice he had on him. Like Joe Pesce after sucking half a balloon's worth of helium. Downright Lollipop Guild. Paulo was definitely a lot more attractive when I was five foot three, and he kept his cakehole closed, and didn't follow me around 505 Richmond like a beagle in heat.

He tailed me through three entire offices, doing most of the work (which was nice) and chattering all the way (which wasn't). Finally, I dropped several hearty hints that I was of the lesbian persuasion, which succeeded in sending macho Paulo scuttling back to his broom closet.

Good.

Unfortunately, by the time I made it to the Malcolm Anders Agency, it had pretty much cleared out. There was one guy working late, typing at his computer and eating from a bag of mini-carrots. He had a buzz cut, long sideburns, and 1950s-style horn-rimmed glasses. He was wearing a tank top and a curling cardigan with plastic buttons in the shape of curling rocks. I couldn't tell if he was ultra-groovy or gay or both.

"Excuse me," I said, stopping my cart at his cubicle.

"Yes?"

"I guess Fiona has left for the day, huh?"

"She's actually out of the office this week. But she'll be calling in." He studied my face as if we had met and he was trying to place me. "Is there something I can help you with?"

"Um, she gave me her card and asked me to get in touch with her."

"Cleaning lady!" he said, pointing to my cart. "You must be . . ." He sifted through the papers on his desk, locating a lime green Post-it note. "You must be Allison Penny."

"How did you know?"

"I'm Brendan, Fiona's assistant. She told me you might be calling, and that you were stunning and not to let you get away."

I laughed. Then I tried a smile on him, one I had been practicing at home in the bathroom mirror. It started out cutesy, then bloomed into dazzling.

"She was right. You are stunning." He looked me up and down. "But you're gonna have to lose the shirt. Not lose as in topless, just lose as in replace it with something, anything else."

I laughed. My Old Allison sweatshirt was about ten sizes too big.

"Mini-carrot?"

"No, thanks."

"They're organic." He held the bag toward me, jiggled it. I took one.

"You know, Fiona said you were a cleaning lady; she didn't say you were a cleaning lady *here*."

"I'm not. I'm just filling in for a friend. This is my first time at this building."

"Really? That's weird." He devoured a carrot in rapid rabbit nibbles. "So you're just here for tonight?"

"No. I'll probably be filling in for a little while."

"Oh. Hmm. 'Cause you know there's this other agency in the building. And if anyone up there gets a look at you, they'll probably try to sign you. And you're gonna think it's a good idea because their offices are a lot swankier than ours, and they rep a lot of top models—a couple who started here, as a matter of fact—but you shouldn't do it, because it's a big pond up there with a lot of big fish, and Fiona is, like, the best agent you could ever ask for, especially if you're just starting out. She doesn't just get you gigs, she'll totally help you launch and manage your career."

"Is she on vacation right now?"

"Sort of. Not exactly. She spends a week every year volunteering up at Camp Wajakosh. You know the cancer camp for kids?"

"Oh. Wow."

"Yeah. Honest to God, I don't know how she does it. I think I'd just be crying all the time." He looked as if he was about to start weeping just thinking about it. "All right," he said, slapping himself on the cheek to snap out of it, "I'm gonna get you the brochure for the photographer we use."

"Thanks." I felt a glimmer of guilt.

He moved toward the reception area, and I took the opportunity to empty his trash can. I had just finished tipping the contents into the cart when he returned.

"Stop that," he said. "You're offending my sensibilities!"

I tucked the empty container under his desk. "Somebody's gotta do it."

"But not *you*, sweetie. Definitely not *you*! I think you should hang up your duster. Throw in the moist towelette."

"I can't. Not yet anyway."

He shook his head and sighed, a well-if-that-don't-beat-all expression on his face. "Here," he said, waving the brochure and placing it on the corner of his desk. "Her name's Keneisha Clarke. All you have to do is call and make an appointment. Okay? I'll let her know that we're paying for the session."

"Okay."

"She's really nice. And really cool. She's, like, this seventy-year-old woman with dreads down to her ass. She'll tell you what to wear and bring and all that jazz."

"Okay. Thanks." As I continued emptying my way through

the office, I thought: There's no way in hell I'm going to scam free photos from these people—people who feed me mini-carrots and volunteer at cancer camps and call me "sweetie." No way.

But when I left the agency, it was with the brochure folded deep in my pocket.

I headed for the *WUT Up* office, hoping that Andrew McKay would have cleared out by the time I got there. Presumably he wouldn't be taping pictures of Shirley Booth on my cart, but I figured he'd find some way to harass me.

The place was packed, and evidently the staff had been toiling through the weekend. Garbage cans were overflowing and there were stacks of greasy pizza boxes and crushed soda cans and beer bottles containing bloated cigarette butts.

When it was this crowded, it meant that *WUT Up* was in the last stage of production. Every two months there'd be a night or two like this and it was always a drag, having to maneuver around all the bodies and contend with the hostile grunts and groans as I tried to get under desks, past the fabulous footwear, to cart away the crap of the assiduous staff. Typically, it was a pain in the ass, but on this occasion the hipsters were inordinately affable, smiling, getting right out of my way, even handing me their bins and helping me clear (mostly it was the males who did this). Everyone seemed to be sucking on beers and kicking back, and I didn't have the usual trouble navigating my way through the trash-can labyrinth, quite the opposite.

Of course, as soon as Andrew McKay caught sight of me, he had to start something. He sat bolt upright in his chair and bellowed, "Hell-o, Guvner," in an accent worthy of Keanu Reeves in *Bram Stoker's Dracula.* I ignored him. I had perfected my poker face, pretending for ten months to be Portuguese and uncomprehending. Why stop now?

"Hey," he said. "Excuse me, Miss Cleaning Person?"

I didn't respond.

"Hello . . . lovely cleaning-type person?" He said it with extreme faux-earnestness. A few people chuckled as I mutely carried on with my work. Andrew approached my cart and put his hand on my arm. "Hey," he said, more to the group than to me. "Where's our mascot? What have you done with Hazel?" He was flushed pink and slurring his words, obviously drunk or stoned or both.

I stared as if mystified, then voiced one of two phrases I knew how to say in a foreign language: *Na se klotsisi to papee.* In Greek it means: May a duck kick you. My ex-roommate, Elda, had taught it to me.

"Easy for you to say," said Andrew, dimpling, giggling crazy at his self-amusing retort.

"Looks like Hazel's been taken from us," said a pierced-face hipster with mock sorrow.

"Replaced by Claudia Schiffer," said a girl with a Cleopatra hairdo dyed the color of Hawaiian Punch.

"Poor Hazel," said Andrew. "I guess she went back to her swamp."

"Back to her tar pit," said Cleopatra, laughing.

"Yes, walking and waving into the tar pit . . . Good. I'm sick of that smelly troll and her death stare. Hey, Claudia," whispered Andrew, tugging on my sleeve. "You wanna beer? A brewsky?" He weaved over to the makeshift kitchen area and started rattling around in the fridge. "What the fuck . . . are we outta beer, you guys?"

"Afraid so."

"You mean to tell me we've put this baby to bed, and we're outta beer?!"

"Yuppers."

"Damn!" said Andrew. "This calls for measures drastic. Methinks we must repair to my lanai for more libations. What say you people?"

Inexplicably, Andrew's minions seemed keen to follow

him home. Just before the mass departure, he put his hands on me again. "Hey, Claudia, you wanna come for a drink? Come for a drinky?" he said, tipping an imaginary glass to his mouth, grinning cute, giving me the dimples. Even with the supposed language barrier it was impossible to mistake his meaning. I pointed to several desks that required cleaning.

"Oh pshaw!" he said, tugging on my sleeve, gesturing for me to leave it.

I yanked my arm away and moved off.

As he was stumbling out of the office, Andrew turned and shouted, "Yo, Claudia, don't forget to LOCK THE DOOR." He mimed the action so that I would understand.

I smiled and called out the one other phrase Elda had taught me: *"E mana sou einai mounie apo forado."* Your mother is a horse's cunt.

"Absolutely," said Andrew, blowing me a kiss. "I love you, too."

After they left I did something I probably wouldn't have done if I hadn't just been called a smelly troll by that no-good shit smear Andrew McKay. Smelly? I was never smelly. Ugly, yes, troll-like, perhaps, but that was beyond my control. Never was I smelly. As for the "death stare" comment, my God, you think he would've learned something! But no, not Andrew McKay, not Mr. I Can Get Away with Anything Because I'm Cute and Popular and My Parents Are Well-to-Do. Okay, hang on, I'm getting ahead of myself. Back to the thing I did.

For a few minutes, I just rage-tidied, an anti-Andrew tirade flaming hot in my brain. I was clearing detritus off his desk in an angry and haphazard fashion when I accidentally knocked the mouse to the floor, which caused the computer monitor to flicker out of sleep mode. The screen lit up with the nauseating new cover of *WUT Up*, the summer issue; the one that had just been "put to bed." It featured a digital composite of a man-machine—half robot, half full-lipped male model. ARTIFICIAL INTELLIGENCE NOW! screamed the head-line. A small cursor blinked on and off in the middle of the page.

I picked the mouse up off the floor and placed it back on its pad. Then for some reason I kept my hand on the device, rolling it around so that the cursor moved to the arrow in the corner of the screen. I pressed the left button and began scrolling down. The next two pages came up side by side, as if the magazine was open on the screen. It was an advertising spread for something called Frog March. Those two little words appeared tiny and green in the corner; the rest of the image was a panoramic close-up of a naked young woman lying on her side. Just her torso made it into the two-page spread. Her nipples and pubes had been airbrushed out. Exactly what Frog March was, I couldn't tell you.

I continued scrolling, and the laid-out magazine went slowly by. More ads, at least eight glossy full-pagers, all of which featured starving, inadequately clad teens draped in or around ostensibly must-have products. Next up was the table of contents, followed by Andrew McKay's column—an insuf-ferable block of vainglorious drivel called "True Confes-sions." Above the text was a picture of Andrew, laughing and holding out his hand as if to block the lens and hide from its prying eye. Of course, it was a shamelessly premeditated pose. You could tell by the careful positioning of the hand and the way the fingers were spread just wide enough to reveal his dimpled, allegedly bashful cuteness.

This is where I stopped.

The "True Confessions" page appeared in every issue of *WUT Up.* In it, Andrew McKay would stray from the digital-culture mandate of the magazine and simply divulge his guilty pop-culture pleasures to readers. I had read one in which he "confessed" to harboring libidinous feelings for the stern host of *The Weakest Link,* and another in which he'd admitted to reading *InStyle* magazine in the bubble bath. As if anyone gave a flying fuck. In the new issue Andrew claimed that he felt a grave and overpowering need to unburden himself. He confessed to having an addiction—a junk-food addiction. Gasp! He then went on to list and tally up his daily intake of empty calories.

Gee, what a load off. No doubt, peace of mind and restful slumber were immediately restored after that powerful unbosoming.

As usual, the faux-dramatic cuteness of the piece galled me. And as usual I thought: Yeah, right, he feels the need to get this inanity off his chest, but Andrew's real sinister secret can stay hidden forever without any deleterious effects on his mental or physical well-being. Then, suddenly, I felt a tingle of brave in the fingers and the back of the skull as I fantasized about revising the text and offering up a truly true confession from Andrew McKay.

Yes.

And I wasn't afraid of being found out or losing my job. I realized that, looking the way I did, it probably wouldn't be difficult to get another job. Hell, maybe I could even try out the modeling thing, just for laughs. Didn't Fiona say the money could be very good?

The first paragraph I left almost unaltered:

> Gentle *WUT Up* Reader,
> There is something I must share with you, something I am deeply ashamed of but can no longer conceal. For years, I told myself that I was fine, that I didn't have a problem, but lately my secret has been weighing heavily on my mind, even affecting my mood and performance (or so friends and loved ones tell me). Therefore, I must have out with it: I am an addict . . . a junk-food addict.

I moved the cursor into the body of the text and clicked in after the colon, just before *I am an addict . . . a junk-food addict.* I hit the insert button and typed, *I am a liar . . . a liar and a killer.*

I was able to retain the first sentence of Andrew's next paragraph: *It all started years ago when I was just a lad.* I clicked in after that and continued typing.

It was back in high school. As you may have guessed, I was wildly popular (please see photo above). I was captain of the intramural hockey team, Student Council president, and a member of the Special Events Committee. I was also senior co-editor of the yearbook, and if it hadn't been for Miss XX, my Theater Arts teacher, I would have undoubtedly played the lead opposite Nicole Mackenzie in the school's award-winning amateur production of *Oklahoma!*

Miss XX wasn't always my enemy. Initially, I was one of her pets (probably because I flirted with her in spite of her disfigurement). Yes, Miss XX possessed an unfortunate facial distortion: seriously protruding eyeballs, which made her appear perpetually horrified and rather insane. Of course, students made fun of her, but I was one of her staunchest defenders. That is, until she made the grievous gaffe of casting Robbie Kerr as the lead in *Oklahoma!* I was flabbergasted and irate (even though it was widely acknowledged that Robbie was truly talented—a natural actor with a big voice). But I looked like Curly. Hell, I *was* Curly—handsome, strapping, and heterosexual. Robbie was a bone rack, he had acne, and he was gay. I'd like to add that Nicole Mackenzie, the beauty chosen to play Laurey Williams, happened to be my girlfriend, so it would have been perfect for us. Honestly, I found it hard to believe that after months of smooching Miss XX's ass, she actually wanted me to accept the role of Jud Fry. The villain!

I dropped out of the production and went on a bitter campaign against Miss XX, dreaming up a raft of new and spectacularly cruel jokes about her visage (my anonymously authored list "Top Ten Reasons Miss XX's Eyes Are Popping" circulated for weeks). I also started the rumor that she was a lesbo. After all, she never wore dresses, she had her hair cut short like a man's, and she picked Robbie Kerr to star in the play. Clearly it was a gay-solidarity thing. Clearly if she was immune to my prodigious charms, it was because she preferred fish to meat.

My campaign of ill will gained momentum, and I can assure you Miss XX was not unaware of it. Still, nothing tragic would have happened if I hadn't gone that one step further. Had I not been a total scoundrel, Edwin Fung would still be alive.

Edwin Fung was co-editor of the yearbook, a grade-twelver. There were five or six of us on staff, but Edwin and I were the top guys. I was the content side; Edwin was the technical side. He also snapped most of the photos. Edwin was a quiet student in the Enriched Program. He planned to study science and become a medical researcher (I know because I read it in his obituary). His parents were immigrants from China, very conservative and strict. Edwin must have been deeply afraid of shaming them, because after the police came to the school to interrogate him, after they tried to extract a confession by suggesting that only he had the technical expertise to alter the yearbook at the last minute, after they informed him that he would almost certainly be expelled, Edwin panicked. And that night Edwin, who obviously took things much too seriously, jumped off the Bloor Street viaduct.

Of course, anyone with a smattering of brain cells knew that it was I who had altered the yearbook—specifically, the quarter-page photo of Miss XX leading the relaxation exercises that took place at the beginning of each drama class. Edwin had taken the snapshot of her hovering over the prostrate forms of Jessica McBain, Debbie Alexander, and Christa Vukovics. But it was not Edwin who drew the squiggly lines to make it look as if rays were coming out of Miss XX's eyes, and it was not Edwin who added the offensive caption to the bottom of the photo: *Miss XX incapacitates the gals with her gorgon death stare before dragging 'em to the portables for some alternative-lifestyle lovemaking.*

Naturally, the cops interrogated everyone on the yearbook staff, including moi. But I played it cuke cool. I knew that our headquarters had no lock on the door. So anybody could have fucked with the program, right? The bozo cops were throwing their weight around, but I knew they had no proof. And I knew all about the burden of proof. My dad's a hot-shot attorney, don't you know, practically a celeb in this town. Still, there was something of a case to be made against me: my position on staff, my public beef with Miss XX, the fact that it was my responsibility to check the layout and copy before the yearbook went to print (I claimed I was so sick of looking at it, I just skimmed it, and that all I was guilty of was sloth and inexperience).

The funny thing is, the day after Edwin took a long walk off a short viaduct, everyone expected me to be so filled with remorse that I would come forward to clear his name. But I figured as long as he took the plunge, he might as well take the blame. Of course, Miss XX was pressuring the school to expel me. The police were threatening to launch a thorough investigation (although they themselves were being scrutinized for leaning too heavy on Edwin and frightening him, literally, to death). I tell you, it was quite the kerfuffle. In the end, strictly as a show of good faith, my dad offered to pay for a reprint of the yearbook. A generous gesture appreciated by all. And that was that. I finished up the year and returned the following September to do my grade twelve. Miss XX didn't return, though. Miss XX was pretty much forced to seek employment elsewhere.

So you see, even though she was right, even though I would have been perfect for the role, I never did end up playing the bad guy after all.

I hit Control S on the keyboard to save the document. I read it over, corrected the typos, and re-saved.

It gave me satisfaction to know that Andrew would read it and have to once more erase the story from memory. At best,

I figured one or two others in the office might get a look at it and force him to dredge up the past. I had no idea that the magazine would go to the printer that way, and that because I had left the first paragraph almost entirely intact, and the length of the text virtually the same, nobody would pick up the difference at the proof stage, and that the new true Andrew McKay confession would be noticed only once seventy-five thousand copies of the magazine had been printed and bound with glue. But several weeks later I learned that that's exactly what had happened.

Alas, the mags never made it to the stands, but someone at *WUT Up* leaked a copy to *Scoop* magazine and soon after, the mainstream media was gleefully reporting the story. Of course, Andrew denied any involvement in the original incident and threatened to sue the perpetrator of this one once he was found. The funny thing was, he had to admit that, as in the earlier scandal, it was he who had "proofed" the offending issue before it was mass-printed. And once again Daddy had to come to the rescue, tapping the capital to pay for a brand new print run.

This time to the tune of $112,000.

I took the service elevator to the fourth floor. Time for one more office before my break. Contrary to Brendan's fears, nobody at IZ Talent Management tried to sign me up or offer me the world. Mind you, the place was deserted, so maybe someone would have if they'd been around. Maybe if Peter Igel had been "working" late, he would have told me that I had a special quality, and maybe he would have put the jazz music on and tried to rip my clothes off. Maybe I would have stapled his penis to the desk.

His lamp was on, but Igel was long gone. He had left a Post-it note stuck to the door of his office: *Please Windex and wipe.* An arrow pointed to a greasy handprint on the glass. Igel often left these notes for the cleaning staff. *Please dust* stuck to the Art Deco figurine that stood atop his filing cabinet, or

Please vacuum stuck to the seat cushions of the sofa. As I lifted his trash can to empty it, I saw that it contained his usual sloppy mess. That night it was a half-eaten bratwurst, sauerkraut spilling from the bun onto a photo of a smiling wanna-be, the left side of her face almost entirely obscured by mustard and cabbage. I fished out the fat brat and balanced it in my palm. Then I opened a sliding drawer on the metal cabinet behind Igel's desk and filed it away. Under *S* for sausage. I replaced the can without rinsing it. Then I wrote, *Please fuck yourself up the ass* on a Post-it note and stuck it on the December page of his Annie Leibowitz calendar.

I figured wherever I was seven months from that night, I'd have at least one thing to smile about.

When I got to the patio, all my New Allison audacity began to melt away. My stomach felt flippy and I had to resist the urge to gnaw on my nails.

Nathan always came to the patio on Mondays. We'd blab about our respective weekends, and he'd fill me in on the new films he'd seen. I invariably looked forward to these encounters, but on this night the impending tête-à-tête filled me with equal measures of anticipation and dread. On the one hand, I was itching to test-drive my charms on the object of my affection for the last eight months. On the other hand, I was sure that Nathan would recognize me as the chick who had blundered the Antonioni title. Would he think that I was stalking him, following him from workplace to workplace? Probably he'd just think it was a coincidence, and that I was a bonehead. But even if he didn't think that, what about the Paulo Effect? Now that I was growing accustomed to my status as stately long-limbed goddess, would Nathan suddenly seem lusterless? Would the crush crumble and the fancy fade when I next set my new blue eyes on him?

As it turned out: no. My heart did the usual triple lutz/double salchow combo when Nathan stepped onto the dark patio and I caught sight of his balding, curiously shaped head glinting in the moonlight.

"Hey!" he said, coming to an abrupt halt when my presence registered. "Oh, sorry. I thought you were someone else."

I am someone else. "It's okay," I said. "Plenty of room and the weather's fine."

"I was just— I thought my friend was out here."

Friend! I loved that he called me that. "Who, Allison?"

"Yeah. Is she around? I saw her cart at the door."

"No. I left the cart there. I'm filling in for her tonight."

"Oh."

"She's a friend of mine, too. A good friend."

"Oh, really?" He appeared confused and I couldn't tell if it was because Allison had a friend who looked like me, or because someone who looked like me was scouring offices, or because someone who looked like me was standing up and advancing toward someone who looked like him, with a long arm outstretched for a shake.

"I'm Allison as well."

"I'm Nathan."

"Right, Allison has mentioned you. Nice to meet you." I held on for a second longer than appropriate. Then I gave him the smile, the one I had been practicing, but it just seemed to unnerve him.

He took a step back. "So, is Allison sick or something?"

I told him the tale about the father ill in Los Angeles, adding a coma element and a bedside vigil to zing it up a bit.

"Oh, boy. I'm really sorry to hear that. Holy cow." He did look sorry. "Well, if you speak to her, please send my best wishes."

"I will, thanks."

"I guess I should . . ." He gestured toward the building, then executed a move in which he tried to back away and turn around simultaneously, resulting in a small stumble. He laughed self-consciously. "Nice meeting you," he said, and disappeared inside.

So much for test-driving my charms. Clearly, I made

Nathan uncomfortable. In the video store, he'd gone out of his way not to look at me. Now he couldn't wait to get away. He probably felt intimidated, considered me out of his league (the way I felt about him just a few days earlier). It occurred to me that, so far, only handsome/successful men and sleazebags had come on to me. Would it be possible for New Allison to hook up with a balding, insecure video clerk? Would that make sense?

Nathan's rapid retreat left me a little lugubrious. Or maybe it was the patio working its melancholy magic. For the first time since the Big Change I felt like singing. I began. "'When the wind howls in—'" I stopped. Cleared my throat. Started again. "'When the wind howls in from the north—'" Holy shit! My voice! My voice was gone! Well, not gone, but different. Not nearly as good. I stood up. Paced. Cleared my throat and tried again. "'When the wind howls in from the north. And the stars are hiding inside. When you know your baby ain't coming home—'" I couldn't hit the high note! My range was kaput! I took several deep breaths to calm myself down and then tried something less octave spanning. "'No moon, no June, no prairie sky. No lips, no eyes, no gentle sigh . . .'" Bizarre. My pitch was still accurate, but the range and nuance had vanished. Clearly, the transmutation had caused my vocal cords to shift and reshape. Of course. It was understandable.

I sang a bit more, trying to get used to the second-rate sound, and the fact that my best Old Allison virtue had vanished. I tried telling myself that it could have been worse; at least I could still carry a tune, and I reasoned that a trade-off was probably in order. I mean, was I not still way ahead of the game? So my lovely lilt had flown. So what. It's not as if it was doing me any good anyway, right?

Still, it troubled me. And as I sat there alone in the not-quite dark, I couldn't help wondering if anything else had been lost.

6

Model portfolios. Actor headshots. Aside from her name, address, and phone number, that was all the text in Keneisha Clarke's brochure. I sipped my coffee and eyeballed the well-composed, attractively lit photos in her promo piece. Usually, I'd be reading the morning newspaper, but few things were very usual anymore.

George had called earlier—in mid-squash game—to invite me to spend the day at his club. I could hear ball smashing wall as he breathlessly, reverberatingly told me to take a cab, and provided me with his father's account number so I wouldn't have to pay for it. He advised me not to wear jeans.

I had called the taxi. Now I had my hand on the phone again.

"Keneisha speaking."

I hung up. *Fuck it. I'll just go to the photo booth in the subway.* I drained my coffee. Stared at the brochure. *Of course, even if the booth is working, the lighting is ghastly, and I'll only get my head in the shot . . .* I couldn't help but notice that the female models in the brochure weren't nearly as beautiful as I was, and surmised that they were probably outearning me by a ratio of at least ten to one.

I picked up the phone.

George was waiting outside when my cab arrived at the swanky old-dough digs. He looked tanned and healthy in his squash outfit, the sun shining all over him.

"Hey, babe. I'd kiss you but I'm all sweaty."

"It's okay." I didn't detect any evidence of sweat. Perhaps even perspiration was tasteful and understated around here.

George escorted me past various riffraff screening posts to the interior of the club. I got spooked by a sign that said WHITES ONLY, until George assured me that it referred to nothing more than racket-sport garb. Still, the notice could have easily applied to the members I saw milling about as George took me on a tour through the luxe labyrinth.

"And this, finally, is the entrance to the women's spa area."

"Uh-huh."

George smiled. "I took the liberty of booking you some treatments."

"Really?"

"You're into the spa thing, aren't you?"

"Um . . . sure." The closest I had come to the "spa thing" was when my toilet malfunctioned and sprayed like a bidet for two hours.

"Well, I'm doing a massage, facial, and manicure. I timed your stuff so we could meet for a late lunch in the atrium. Around three. That all right?"

"Of course. Thanks."

"Eva's expecting you. She helped me pick the treatments, but feel free to substitute."

"Um, do I need anything . . . ?"

"Nope. They have robes, combs, shampoo, hair dryers, body lotion, shavers—"

"Wow."

"Yup," said George. "Everything you need."

"Everything I need" included having my face exfoliated with a kiwi-pineapple peel and hydrated with a truffle-butter mask. In between those two procedures, my pores were coaxed open with an orchid-infused steam, only to be shut tight with glass wands full of antifreeze gel. I had my hands "polished" with ground Thai rice, then massaged with fragrant oils. I had my feet dipped in a mixture of hot paraffin wax and something called fango mud, then wrapped up like take-out sandwiches, in paper-lined foil, and set under heat lamps for fifteen minutes. After that, I was bathed by an attendant in a dimly lit chamber that smelled of cedar and citrus—the first part of my Ayurvedic body wrap. I was then slathered neck to toe in heavy cream mixed with cocoa, and rolled up, I kid you not, in banana leaves. Giant banana leaves. I was like a human fajita, like a five-foot-nine-inch packet of dim sum sticky rice. It took two attendants to peel, rinse, and rouse me—I was relaxed practically into a coma. I took a steam bath and a shower, drank peppermint tea, lounged in a wicker recliner in a terry-cloth robe, and flipped through *People* magazine's 50 Most Beautiful People issue until it was time to get ready and meet George.

"There she is," he said as I glided around members lunching lovely in the atrium. "How do you feel?"

"Wonderful."

George was seated with two friends who rose to shake my hand. "Glen, Doug, this is Allison."

"Pleased to meet you," I said.

Glen and Doug were clean-cut, propitiously born, Delta Kappa Epsilon types in their late twenties. I wasn't expecting a group meal, and I gleaned pretty quickly that I was there to be displayed, like a pretty new Patek Phillippe. After polite preliminaries, the boys launched into a conversation that, while often meant to impress me, was never really intended to include me—joshing about mutual friends, boasting about business matters, spewing sports statistics, etc.

Now, here's where you expect me to get all boo-hoo and indignant, right? I was supposed to feel exploited. The browbeaten bauble. Well, the fact is, I didn't mind. For one thing, the concept that someone would want to show me off was so novel, I was clam happy to play along. More important, I was far too detached from the experience to feel put out by it. After all, I was only *acting* the part of George's new ornament, and frankly, it was a pretty enjoyable role. The spa treatments had been amazing; every cell in my body was sighing sweet. Did I really need to assert my intelligence, and have Doug or Glen get to know the real me? No. What I needed was something good to eat. I ordered a grilled lamb burger and sweet-potato fries. Glen and Doug and George opted for high-protein low-calorie salads. When I endeavored to pass the breadbasket around, they all but recoiled (as if the thing contained anthrax, or an economy-class airline ticket). I happily swallowed two rolls with butter before engulfing the rest of my meal like a starving velociraptor.

"Jeez," said Doug (or maybe it was Glen, I can't really remember), "where *do* you put it, Allison?"

"Here," I said, jutting out my chest. There was a moment of silence before Doug and Glen burst out laughing.

"And she's funny, too!" said Doug. Then George laughed as well, but it seemed to be with relief. After that I kept quiet and finished my lunch, which was actually my breakfast, and much, much better than half a row of saltines. The food at the club was good. Very good. After I had polished off a slab of chocolate mud cake with warm liquid center, I let George take me back to his condo and come on me. He wanted me to hang around and have dinner with him later, but I invented an excuse since I had to go to work.

Strange that after all that swankiness I had to hustle off to my scrub gig. As I went along my route—a quiet, Nathan-less night—I calculated that I would have to empty trash cans for a week to pay for one of those glorious banana leaf treatments.

When I got home, I found Virginie and Fraser cuddling on the sofa, watching *Late Night with Conan O'Brien*. Normally, I would've headed straight to my room and stayed there, but I had a mission to complete. So I changed into my Le Château slut dress—sans bra and panties—and returned to the living room to inflict friction and induce dissension.

"Mind if I join you?"

Virginie shrugged. Fraser said, "Why, are we coming apart?" a rejoinder that left him with a satisfied grin.

You will be, I thought. Then I forced out a chuckle at his joke attempt, sat on the love seat opposite them, and crossed my legs high, giving them a nanosecond flash of naked crotch. "You're a real card," I said flirty to Fraser. "You ought to be dealt with."

He blushed and guffawed. Virginie smiled tight. "George called," she said, trying to pinch off the jovial exchange and get me the hell out of there. "He said to call him when you got home."

"Well, it's kind of late. I'll call him tomorrow."

"So you and George are together, eh?" said Virginie.

"Well, we're dating." I looked squarely at Fraser. "But, you know, not exclusively."

"So, um, George sent all the flowers?" said Fraser.

"Yeah."

"It's a bit much," snipped Virginie.

"Feel free to chuck some," I said. "I'm not really a rose person anyway."

"Oh, really?" said Fraser.

Virginie glared at him for giving a shit, or pretending to.

"I'm more of a tulip person," I confided. Then I looked at Virginie. "Roses are pretty, but sort of common, you know." I looked back at Fraser and crossed my legs as high as I could go without getting gynecological. "Tulips are much more stately and beautiful, don't you think?"

"I guess." He put his hands over his crotch.

Virginie cranked the volume on the TV.

All three of us stared at it then, at Conan O'Brien interviewing Gisele Bundchen, but none of us was paying attention. I could tell. The room was vibrating with a hot preoccupation. Our TV viewing was like a flimsy sheet tossed over a tangle of wrestlers—a thin veneer atop the pulsing horniness and sexual jealousy raging big and silent in the room. Three people ostensibly focused on giggly Gisele, but clearly preoccupied by pudendum. I was so close to a full and deliberate flashing, mere millimeters away from seriously breaking the social code, that it was impossible not to obsess about it, each one of us in a different way. It was tantamount to having the coffee table burst into flames, and the three of us just sit there, gawking at the tube as if mesmerized.

At the commercial break, Virginie made a big show of

stretching cute and yawning drowsy. "I'm so sleepy," she said in her little-girl voice. She rubbed a fist in one eye and rested her head on Fraser's shoulder. "Time to hit the hay, babe?"

"Um, I don't know. I wouldn't mind watching the rest of the show."

"Really?"

"Might as well see it all," I said, flexing the foot of my crossed leg.

Virginie gave me a dagger look. I thought she was going to tell me to fuck off or mind my own beeswax, but instead she just swallowed hard—I could practically hear the constricted gulp. She snuggled in closer to Fraser, coiling herself around his arm, becoming appendage.

"You can go if you want," he said, kissing the top of her head. "I'll be in in a few minutes."

Sure. Like that was going to happen.

"No, it's okay. I'll stay for a bit."

Of course, the moment Conan began bidding viewers good night, Virginie collected her smoking paraphernalia and stood up. "Ready?" she said, more command than inquiry.

"Um, yeah." He had no choice.

Virginie pitched the remote at (not *to*) me. " 'Night," she snipped begrudgingly.

" 'Nighty-night."

"See ya," said Fraser, following her out, but turning back for one last oafish ogle.

I obliged by lifting my skirt and spreading my legs. "Sweet dreams," I said.

I waited to see if he would return. But no go. As I passed their door on the way to bed, I could hear Virginie's voice, pinched with restrained rage, rising and falling. Well, I thought, this is going to be easier than I imagined.

Again I slept inordinately deep and long. But when I awoke I felt slightly nauseous, which was strange since I never got sick to my stomach. I lay in bed until it passed, then headed to the bathroom for a pee. I found the door locked and the shower going. Who? I tiptoed to Virginie's bedroom door and listened. I could hear someone moving around inside. I stood there until I could identify—via throat clearing—which one it was and then opened the door. Fraser was getting dressed. Just finishing.

"Oh," he said, startled, buttoning his jeans.

"Good morning."

"How's it going?"

I opened my robe.

"Whoa," he said, staring hard.

"Come here for a sec."

He hesitated, nervous.

"It's okay," I said. "She's in the shower." What I didn't say was: *And you know as well as I do that the cow will stay in there until every last hot-water droplet is down the drain.*

He moved to the doorway and peered past me into the hall. All clear. We put our hands on each other. "Oh, wow," he said. "Wow." He tried repeatedly to kiss me, but I kept dodging his efforts, sliding my mouth away as if I absolutely had to keep sucking on his neck and ear (the thought that he may have recently laid lips on Virginie's gob or any of her equally odious orifices had turned me off smooching).

"Not now," he whispered hotly. "Come to my place later."

I went for his blue-jean buttons with both hands.

"No," he said, catching me by the wrists, pushing my arms above my head, and thrusting me up against the door frame. "Meet me later. Seriously."

I wrapped one leg around him and then, with a little hop, the other. I squeezed hard around his hips and clung tight. He was holding me in the doorway like that, whisper-pleading for me to let go and visit him at home later on, when I heard the scream—a banshee blast, like a cross between air-raid siren and wounded manatee.

"Shit!" shouted Fraser right in my ear. And the next thing I

knew, we were shoved through the doorway by an enraged Virginie, toppling ass over teakettle onto the hard bedroom floor.

"Salaud!" shrieked Virginie. *"Chien sale!"* She kicked and clawed at Fraser, losing her bath towel in the process. "Get the fuck out of here! Now! *Crisse ton camp!"*

He pried himself from my leg grip and, under a rain of furious blows, struggled to his feet. "Just chill for a second! Calm down!"

"Va chez l'diable! Tu m'ecoeures!" she screamed, firing fast punches—à la Sonya in Mortal Kombat—at his kidney/pancreas, neatly pounding the crap out of the boy's endocrine system. *"Dehors!* Now!"

"Wait! Can we just talk about this?!"

She grabbed his jacket and used it to thrash him repeatedly until he caught hold of a sleeve, wrenched the thing from her mad hands, and stumbled into the hallway.

"I'm sorry," he said, making for the door. "I'll call you later."

"Va donc baiser ta guidoune, you pig! *Va te faire foutre!"*

Well, that doesn't sound very promising, I thought as I stood, closed my robe, and tied the belt tight around my waist. I decided it was a good time to clear out of there, but Virginie blocked the bedroom doorway, sealing me in. She was naked and hyperventilating. She looked truly bananas. I made the mistake of smirking.

I said, "Out of my way, nutsy."

"Ma Calisse," she hissed, coming at me. *"Ma maudite putain!"* She grabbed a handful of my hair and wrenched hard.

"OW!" I yelled. "Let go!" I clutched her arm with both hands and sunk my nails into her flesh.

"Ma tabarnak!" She yanked harder.

Not wanting to lose a piece of my scalp, I had to move in the direction of the pull. When my head was halfway to the floor, she shoved me back onto the futon, jumped on my chest, and pinned my shoulders down with her knees. She grabbed a fresh hunk of hair in each hand.

"You stupid bitch!" she screamed. "I AM GOING TO RIP YOUR STUPID HEAD OUT!"

Uh-oh, I thought. I have to go to the photographer's in less than two hours, and it probably won't do to show up with the equivalent of crop circles on either side of my skull like some kind of *Bizarro World* Princess Leia.

"Get the fuck off me!" I yelped, digging my nails into her forearms. Her shaved vagina was right in my face, the denuded parts covered in tiny white bumps. Like plucked poultry. Thank God it was freshly scrubbed.

I dug as hard as I could into her arms with my nails, even felt blood oozing around my fingertips, but the demented bitch didn't flinch; if anything, she pulled harder.

Plan B. I reached out my right hand to try to grab a weapon. I caught hold of the bedside lamp and brought it crashing against her head. The thing crumpled like a paper bag full of air. Fucking Ikea! I reached out again, trying to locate an ashtray (or preferably a ball-peen hammer). Instead I got hold of what turned out to be a sex toy, a giant rubber dildo, which I used to pummel her about the face, head, and neck. After sustaining eleven solid blows to the temple, she let go of my hair, rolled off me, and crumpled into a sobbing heap at the end of the futon.

"Fucking psycho," I said, scrambling to my feet. "I should have you charged with assault!" I dropped the rubber penis on the floor. *Thud.*

"I want you out of here," she shrieked, pulling the duvet up over her body. "I want you out of my apartment!"

Yeah, I thought, now you know how I've felt ever since you arrived on the scene.

"I don't give a rat's ass what you want," I said. "Guess whose name is on the lease? Yeah, that's right. As far as I'm concerned, this is *my* apartment now."

Down the hall I swept, all adrenaline and triumph, already framing the story in my mind, and how I would tell it to Isadora. Then I remembered, no, Isadora was finished. The cold shoulder. Over.

I closed myself in my room, exultation sliding away like sand through fingers.

7

I am asleep when the call comes in—an urgent one from the Bone Marrow Registry. They think I may represent the last hope for a forty-year-old woman suffering from leukemia. I rush to Blood Services and offer up a vein. It turns out that I am a perfect match for the anonymous patient. Without a thought for my own well-being, I agree to undergo the surgery/harvest. During the painful and lonely recovery period, a letter arrives from the recipient of my marrow. It is an eloquent missive full of gratitude and grace. She promises to get in touch with me if all goes well. All does go well. The recipient makes a full and splendid recovery. I receive another letter, in which she reveals her identity: Miriam Louise Bennett. She is a physician with Medecins Sans Frontieres (Doctors Without Borders). Soon she will be returning to her post in war-ravaged Somalia, but first she believes it is imperative that we meet. As a medical expert, she knows that the chance of a complete stranger having identical leukocyte antigens is next to nil. She thinks we may be related. She asks if I was adopted. . . .

A poignant reunion ensues. We recognize each other instantly, and marvel over the miraculous way in which we have come together. I, Allison Penny, have returned the gift of life, and by extension, saved countless cholera, malaria, and war-injury patients in Africa. My mother invites me to accompany her to Somalia, in the capacity of nurse. By day, we toil at the ramshackle hospital. At night, we sit around an open fire, drinking Amarula and getting to know each other. We wear handsome khakis and starched white blouses. Birth Mother Fantasy #6. In the updated version, I tell my mother about kicking Virginie's ass. She laughs and laughs.

"There's the smile I've been waiting for." *Pop.* "Lovely." *Pop.* "Whatever you're thinking, keep thinking it." *Pop.*

I was seated under a large, square lighting device called a soft-box, trying to smile naturally for Keneisha Clarke. Fantasy #6 was helping, but it still wasn't easy. I felt like a newscaster with lockjaw, and every time Keneisha snapped a photo, the flash would pop and my eyes would involuntarily close. I was a bit sore from my battle with Virginie; I had lost some hair (not enough to be noticeable) and sustained bruising to my left hip and upper thigh, but most of my discomfort stemmed from having to glam for the camera. After twenty-two years of larva, it was difficult to butterfly.

"Okay." *Pop.* "That's good." *Pop.* "Now let's try sultry. Think of something hot. Something *sexy.*"

"Um, okay . . ." I thought about George standing over me in bed. Then I had a flash of him going to get the Kleenex box.

"Hmm," said Keneisha. No pop.

"Sorry."

"It's all right. Why don't I change the music. You want a little more Scotch?"

"Sure, thanks." When we first began, I was so rigid that Keneisha had resorted to Glenfiddich to loosen me up. Now she was putting on "Sexual Healing" by Marvin Gaye.

"How's that?" she asked, swaying a little.

"Um . . . maybe a tad over the top."

Keneisha laughed and switched CDs. Then she dimmed the ambient studio lights, poured another drink, and had me change into something slinky. Between the warmth of the booze, the cool of Diana Krall whisper-singing "The Look of Love," and Keneisha's patient prompting, I was able to unwind and start posing. *Pop, pop, pop* went the flashes. "Great, beautiful, lovely," went Keneisha. I was just starting to really diva it up when she told me she had what she required, and the session was done.

"So listen," I said as I gathered my things. "You're going to get paid for this regardless of whether or not I get work, right?"

"That's right," she said. "The agency pays me now, and when you book your first job, they'll take it out of your check."

"So if I never book a job, the agency just swallows the cost?"

Keneisha laughed. "Are you kidding? You'll book plenty of jobs. Honey, you've *got* the supermodel look, very distinctive, you just need to be confident and *become* the thing. You can do it. I just saw you do it."

I felt a little surge of nausea then.

"Are you okay?" she said.

"Yeah. I think I just need to sit for a second."

"Uh-oh," she said. "Is it the whiskey?"

"No, no. I had this this morning. It'll pass."

"Well, don't rush off. Sit for a bit."

"It's weird, you know, I never get nauseous."

"How about some tea? You want a cup of tea?"

"Thanks," I said. "And sorry. This isn't like me. This really isn't like me. . . ."

When I got home Virginie was in her lair, blasting misery music and nursing her wounds. Fine. Big deal. It was a pleasant switch to be roaming freely around the apartment while she did the holing up and hiding out. I scrubbed the pancake makeup off my face—Keneisha had done my makeup—and changed into work clothes. I was somewhat distressed to find that the bruises on my left side had spread into a horrible Rorschach of blue and purple, but I took comfort in the fact that they'd be gone in a week and then I'd be perfect again.

"Perfect," I said as I touched up my lipstick in the hall mirror before leaving. Nathan would be working that night and I wanted to look nice. As I was walking out the door, an FTD man came hustling up the walk with a small arrangement of flowers—yellow daisies in a glass bud vase. Definitely not flowers by Marco; presumably not flowers from George.

"Allison Penny?" he said.

"Yes."

"Here you go." He handed me the arrangement, smiled politely, and skedaddled.

I ripped the cellophane open with my teeth and fished out the enclosed card: *Allison, We need to talk. Call me. 555—4083.* I realized that the flowers must have come from Fraser, and that he actually thought we had something to jaw about. What a galoot. Oh, well, at least this time I didn't have to hunt for a vase. I set the daisies on the kitchen table and put the card face up at the base of the container where it was certain to be seen by Virginie.

8

"Hey."

"Hi." I was hoping that Nathan would make an appearance on the patio, and he didn't disappoint. "How are you?"

"I'm okay," he said. "I just thought I'd see if you'd heard from Allison, how her father was doing and whatnot." He seemed unusually ill at ease.

"I spoke to her today. He's a bit better," I said. "Still unconscious, but the vital signs are improving."

"Oh, that's great!"

"Well—"

"I mean, not 'great'—the man's in a coma—but you know, it's good that he's better—I mean, slightly better—um, improving, that is."

"Yeah." I had no idea how endearing Nathan could be when nervous.

"Anyway . . ." He looked as if he was about to bolt, but this time I wasn't going to let him get away so fast.

"So," I said, "Allison told me you're quite the film buff."

"That's true, I am."

"She said you do reviews."

"Yeah. Occasionally I'll do a piece for the dailies. But mostly I review—well, and also sometimes do columns or interviews—for *Savoir-Vivre.*"

"Oh, yeah?"

"It's just a dinky little bimonthly."

"I've seen that paper. It's good. Good writing."

"It is pretty good." He didn't take a seat beside me as usual, but he did lean back and rest against a barrel full of flowers—white tulips that were past their prime and hanging on by a breath. The slight intrusion caused half a dozen of them to completely drop their petals, leaving the ramrod stems bare. "Oops," he said, surveying the damage and readjusting his position. He looked unduly embarrassed.

"I love tulips," I said. "Especially the white ones."

"Yeah, they look good in the dark. Or they did until I sat on them."

I laughed. "So when you're not taking care of the plants here, you work at a video store, right?" I sensed a blush, but I couldn't really tell in the dim light of the patio.

"Yeah," he said. "At Art & Trash. It's, uh—it pays the bills."

"You know, I popped in there the other day, on Saturday. I think I saw you."

"Yeah, I was there Saturday."

"You were watching that Bruce what's-his-name documentary. *Chop Suey.*"

"Bruce Weber. And you were looking for Antonioni's *Love in the City.*"

"Right."

An exchange of shy smiles acknowledging the mutual recognition.

"But you didn't have it," I said.

"Not at the store, no. But I have it at home."

"You do?"

"Yeah. On VHS. I could bring it on Friday, and lend it to you if you like?"

"Or maybe I could come over sometime and watch it?"

"Um, sure. Really? I mean, yeah, if you want to." He looked confused, almost suspicious.

"How about tonight? After work."

"Tonight? Oh . . . um—"

"We don't have to. Sorry. I didn't—"

"No, it's okay. I was just—"

"It's kind of late—"

"No. It's not too late, it's just, um, it's just that my place is, well, it's a bit of a pit. Not exactly designed for entertaining. Pretty much a dump actually."

"I'm sure you're exaggerating. I bet it's fine."

He laughed. "It isn't really."

"Well, if you don't want me—"

"No, I do, it's just—"

"I'm sure it's fine. And even if it's not, I don't care. Honestly."

"Listen," said Nathan, "this isn't some kind of a joke, is it?"

"Joke? No. What do you mean?"

"Nothing. Never mind."

"So, tonight it is?"

"Tonight it is."

He was not exaggerating. The place was a dump. A tiny fart of a bachelor apartment on the twenty-second floor of a dilapidated high-rise in the pawnshop and biker gang district.

Grim.

"Well, this is it," said Nathan, flicking on the overhead light (a bare bulb dangling dangerous from a bulge of escaped ceiling wires). "My crumble abode."

I was relieved to find that the fetid stench in the hallway ended abruptly when we stepped inside the apartment. "It's not so bad," I lied. But it was bad. One small room that served as bedroom, living room, dining room, and office, crammed with plastic milk cartons and Salvation Army castoffs. Nothing matched. The cracked plaster walls were painted (long ago) in sick apricot; the milk cartons were orange, scuffed and stuffed full of books, videos, and DVDs; the sofa was an abomination of floral velveteen sheen in purples, grays, and black; the computer desk/kitchen table was fake wood-grain with rusted chrome legs; the computer chair was chocolate brown; the unmade bed—a double mattress and baby-blue box spring in the corner on the floor—had a burgundy duvet, two faded pillows (one pink, one beige), and a threadbare sheet with green and yellow stripes. The only apparent nod to decor was a large shrink-wrapped movie poster for *Young Frankenstein*, hanging outside what I assumed to be the bathroom. Other than that, the only objects that appeared to have been purchased new, or purchased at all (i.e., not dragged out of a Dumpster), were a snazzy widescreen-format television set and a gleaming DVD player.

"Do you want me to take off my shoes?"

"Don't be absurd." Nathan got down on his knees in the corner where the stereo and TV were and started mucking around with an octopus of cords all leading to one stressed outlet. He unplugged something, plugged in a standing lamp, then switched off the overhead bulb. Better. "Um, sorry about the noise," he said. Annoying techno music vibrated through the south wall of the apartment: *Ging-gda-ging-gda-ging-gda-ging. Ging-gda-ging-gda-ging.* "My neighbor's a crack whore."

"Seriously?" I laughed. "Is she really?"

"*He.* I suspect so. From what I've seen. I try to avoid going over there, usually don't ask him to turn it down unless it's really late."

"That's understandable."

"So . . . would you like something to drink?"

"Sure. Thanks."

A counter separated the main room from a galley kitchen. Sad linoleum. Gruesome wallpaper. Evil lighting. I followed Nathan into the teeny green space.

"Let's see . . ." He opened a double cupboard above the sink. It was almost entirely full of videotapes. One tenth of the shelf space was devoted to foodstuffs: instant oatmeal, Ichiban noodles, Kraft macaroni and cheese. He pulled out a dusty bottle of Jack Daniels.

"Unfortunately, all I have is bourbon. Or I have Wink if you prefer nonalcoholic?"

"Bourbon's fine, thanks."

He opened the bottle and sniffed it. "On the rocks or neat?"

"Rocks, please."

He opened the fridge. Inside was a tiny tin freezer in critical need of defrosting. The four walls were thick with bulging ice, leaving a space just big enough for the one ice-cube tray contained therein (the cubes were covered with a half-inch of crusty snow). He tried to slide it out, but the thing was wedged in tight, frozen in place. He pulled harder. A squeaking sound, but the tray barely budged. I noticed there were a couple of shriveled green peas and what looked like a pubic hair suspended in the left wall of ice.

Nathan blushed. "Guess it's time to defrost."

I laughed. "Don't worry about it. I can take it straight."

"No, it's okay. I got it." He yanked harder. "Pass me that screwdriver."

I handed him the tool and he went at the ice. A mad crunching sound as he chipped violently until the tray was free. "There we go. Piece of cake." He wiped some sweat off his curiously shaped forehead and rinsed the tray under the tap to clear off the frost.

"I love it when you're defrosting," I said, "and you get to the point where you can wedge a butter knife between the bottom of the freezer and the coating of ice that covers it, and the whole chunk comes away in one freezer-shaped piece."

"I love that moment!" he said, fishing two tumblers out of the dish rack. "It's so satisfying. Better than bubble wrap." He cracked the cubes and poured the bourbon. "Sorry. I don't really have proper glasses." One tumbler had a *U-Bet Chocolate Syrup* logo on it; the other was plain blue, but smacked of gas station giveaway. He handed me the plain one.

"Thank you."

"Cheers."

We clinked and sipped. "Antonioni," said Nathan, moving past me into the living room. "Have a seat. Make yourself comfortable." He set his drink down on one of two upended milk cartons that served as a coffee table and began looking for the tape.

I perched on the hideous velveteen sofa (comfortable it was not) and watched Nathan hunt for the movie. *Ging-gda-ging-gda-ging-gda-ging. Ging-gda-ging-gda-ging*, went the music from next door.

"Unfortunately, they're not in any particular order," he said, scanning the shelves. He seemed nervous. Distracted.

"It's okay," I said. "Take your time."

He went back into the kitchen to search. I got up and started nosing around, looking at all things Nathan. His shoes: five nearly identical pairs of Adidas lined up by the front door, the tops all sloping outward off the heels from the odd way he walked. His books: one milk carton full of dead authors—Nabokov, Lawrence, Austen, Greene—and half a dozen more cartons crammed with film tomes: *The Dark Side of Genius: The Life of Alfred Hitchcock; The Cinema of Ken Loach; Digital Babylon: Hollywood, Indiewood and Dogme 95; Easy Riders, Raging Bulls;*

Close Up: Iranian Cinema, Past, Present, and Future; Tokyoscope: The Japanese Cult Film Companion; Peckinpah: The Western Films: A Reconsideration; Movie Love: Complete Reviews, etc. His desk was heaped with notebooks and magazines and yellowing newspaper clippings and at least half a dozen tubes of cherry Chapstick. My attention was drawn to a couple of hand-scrawled quotes stuck to his computer monitor: "Photography is truth. Cinema is truth twenty-four times per second."—Jean-Luc Godard; " 'Kiss Kiss Bang Bang,' which I saw on an Italian movie poster, is perhaps the briefest statement imaginable of the basic appeal of movies."—Pauline Kael.

"You know, it's not really an Antonioni flick," Nathan called out, sounding like his head was deep in a cupboard. "It's actually a bunch of different segments directed by different people. Um, Fellini, Dino Risi, Lizzani, Lattuada . . . Maselli, Zavattini."

"I love it when you speak Italian," I said. I was right behind him now. Close. He wheeled around, shocked at my proximity. He was holding the video.

"Found it," he said, blushing.

"Good," I said, noticing, under the harsh fluorescent light, three barely visible freckles on Nathan's lips. We stood there smiling at each other for a long moment. *Ging-gda-ging-gda-ging-gda-ging,* went the trance music from next door. I wanted to lunge but couldn't seem to move. There was a buzz of electricity crackling between us. A surge of heat spread from my solar plexus through the rest of my body, and I could hear Nathan's breath getting faster and heavier. *Ging-gda-ging-gda-ging-gda-ging,* and my heart a mad hammer as we stood there suspended. Then my mouth said, "Kiss kiss bang bang . . ." And a moment later we were in a lip lock, and don't ask me how it happened or where the tape Nathan had been holding got to, because I have no idea. All I know is that we ended up groping our way into the main room and crashing down on the mattress in the corner.

"One sec," said Nathan. His glasses were askew on his nose

and jabbing into my face. He plucked them off and chucked them on the floor—they skidded halfway across the room. We resumed clutching. Bourbon tongues. Hungry hands. Delirious dizzy goodness for who knows how long until I whispered, "Let's get undressed," at which point Nathan pulled away and sat up and said, "Hang on. Can we just pause for a moment here?" I noticed then how different he looked without his glasses, the eyes smaller and more tired.

"What?"

He sighed deeply. "It's just—well, before we—um, I'd just like to know what the deal is. I mean, is this some kind of joke or what?"

"It's not a joke. Why do you keep saying that?"

"Because . . . Well, I realize that this may be hard to believe, but it's not every day that gorgeous young women invite themselves over to my apartment—and then want to stay and get naked once they've seen it."

"Well . . . maybe it should be."

"Oh, yes, I agree, it should. Absolutely. But it isn't, trust me. So either this is some kind of elaborate joke for which you're presumably being compensated, or you're a supremely misguided con woman, or else you've recently escaped from a mental institution and you're about to get all Glenn Close on my ass."

I laughed. "I'm a friend of Allison's, we've been pals since we were tykes. Don't you trust her judgment?"

"Okay, so what, you have some kind of ugly-man sexual fetish, s'that it?"

"Boy, oh, boy. Self-esteem issues?"

"No, actually. In fact, most of the time I walk around harboring a secret superiority complex. You just happen to be testing its limits right now."

I laughed. "Listen," I said, "I'm attracted to you, okay?"

"Hmm."

"I think you're very cute—"

"Uch," he bristled. "That word."

"You know what I mean. And I feel as if I know you a bit, based on stuff Allison has told me. . . ."

"Like what?"

"Well, you know. . . . That you're great."

He laughed. "I miss her," he said.

"Me, too," I said reflexively, but it was true, in a way. And I realized that this was the first time since the Change that I truly felt like her/me. The real me. Content at the core, just to be alone and quiet with Nathan. "Listen," I said, pinching the rough flap of skin at his elbow, "why don't we just watch the movie, then maybe in the next little while we could go out a few times and get to know each other better before we . . . you know."

He chewed on a hangnail and thought it over. "Nah," he said, breaking into a wonky smile. "Let's just get undressed."

We did. We did get undressed, and there was much touching, licking, kissing, and squeezing, and Nathan brushed his lips softly over the bruised area around my hip and said, "Poor you," which I thought was very nice. Before long he was excusing himself to go fish out condoms from the bathroom medicine cabinet, and I thought, Well, this is it, after twenty-two and a quarter years it's finally, finally going to happen. I ran my hand over the ugly sheets on the mattress in the corner on the floor; it didn't seem like such a grand bed in which to lose one's virginity. The crack whore's music was still vibrating through the wall of the grim apartment, and when Nathan emerged from the bathroom, I saw that he was not as muscular as I'd imagined he would be. His body was pale and freckly, and he had a bit of a belly hanging soft and white. When he ripped the condom packet open with his slightly snaggled teeth and rolled the latex onto his birthmarked penis, I noticed that his balls sagged loose and lopsided, and I couldn't help but reflect on how much better looking

George was, especially from that low angle. But just as I was thinking that about George, Nathan got down on the bed and positioned himself on top of me, and slowly, slowly we started to slide together and actually do the thing, and it hurt a bit but also felt stupidly good. And a cliché popped into my head, which made me smile and grip him a little bit tighter with my arms and legs: *It's what's inside that counts.*

I didn't sleep well. The music from next door went on forever, sirens and drunken screams punctuated the night, and the mattress on the floor proved to be terribly lumpy. But when I awoke, I was tangled up in Nathan, a lovely way to start the morning, especially since it was crazy pouring outside and there was a breeze coming in, smelling fresh like ozone and wet cement, and the apartment was almost dark behind curtains in the gray day. Nathan gained consciousness a second after I did. He rolled slowly onto his side to face me. His eyes were puffy from sleep, and I was reminded of a tortoise, a friendly cartoon tortoise moving sluggish.

"Hey," he said.

"Hi."

A thunder rumble followed by silence awkward between us. Nathan was looking at me with a mirthless grin on his face. He appeared resigned, as if he was waiting for me to turn all cold, get briskly dressed, and hightail it out of there. I ended the moment by moving in for a kiss. After a bit of tentative smooching, I worked my tongue into his mouth and wrapped my hand around his cock.

"What time is it?" he said, propping himself up on an elbow and squinting blind at the digital clock on his desk.

"Ten twenty-eight."

He laughed. "I'm supposed to be at work in . . . seventeen minutes."

"Something tells me you're not going to make it."

"Something tells me you're right."

We had sex again. This time it hurt less and felt better. After, Nathan got up and took an absurdly long piss. I'd never heard anything like it; it went on and on. I lay in bed, listening to the wild weather and the hilariously endless urination, and I felt finer than I'd felt in a long time. The only thing that could have improved my mood would've been a cappuccino soak in a claw-footed tub like at George's place, but it was not to be. Nathan's bathroom was a disaster. All calcified faucets and cracked green tiles, bare lightbulb and murky medicine cabinet mirror. A shower-massage device with a broken-off head—essentially just a beige plastic hose—dangled down into the poorest excuse for a tub I'd ever seen. It was about three feet long and no more than nine inches tall, designed by sadists to do nothing more than catch shower water. Impossible for anyone other than a child, midget, or double amputee to bathe in. It really was a grotesque apartment, and the cockroach traps under the sink were creeping me out. I quickly emptied my bladder and, while the toilet was flushing, quietly squeezed out a few farts I'd been holding in since I woke up. Then I burrowed back into bed and watched Nathan prepare coffee and breakfast in the hideous kitchen.

"I just remembered my dream," he said.

"Oh, yeah, what was it?"

"It was about you and Allison," he said. "We were in a pool. I can't remember exactly what was going on, just that we were all swimming together in a pool. I think we were at some actor's house."

"That's weird."

"Yeah. Actually, you remind me a bit of her."

"I do?"

"Yeah, your mannerisms, your way of speaking. Your sense of humor."

"Hmm. So you guys are pretty good friends, huh?"

"I guess."

"What do you mean, 'you guess'?"

"Well, we're definitely friends, but we generally just see each other at work."

"Why is that?"

"I don't know."

"I mean, you like her, right?"

"Yeah. I like her a lot."

"So, did you ever think about dating her?"

"Dating? No. I mean, Allison's great, there's just no chemistry there."

"Chemistry?"

"Right."

"So, do we have chemistry?" I asked, miffed that Nathan had confused chemistry with physical appearance, but relieved that he hadn't insulted the way I looked.

"Oh, man . . . we're a regular Dow or DuPont. We're Union Carbide." Nathan unplugged the kettle and poured. "I like Allison, though. She's sweet."

"Sweet?!"

He laughed. "Well, you know, she's pretty cynical, but yeah, I think she's sweet. She has the most amazing voice. But I guess you know that."

"Yeah." A stab of sadness for my lost lilt. I wanted it back. Not at the cost of "no chemistry," but in addition to the new attributes.

Nathan carried in mugs of Nescafé lightened with non-dairy creamer, and small plastic bowls of instant oatmeal. Both substances looked gray and objectionable. I managed to gulp down most of the coffee but couldn't get through the gummy porridge.

"Thanks." I set the dishes down on the floor beside the bed.

"Sorry. If I'd known I was going to have company, I would've had eggs or something. At least milk and cream."

"It's okay," I said, picking a bit of lint out of his navel, examining it, and tucking it into mine. "Next time."

Waking Beauty   165

He liked that. He said, "You know what, I don't feel like going to work today."

"I think you should call in sick and hang out with me some more."

"I think you're right."

We lay in bed for a long while, savoring the storm and the daytime darkness. It was conducive to asking questions personal and I posed ones that Old Allison would never have brought up during a brief patio confab. I managed to learn quite a bit about Nathan's family. His parents were originally from the U.K. Father: a Scottish Jew from Glasgow. Mother: a Welsh Catholic from Cardiff. Both avowed atheists, but according to Nathan, each secretly in love with their own religion. He said they got along well but bickered constantly—mostly for sport and pleasure. His dad was a pharmacist who played and collected tubas. His pride and joy was a giant tuba that was eight feet tall and, ostensibly, forty-five feet in length if uncoiled. He told me that his mother was seven years older than his father, and was forty-one when she had her first child. Evidently, at the age of seventy-three she was still ridiculously spry—swam one hundred laps every morning at the local community center—but attributed her excellent health to the two ounces of Danzy Jones Whiskey Liqueur she enjoyed each evening before and after dinner. Nathan's father didn't drink or swim, ordered his corned beef with extra fat, and drove everywhere—even to the corner store. A former cigar smoker, he had been on the nicotine patch for six years running (much to the horror of his GP). I already knew that Nathan had a younger sister named Kate who had gone back to school to get her law degree and was now articling with a big firm in the city, but I hadn't known that she had recently come out of the closet and was planning a wedding to her girlfriend, Gwen, a woman who designed children's clothing for the Roots retail chain. Apparently, after the initial shock faded, Nathan's folks were fine with the nuptial news and actually seemed relieved that thirty-year-old Kate was finally getting hitched (although they were against her plan to wear a lavender tuxedo to the wedding).

As far as my own background went, I tried to deflect questions and keep things vague. I found that I could distract Nathan by steering the conversation toward cinema, a topic he was endlessly eager to discuss. I had the advantage of ten months of patio movie blab, and in order to compensate for my ditsiness at Art & Trash, I regurgitated many of Nathan's cogent views on a number of films. He was obviously impressed with my intelligence and good taste, and when I told him that the original version of *The In-Laws*—a film I still hadn't seen—was my favorite comedy, he fairly glowed with pleasure.

I did end up divulging a bit about my personal life. At some point I admitted to being adopted and feeling disconnected from my parents. It felt strange to discuss it openly with another human.

"So you don't get along with either of them?"

"Well, it's possible that I might get along with my adoptive dad, but I've never had the chance to find out. He split when I was a kid, and didn't keep in touch. As for my mom, well . . . it's like she's been in an absolutely foul mood for about twenty years." I laughed. "She's hard to please."

Nathan didn't laugh. He said, "So you feel like you're always trying to please her?"

"Um . . . maybe when I was little. Not anymore." *Sometimes just the opposite.* It occurred to me then, in a moment of clarity, that perhaps my overeating had been a kind of weapon, that maybe I had fattened myself to antagonize the impossible-to-please Miss Beef and Barley.

"So what about your birth mother? Have you ever thought about trying to find her?"

"Oh, God, yeah. But I was always too afraid to go through with it."

"Afraid of what you might find, I guess."

"No. Not at all. Afraid of being a disappointment, you know."

"What? That's nuts. You're lovely. Why on earth would she be disappointed?"

"I don't know," I said, turning away to hide the tears inexplicably welling in my eyes. Maybe she wouldn't be . . . now.

"Well, anyway," said Nathan, curling himself around me, spoon style, "if you're ever feeling masochistic and craving a dose of family, you're welcome to come with me to my folks' for dinner."

"Really?"

"Not that you'd want to. My mother would force you to consume Danzy Jones Whiskey Liqueur, and the first thing my father does when a new person comes to the house is take them down to the basement to show them the Majestic Monster Tuba."

I said it sounded fine to me.

Eventually the rain subsided and the sun struggled to make an appearance. Valiant but veiled. Pale and hazy. Nathan suggested that it would be a good day to catch a matinee. As I was leaning over his shoulder, checking the local movie listings on the Internet, my gaze wandered to the far corner of his desk and settled on a yellowing manuscript covered in overlapping coffee rings. Through the Spirographic pattern of java circles I could make out the following laser-printed words: *An Honest Man, an original screenplay by Nathan Billyack.*

"Hey," I said. "I thought you said you weren't interested in writing movies."

"I'm not," he said. "But did I say that? I don't remember telling you that."

"Oh, um, I think Allison told me. So, what's that?" I gestured to the stained script.

"That is a coaster."

"No, seriously."

"I am serious." Nathan continued to scan the listings on-screen. "I use it to set my hot beverages on while I type. It reminds me not to be too harsh, particularly to screenwriters."

"Can I read it?"

"God, no! Hey," he said, "how about 'Rivethead,' the new Linklater film?"

"Oh, come on." I spun his ugly swivel chair around to face me. "Can't I read it?"

"I don't think s—"

"Please?" I settled lightly in his lap and tried a Virginie-style pout.

"Yes. All right," he said. "If you want. But let me read it again first. Make sure there's nothing too embarrassing in there."

We bought popcorn, a jumbo container hot and buttered, and devoured every kernel, even the semi-popped at box bottom, before the conclusion of the coming attractions. Then Nathan held my golden topping—covered hand tight and greasy in his lap through the rest of the movie, and it seemed as if what was happening on-screen was the peripheral experience. Afterward he walked me to the subway. He kept hold of my hand on the way there, and I noticed people giving us the what's-wrong-with-this-picture? look as they passed by. When we got to the station, Nathan walked me down the stairs, right up to the turnstiles.

"Well," I said, "I guess I'll see you at work tomorrow night."

"Definitely."

"Okay . . . See you."

We stood there kissing until a stout woman came barreling by and shouted, *"Hello!"* right at our heads because we were semi-blocking one of the turnstile entrances. We laughed and moved out of the way.

"Um, before you go, why don't you give me your info?" said Nathan, fishing out a pen and notebook from his khaki knapsack.

"All right." I scrawled my address and phone number, and took his, even though I knew he was in the book because I had looked him up months ago for no practical reason.

"So, listen," he said. "I know this is a long shot, but are you by any chance free on Saturday night?"

"I have no plans," I said. "Except to read your script."

"I've got a much better idea. Why don't you come over for dinner? I'll cook something, we can watch the movie . . ."

"That sounds good."

"I make excellent lasagna. You like lasagna?"

"What's not to like?"

"Good. 'Cause I have an amazing recipe from an old Italian woman who used to live on my parents' street."

"Oh, yeah?"

"Yeah. She made an industrial-sized pan of lasagna once for some local community event, and everyone went gaga over it. For years people begged her for the recipe, but she refused to give it out until she was, like, a hundred and three and on her deathbed."

"So her last words were 'Bake at three seventy-five for sixty minutes?' "

Nathan smiled. "I'll never tell." He stuck the notebook and pen back into his knapsack and slung it over his shoulder. "I should probably make the sauce tonight; it's better if you prepare it in advance. Oh, do you like artichokes? The recipe involves fresh artichokes."

"I do. I do like artichokes."

"And you eat meat?"

"Anything with a face."

"Okay, great. So I'll see you on the patio at break tomorrow night?"

"Definitely."

A quick kiss and he was off, backpack bobbing as he dodged jaunty through the early rush-hour crowd that was starting to stream in, weary and purposeful, from the street.

Un grand surprise when I arrived home. Virginie was gone. And so was her stuff. The apartment was a shambles and the daisies that Fraser sent had been neatly decapitated. A new note sat at the base of the vase, next to the two snapshots of Old Allison snoozing on the sofa. The note said: *Fuck You! Fuck your fat friend also!!!* I crumpled the note and tossed it in the trash. I was going to throw the photos away, but something stopped me. I guess I couldn't completely part with my old ugly self. I folded them in half and stuck them in my pocket.

My next impulse was to bolt into my room to check for wreckage. Happily, everything in there appeared intact (it wasn't until the following afternoon that I discovered the bitch had taken a malicious knife to my Le Château slut dress and deposited the shredded remains under my futon). Then I went to check the answering machine. But there was no answering machine. And no microwave and no thick-slice toaster and no coffee table and no VCR and no DVD player and no hall mirror and no bath mat and and and . . .

I didn't have time to deal with it. I would deal with it when I got home from work. With rent looming, and no Virginie to pony up half of it, I couldn't afford to be late.

Oddly enough, impending bankruptcy didn't squelch my spirits. I was in a fab mood when I said sayonara to Nathan in the subway, and was still in an elated state as I went along my route, blithely ridding 505 Richmond of its garbage. I felt especially cheered when I entered Peter Igel's office and found that it was beginning to smell quite strongly of decaying meat. He had erroneously identified his garbage can as the source of the stench and placed it just outside his office door with a Post-it note attached: *Please empty and scrub out.* God, I was sick of those notes. I dumped the can, took it to the IZ Talent Management kitchen, and washed it in the sink.

As I was returning it to where it belonged, I stopped to peruse some photographs laid out on Igel's desk: two female models, one of whom I recognized from billboards or television. Both of them were exceptionally beautiful, particularly Amber, the one on the left. A handwritten note clipped to her head shot said: *Peter, what do you think? Just Natasha? Can't we include Amber or Geneva?* A corner of paper was sticking out from under the smiling Amber photo. I lifted her up and found a sheet of cream-colored paper embossed with the Calet fragrance logo. WORLDWIDE SEARCH FOR THE NEW FACE OF CALET #7, it said in bold across the top. *We Are Currently Conducting a Worldwide Search for the Next Star of an Exciting New Campaign Featuring Celebrated Directors from Three Continents!* The concept of the promotion was to have a trio of hotshot movie directors each film a television commercial in and around the Getty Museum. The idea was to evoke one of the following attributes of Calet #7: Femininity, Timelessness, Sophistication. I recognized two of the directors' names: Jason Soderman (who would be shooting the Sophisticated element) and Lucas Masson (who would be handling Timeless). The Asian one I'd never heard of: Kwan Shui-Mei (Feminine).

I put the photos back the way I'd found them and collected my cart. As I was leaving the agency, I noticed another one of Igel's Post-its stuck to an IZ Talent envelope at the reception desk. A closer inspection revealed that the envelope was addressed to the Calet people. When I ducked behind the desk and ripped it open, I found a cover letter from Igel, plus a résumé and photo for Natasha (apparently, Amber and Geneva hadn't been deemed Feminine, Timeless, or Sophisticated enough for the gig). After reviewing her résumé and concluding that she was not hurting for cash, I tore her in half and tossed her in my trash bin. Then I dug out the blurry snapshots of Old Allison from my pocket, smoothed them out, and stapled them to Igel's cover letter. I slid the thing into a fresh IZ Talent envelope, sealed it, copied out the Calet address, and placed it back on the reception desk with Igel's Post-it note on top: *Please FedEx ASAP!*

A blue sports car . . . yes, George's baby-blue Vanquish parked illegally on the curb when I got home from work. Who knows how long he had been waiting for me.

"You're alive," he said, jumping out of the automobile.

"Just barely. I'm kind of bagged. How are you?"

"I've been trying to get in touch with you since yesterday afternoon. Didn't you get my messages?"

"I didn't. And there's a good reason for that. Come on in," I said reluctantly. I would now have to do something I had never had the opportunity or misfortune to do before. Break up with someone.

George followed me up the walk and onto the porch. "What are you wearing?" He seemed puzzled by my massive Old Allison T-shirt. My greasy hair was tangled in a topknot, and my only pair of jeans were getting grungy, and starting to smell alarmingly like Frito's corn chips.

"I was at work," I said.

"Work? What work?" He followed me inside.

"I've been filling in for Allison while she's away."

"Filling in where? Hey, what the hell happened to this place?"

"Virginie bugged out. Just took her stuff and split. Including the answering machine, which is why I didn't get your messages." I dropped my keys on the kitchen table. "I think she may have moved in with Fraser."

"Like hell she did. I spoke to him two hours ago and he was all distraught because she left this wicked message on his cell."

"Really? What message?" I hid my smile by turning away and opening the fridge.

"That she never wants to speak to him again and that he can forget about getting his camcorder back."

"Jesus, she took the food, too." The fridge was almost entirely stripped of its contents. "I guess I can't offer you anything, except for some Sunny Delight, or a glass of salad dressing . . . some bacon fat in a jar."

"I'm fine. Is there any water?"

"Tap water."

"Never mind, I'm okay." He was pacing around, restless.

I carried the Sunny Delight to the table and sat down. "So did he say anything else?" I unscrewed the lid and took a swig. Did George know about my libidinous doorway clinch with Fraser? Was he here to break up with *me*?

"Just that they'd had a big fight, I don't know. I don't really know him that well. Don't you want a glass?"

"Does this bother you?"

"Not especially."

I took another swig.

"So what's this work you're doing?"

"Oh, just filling in for Allison, helping a family down the street clean an office building downtown."

"Are you kidding me?"

"No. Why?"

"That's ridiculous. You shouldn't be helping families clean office buildings. That's absurd." He laughed.

"Why? I'm helping out my friend and I'm earning some money."

"I thought you were on vacation?"

"Well, I'm thinking I might stay for a while."

"Oh, good. That's good. I'm seeing many weekends at the cottage. Whi—"

"Oh, that reminds me. About the Cecilia Bartoli thing on Saturday—"

"Forget that. I gave the tickets away."

"Oh . . ."

"That's why I'm here," said George. He smiled and

handed me a rectangular white card. It was embossed with a stylish silver logo: *H&E.*

I read: *You are cordially invited to the opening of Heaven & Earth.* "What is it?" I asked, flipping the card over. *This invitation is nontransferable.*

"A new club, the *only* decent nightclub in Muskoka. I mean, this ain't some country club with a dance floor and a deejay. This place was über-designed from the ground up. They've been working on it forever. And it's going to be an amazing party, impossible to get into and probably crawling with celebs that have places up there. Kurt and Goldie, maybe Kate Hudson, and I heard Steve Martin, and Matthew Broderick, who's shooting a movie in the area." George was all excited, pacing, pacing. "Anyway, the guy who owns it designed some offices for Father last year. Hence the invite."

It was then that I noticed the name of "the guy who owns it" on the white rectangle, and realized, with a small shiver, that what I was holding in my hand was not just an invitation to the grand opening of the *only* decent nightclub in cottage country, but also a direct-access pass to my adopted father, the elusive Simon Penny.

"So I was thinking, you should come with me for the weekend. You could pack up now, spend the night at my place, and we could leave in the morning."

"What, *this* weekend? I can't." Saturday night. Nathan. Deathbed Lasagna.

"Why? You'd love it up there. We have a brand-new hot tub overlooking the lake, boats galore, and this party is going to be amazing, seriously."

"It's just—well, for one thing, I have to work tomorrow night." *So I'll see you on the patio at break tomorrow night? Definitely.*

"Cleaning the building with the family?" He laughed. "Just call in sick, quit!"

"I don't think I can do that." He's making the sauce in advance. Fresh artichokes are involved.

George was incredulous. "You're telling me you can't get a better job than that?"

"No, I intend to. It's just—well, I don't really have any marketable skills, and this job was handed to me."

"Well, hand it back. I don't like you doing that, anyway. You don't need to be doing that." He waved his hand dismissively.

"But I do need to be doing it. I have to pay Allison's rent at the end of the month. Now that Virginie has taken a powder, I'm going to have to pay her rent, too. Plus, my credit card is smoking, I have about twenty-seven dollars to my name . . . so, yes, I'm afraid I do need to be doing it."

"Well, cripes, Allison, I can lend you some money. Why didn't you just ask? What do you need? A couple thousand?"

"You would do that?"

"Sure. No problem. What do you need, a few thousand? How about three? Would three tide you over?"

I hesitated. "You want to just lend me three thousand dollars?"

"I have a checkbook in the glove compartment. I'll go grab it. And listen, I'm supremely confident that, skills or no skills, a gal like you could walk into any number of establishments tomorrow and get hired like that." He snapped his fingers. "Any bar, any makeup counter, any clothing boutique . . . I mean, think about it." He snapped his fingers again. "Like that."

It was true; a "gal like me" could get hired pretty easily. And with three thousand dollars in my pocket, I wouldn't have to go back to 505 Richmond. No more garbage carts, no more Peter Igel, no more Andrew McKay and *WUT Up* magazine. Also, no more patio breaks with Nathan, but I no longer needed 505 Richmond to rendezvous with him. I felt a strange comingling of relief and nausea as George strode back into the apartment, sat down at the kitchen table, and began filling out the check.

"This is good. Now you can come with me, right?" He

ripped the check out of the book and held it up. "It's really beautiful up there."

"Um . . ." I stared at the name on the invitation. Direct Access. Real face time with my adoptive father. Maybe I could chat him up and ask him about his past, find out why, after battling for custody, he hadn't kept in touch with his daughter. Maybe I could even tell him who I was; after all, he hadn't seen me since I was five years old. Wasn't it possible that I had blossomed into something beautiful? Maybe we'd hit it off, really like each other. He'd invite me to visit him in L.A.; I could stay in the guesthouse by the pool. . . .

"Hot tub overlooking the lake," said George. "Boats galore."

I have to admit it sounded good. I'd never been to a cottage before. "How about this," I said. "How about I come with you, but instead of leaving tomorrow morning, we leave Saturday morning? That way I could finish out the week for Allison, give the people a couple days' notice to find a replacement by Monday, and collect my pay." More important, I could see Nathan in person and tell him that I wouldn't be able to make it on Saturday night. I could kiss and reschedule (I was pretty sure lasagna could be frozen).

"That's not going to work," he said. "I've invited a couple friends to join us, and they'll be showing up early Saturday morning. I want to have the fire going, breakfast ready. . . ." He slid the check across the table.

I didn't pick it up. I said, "But if you have friends coming, why do you want me to go?"

"Because it'll be fun! Besides, Don and Dawn are a couple," he said. "I don't want to play gooseberry all weekend."

"Gooseberry?"

"Fifth wheel. Odd man out." He pushed the check closer toward me. "What if we leave tomorrow night? Does that suit you?"

"After my shift?"

"Sure. What's the earliest you can get out of there?"

"If I hustle, I could be done by eleven-fifteenish."

"All right. Driving will be easy at that time of night. So bring your stuff to work and I'll swing by and get you around eleven-fifteen, all righty?"

"Okay. Thanks."

"Hey, why so glum, babe?" George leaned over and kissed me on the ear. Then he slid the Heaven & Earth rectangle from my hands and put it in his pocket. "You know, there are people who would kill for this invitation."

10

Friday. I woke up early to hit the Laundromat. As usual it was an odious experience. Four of the eight washers were taken, one was out of order, and another was rendered (to my mind) unusable after I discovered a washed Kotex pad inside. To top it off, the rude woman with the snot-nosed triplets was there. So was the asshole student with the orange jeans. The rude woman had once caused me great embarrassment after one of her mucus-encrusted children who'd been staring slack-jawed at me for ten minutes said, "Mommy, why is that lady so fat?" "Well," said the rude woman in a singsongy voice, "I guess it's because she eats too much."

But the rude woman was nothing compared to the asshole with the orange jeans. This guy was a real Laundromat prick. The kind of guy who would hang on to and refuse to temporarily relinquish one of the rolling baskets even if you needed it at that moment and he didn't. The kind of guy who wouldn't give you twenty seconds of grace after your cycle had ended, who would fish your freshly washed undies out of a machine with his grubby mitts and toss them on any available surface no matter how filthy, if you happened to step outside for some air and weren't back to empty your machine the instant it stopped spinning. The kind of guy who would fold his clothes slowly and meticulously, one item at a time, out of the dryer, even if you were standing there with an armload of soaking sweaters. A real Laundromat scourge. Except on this day. On this day, he was far from infuriating. On this day, he enthusiastically offered me the use of his rolling basket. On this day, he cleaned his disgusting cat-hair-spiked lint out of the dryers when they finished spinning, and removed his clothes unfolded to free up the machines for me. And when the rude woman ran outside to chase after one of her shrieking rug rats, and I opened her dryer and plucked out a fluorescent pink bathing suit, secreted it under my sweatshirt, and restarted her machine, he just laughed and winked at me as if we were old friends sharing a grand joke.

Hmm.

I got the clothes home and changed. Then, for the eighteenth Friday in a row, I took the subway to my mother's house to drive her around and help with her errands. It wasn't that I was so inclined to assist; I had my own agenda to pursue: pick up adoption papers.

She looked confused when she opened the door and caught sight of the New me instead of the Old me.

"Mrs. Penny?" I said.

"Yes?"

"Hi." I smiled sweet. "Allison sent me to help you out today."

"Oh," she said, looking even more confused, but a smile beginning to blossom in response nonetheless.

"She's not well, so she arranged for me to take over, if that's all right with you?"

"Um . . . I suppose so." She cocked her head to the side. "You're a good driver, right?"

She said it kind of jokey, and I thought, That's what you want to know? Not what's wrong with your daughter? "I'm an excellent driver. I've been driving since I was sixteen and I've never had an accident." *Neither have I backed up over a helpless animal while toddy sodden, you cow.*

"Well, that's reassuring," she said all perky. "Come on in for a minute, I'll just put myself together." She ran her fingers self-consciously through her crispy hair. "I'm running a bit late this morning."

I followed her down the hall into the kitchen. I could tell that she had already put herself together but felt the need to spruce up now that she had seen me. I said, "Nice place, Mrs. Penny."

"Oh, please, call me Diane, you're making me feel old!"

"Sorry."

"And you are?"

"Allison, actually."

"Oh, that's funny. Well, as long as I have an Allison helping me out, ha-ha-ha."

How cheerful she was. How friendly and effusive.

"Would you care for a cup of coffee, Allison?"

Care for coffee? She never offered coffee. "Sure. If it's not too much trouble."

"No trouble. It's made. I just haven't had a moment to drink it yet. I slept scandalously late. It was glorious." She poured out two mugs from a white thermos carafe and brought them to the table. "Do you take milk or sugar?"

"No, thanks. Black is fine. I just have to . . ." I was chewing gum. I took it out of my mouth and held it between thumb and forefinger.

"Under the sink," she said, pointing.

When I pitched the wad I noticed a heavy sprinkling of beige tablets amid the coffee grinds and cigarette butts. She had dumped at least half a prescription of ReVia into the trash. The insomnia and dizzy spells must have been getting to her. I closed the cupboard and returned to the table. I smiled and sipped my coffee. "Mmm," I said, "good coffee."

"Thanks. So, this is very nice of you, helping out today. Have you and Allison been friends for a long time?"

"Well . . . not exactly. I'm the new roommate. To be honest, I don't really know her that well.

"Oh, okay. I was wondering." She smiled as if something she'd known all along had been confirmed. Obviously, she thought it unlikely that I could be my friend. That pissed me off. I wanted to let her know then that she was a burden.

"Actually," I said, "Allison paid me twenty-five dollars to do this for her today."

"Oh."

"I'm sorry. One of my faults is that I'm painfully honest."

"No, it's fine by me. I was just curious."

"I told her I'd be happy to help her out, that she didn't have to compensate me, but she insisted. She was adamant."

"Yes, well, she probably doesn't want to be beholden to you."

"You think? I got the feeling she wasn't used to asking people for big favors; it made her uncomfortable."

She shrugged.

"Anyway, I'm sure that Allison and I will be friends once we get to know each other better."

She sipped her coffee and smiled small. "I thought you said you were totally honest?"

How quick she was to disparage! I decided to egg her on and let her rip. "Well, maybe not best friends. She is kind of . . . I don't know."

"Look," she said, sighing weary, "Allison is my daughter, and of course I—of course we have that powerful mother-daughter bond, but I know all too well how difficult she can be."

"Hmm. She does seem a little . . . ?"

"She's troubled. Deeply troubled. I wish there was something I could do for her. Unfortunately, there's nothing I can do. She's just a very unhappy girl. Very unhappy and . . . hostile." Sad smile. Resignation.

I tried to appear empathetic. I tried not to dash hot coffee in her face and bring the mug swiftly down onto her skull.

"You must be a model," she said, suddenly chipper, a slight strained quality to the voice.

"Um . . . sort of. I just had photos done."

"Oh, that's exciting. How did they turn out?"

"I won't see them until Monday."

"You know, believe it or not, I thought about modeling when I was young."

"I believe it."

She jumped up and left the room. I knew where she was going. She was going to the living room to get her pageant picture. Moments later she returned with the framed photo pinched between lacquered nails.

"This was me when I was sixteen."

"Wow. A beauty queen."

"Miss Beef and Barley," she said, laughing dismissively, but with obvious pleasure. "Unfortunately, that was the zenith of my career."

"Why didn't you pursue it?" I said, handing the photo back, already hearing the nauseatingly familiar answer in my head.

"I was too short! I was only five foot seven."

I was just two inches away from a totally different life.

"I was just two inches shy of a completely different life." She stared misty and maudlin at the photo.

I used to doubt it when I heard it before. But now it seemed plausible that two inches could entirely alter a life.

I stood up and carried my empty mug to the sink.

"How tall are you?" she said.

"About five foot nine."

"Lucky," she said.

"Yes."

There was no remonstrative "Careful" as I backed the yellow Audi out of the driveway, and before lighting a Salem Menthol, my mother asked me if I minded if she smoked. "I don't mind," I said. "As long as you put the window down." She put the window down; she put it all the way down before lighting up.

First, we went to the bank. She withdrew cash, and I deposited my check from George. Next we went to the Moto-Photo so she could have her passport pictures taken yet again. This time when I asked my mother if she was going on a trip, she didn't hesitate to answer.

"I've been seriously thinking about going to Australia."

"Oh, really?"

"Yeah. I've always wanted to go there, ever since I was a little girl."

"Is that right?" She had never mentioned it before.

"When I was a kid, my grandmother gave me this book called *A Little Bush Maid,* about this girl named Norah who lived on this huge ranch called Billabong." She laughed. "Ever since I read that book, I've wanted to go to Australia. Particularly Victoria. That's where Billabong was."

I remembered the book. It was very old. On the cover was an illustration of a pretty girl riding wild on a horse. I had found it stashed in her sweater drawer when I was ten. Safe and special between cashmere. I remembered that I was not allowed to read it, because she was afraid I would crack the brittle spine or otherwise mess it up.

"I still have the book. A first edition," she confided. "I bet it's worth something to someone."

Our next stop was Boutique Eloquio. She didn't buy anything, but she tried on at least half a dozen outfits. She exhorted me to try things on as well. "Just for fun!" "Actually," I said, "I'm sort of in the market for a new dress." Of course, the well-made clothing looked great on me. And my mother was all animated and buzzing happy to have a real shopping buddy. "Oh, you *have* to try this," she said. "Here, let me zip you up," she said. "Oh, that's stunning with the belt," she said, tightening it around my waist.

It was a bizarre antithesis to the last time she had helped me shop for clothes. Me: thirteen years old, trying to squeeze into the designer jeans she'd picked out. Both of us: miserable and hot with shame when the salesman suggests we try the

Husky department at the rear of the store. Her: digging angry fingers into the waistband of the Husky pants, insisting that I buy them loose so she wouldn't have to come back in a month for a bigger pair. This was nothing like that. This was me as living Barbie doll, and my mother having the time of her life dressing and accessorizing me. "Oh," she said, "I know the *perfect* pair of Pradas for that dress, if you want to pop by Holt's after. . . ."

Did it piss me off that I was suddenly her best pal? Yes. Was I enjoying the attention anyway? Maybe a little.

Tall Job, the snooty saleslady, was there. She wasn't nearly as tall or as pretty as she seemed the week earlier. She was, however, a hell of a lot friendlier to me. I quite enjoyed tossing the rumpled dresses her way, kicking them out of the dressing room for her to pick up off the floor and carefully re-hang. I also liked tossing my bank card on the counter, knowing that there was three thousand dollars in my account, more than enough to cover the shimmery crimson slip dress that weighed about four ounces and cost me $490. There would be no perfect Pradas after that.

We dropped off some dry cleaning and then hit the grocery store. For the first time ever, my mother suggested we have a bite to eat in the Marché area before we shopped. We sat under a striped umbrella in the faux-outdoor café and ate at a small glass table. My mother was extraordinarily chummy and chatty. She asked me if I had a boyfriend. I told her that, unfortunately, I had somehow ended up with two. "Get it while you can!" she yelped, then threw her head back, cackling. She told me that she had recently concluded a short-lived affair with a psychotherapist widower, that she liked him but couldn't handle his fucked-up teenage progeny or his survivor guilt. She provided me with the sweaty particulars of their sexual encounters. She told me she had been trolling the Nerve.com personals online but hadn't found anyone to her liking. She told me she had started the Suzanne Somers diet, and gave me a detailed description of her new food regimen. She had a small green salad and a cup of black coffee. I had a large buttered bagel and a banana smoothie.

Off we went then. Shopping side by side. I picked up some staples for myself and bought expensive cookies to take to the cottage. My mother kept on jawing as we rolled our carts down the aisles. More words than I had heard from her in a decade. When a man who looked like a young Gabriel Byrne smiled at me in the condiment aisle, my mother said, "Holy moly. That guy was a hunk! He looked like that actor . . . what's his name?"

"Gabriel Byrne."

"Yes. Gabriel Byrne. You should go talk to him," she said, nudging me friendly with a rough elbow. "What have you got to lose?" Nudge, nudge. "Just go talk to him."

I was sick of talking. I was sick of her kind of talking—the endless insipid prattle, the humorless blah blah blah. Was this what I had missed out on and craved all those years as ugly Allison? Was this the fabulous persona she reserved for her pretty companions, this shallow, annoying chatterbox?

It sure wasn't much.

Time to take her home and get what I came for.

"I have to tell you," she said, "it's a pleasure to be riding with an assured driver."

"Is Allison not a good driver?" *And am I not Allison?*

"She's a nervous driver. Gets distracted."

I felt my hands tighten on the wheel. "Speaking of Allison," I said, "she asked me to pick something up for her when I dropped you off."

"Oh, what's that?"

"Her adoption documents. She said you have them."

"Oh! Well, how about that." She put down the window and lit a cigarette. She was silent for at least fifteen seconds.

"I guess it can be kind of upsetting when a child wants to find their birth parents."

"I'm not upset, I'm just surprised. She's never wanted them before. And I've offered."

"People change, I guess."

"Well, you're welcome to take them."

"So you don't think it would be upsetting for her father, your ex-husband?" Now was my chance to pump her for info.

She laughed. "He won't know one way or the other. And he wouldn't give a hoot anyway—the prick. Pardon my French."

"So you never talk to him?"

"Never. Unless he misses a payment. Then my lawyer talks to his lawyer." She laughed.

"I guess you were pretty young when you got married, huh?"

"We were both young. I was nineteen, he was twenty-three—no, twenty-four." She took a deep drag. "God, he was gorgeous. You should have seen him. Tall, dark, chiseled features, the whole package. With these incredible blue, blue eyes."

"Is that why you married him?"

"It was one reason." She flicked her cig out the window. "He was also *extremely* determined to marry me." Laugh. "He wooed me like crazy." Sigh. "I don't know. . . . I don't think I made the wrong choice. I just think that circumstances rendered the choice bad."

"What do you mean?"

"Well, I've thought about it a lot over the years, and I'm pretty sure that if I had been able to have children, we'd still be together today."

"Is that right?"

"Mmm. A barren wife just didn't fit into Simon's idea of the picture-perfect lifestyle." Pause. "He's a designer. He likes things just so." She fished out another cigarette, lit it, and blew smoke dragon-style out the nose. "That was one of the things he used to say before we were married. 'Oh, we're going to make such beautiful babies. You and me, kiddo, we are going to make the finest-looking babies in the land.'" She said it sarcastic. "He did not like the fact that we had to adopt. And unfortunately . . . Well, as you can imagine, Allison didn't exactly fit the bill as Simon's picture-perfect child. Although she was very cute when we got her."

I felt a small thump in the solar plexus. Is that how she saw it? Everything spiraling because of me? No. That couldn't be right. Although it would explain how she treated me my entire life . . . But it didn't make sense. He fought for me. In court he fought for me. She told me there was a custody battle. Fierce and protracted. He ran away, yes, but he wasn't running away from me. "Allison mentioned that you were divorced." I swallowed hard, tried to sound casual. "I think she said something about a big custody battle between the two of you."

"Yes." Bitter laugh. Then confidentially, in a lowered voice through mouth corner she said, "But it was a battle in reverse. Neither of us wanted full custody. I mean, I was willing to share it, but he didn't want to have anything to do with it."

I felt a wave of heat pass down over my face, sink into my throat, then plunge to the center of my chest, where it coagulated in a throb of shock and shame, strangling off my ability to breathe deeply or even properly.

"He just did not like that child. Do you know what he used to call her? *Thing.* He'd come home from work and say, 'Where's Thing? Is Thing in bed yet?' I swear, I'd have to stick her in bed two hours early so he wouldn't have his nose out of joint when he got home. And he'd make all these bad-taste jokes like: 'Maybe Thing would like to go play in traffic. . . . Maybe Thing would like to go to the basement and play with matches.'" She laughed and flicked her cig out the window. "Oh, well," she said. "He was happy to pay for his freedom. And I was happy to take his money. As they say: The marriage was a failure, but the divorce was a success!" Big cackle. Small sigh.

I don't remember how I did it, but somehow I moved the Audi through a blur of shifting car shapes and colors; somehow I guided the Audi through traffic to the curb.

"Are we stopping for some reason?"

An outdoor patio came into detached focus. It was like looking at a word disassociated from its meaning. People were laughing with their teeth in the yellow day. I pasted a smile on my face. I pasted one on and I said, "You know what would really hit the spot right now? A drink." I turned the engine off and pulled the keys from the ignition.

"How about you?" I said. "Could you use a drink?"

11

Twenty-four hours later I was lying on a lounge chair on George's boathouse deck, digesting lunch and waiting for warm moments when the patchy clouds would drift away from the sun. George was showing Don and Dawn the charred ceiling beams above the boat slips where old wood-burning engines from an ancestor's steamboat had left their dark mark. I had already surveyed the burned beams, as well as the collection of classic wooden boats—the sporty eighteen-foot Greavette Gentleman's Racer, the sturdy MacCraft patrol boat, the thirty-two-foot picnic boat with its built-in mahogany tables and benches, and the streamlined thirty-six-foot Minette-Shields—all beautiful and gleaming. George had taken me on a tour of the boathouse early in the a.m. to make sure that everything was in order should Don and Dawn choose to sleep there instead of in one of the five bedrooms in the Behemothic so-called cottage. The boathouse was a cottage in its own right, with at least a thousand square feet of living space atop the vessel-storage area. It had two bedrooms with quilt-covered spool beds; a tiny cedar bathroom with a porcelain tub; a cornflower blue kitchen with propane stove, microwave, and dishwasher; and an open dining/living room with peaked ceilings, the exposed trusses and rafters painted creamy white to match the antique wicker furniture below. It also had a sundeck, where I reclined on a heavy Mission-style lounge chair and, feeling rather dyspeptic, mulled over the preceding twenty-four hours.

I had dropped off my mother and departed her place with my shopping bags, adoption documents, and the keys to the yellow Audi in hand (just in case she had any inebriated ideas about taking the thing for a sloppy spin). With juice in her system she had become even more gabby and indiscreet, spilling, on the drive home from the bar, an anti-Allison rant from which I will probably never fully recover. Before leaving, I pretended to go upstairs for a pee, sneaked into her bedroom, and vigorously cracked the spine of *A Little Bush Maid*.

When I was safely out of range of the house, I opened the folded manila envelope that contained my last chance at familial affection. I pulled out the papers creased stiffly down the middle, and scanned the contents until I found what I was looking for. Jeannie Coombes. Jeannie Coombes was the name of my birth mother. My father's name did not appear anywhere on the forms, but Jeannie Coombes appeared. She was there all right. In quaint, old typewritten black and white. Jeannie Coombes, who twenty-two and a quarter years ago lived at 187 Winchester Street. A street that I knew of. A street in a formerly seedy, now sporadically gentrified neighborhood not ten miles from where I resided. Jeannie Coombes, who did not want to keep me with her at 187 Winchester, who had never made the effort to reach me, but who just might be interested, if I happened to track her down and pop by, to see how beautifully I'd turned out. Jeannie Coombes, who might not be disappointed ("That's nuts. You're lovely. Why on earth would she be disappointed?"). Who just might open her arms, fold me warm into her bosom, and say: *Daughter, how I've wondered and missed. Daughter, how I love love love.*

Of course, Jeannie Coombes might slam the door in my face. Jeannie Coombes might have moved out of the city long ago. Jeannie Coombes might even be dead, God forbid.

Thoughts of Jeannie Coombes filled my head as I made my way to the nearest phone booth, as I scanned the directory for a J. Coombes—there were none listed—as I left the booth and started walking. Then I was walking faster and still dreaming of Jeannie as I flailed my arms to hail a taxi, and told the driver to please take me to the corner of Winchester and Parliament. I don't really remember the journey, or the paying and getting out, but I do remember my heart pumping hard as I moved nervous down the street, past yuppies and rummies, until I came to number 187—a tiny single-story row house, bookended by two other workers' cottages. All three houses had been painted yellow with white trim. All three had postage-stamp front lawns that had been turned into English gardens with herbs and flowers bobbing in the breeze, and not a blade of grass in sight. All three had a sweet picket fence, and a darling flagstone path that led to the front door.

Jeannie Coombes, I thought. This is the house where my mother lived. Or possibly still lives? She could be behind that pretty white door right now. Perhaps all I have to do is knock. Just knock.

I lingered on the sidewalk opposite, until a fire engine came screaming down Winchester, blasting its big horn, which I took as a sign to get my ass across the street and up that flagstone path.

I knocked and waited. I could hear activity inside. A few moments later the pretty white door was opened by a pretty brunette woman with a baby in her arms. The woman was short and plump, and for a nanosecond I thought: *Mother?* Then it registered that she was only about ten years older than

I was. She must have been baking. I could smell something good, like warm chocolate-chip cookies, coming from inside.

"Hi."

"Hi. Um, sorry to bother you, I'm trying to find someone who used to live in this house. Jeannie Coombes was her name."

"Oh. Coombes? Hmm, no, never heard of her. . . ."

"Cute baby," I said, to be courteous and put her at ease.

"Thanks! It's her first birthday tomorrow, isn't it?" She said it to the baby in a nursery-rhyme voice.

"That's nice," I said, smiling big at the baby until it was polite to shift focus: "So, you've lived here for quite a while?"

"No, we've only been here about three years, three and a half years. But, uh, the woman who we bought the place from was definitely not the name you said."

"Not Coombes?"

"No. Definitely not."

"You wouldn't happen to remember the woman's name by any chance?"

She studied my face. "Well . . . what is this about?"

"I'm just, um— I was adopted and I'm trying to track down my birth mother." As the words came out of my mouth, I suddenly felt tremendously sorry for myself. I actually had to fight back a swell of tears.

"Oh," she said, giving me an empathetic look. She held the baby tighter. Her right breast started to leak a spot of milk through her T-shirt. "You know what, I think I do remember. Her name was Lewis. Something Lewis. Gosh, I'm sorry, I really can't remember her first name."

"You sure it wasn't Jeannie?" Jeannie could have remarried and become Lewis.

"I really can't remember. But it was definitely Lewis. L-e-w-i-s. And she still lives around here. I see her on the street all the time."

"Really?"

"Should we quickly check the phone book? We can see if there's a Lewis on one of the streets around here."

"That'd be great. Thank you."

"Come in for a sec."

The house was small and pretty. "It's nice in here," I said, imagining Jeannie Coombes/Lewis in the wingback chair by the window.

"Thanks! We did it ourselves. You should've seen it when we got it. Oh, my Lord!" The woman made a face and flipped through the phone book. I looked over her shoulder. There were hundreds of listings for Lewis. "Holy moly," she said, running her finger slowly down the list. The baby, held tight in her left arm, gurgled.

"Sorry to inconvenience you," I said.

"Purvis," said the woman. "There's an M. Lewis at 79 Purvis Street. That's close to here."

"Seventy-nine Purvis." I wrote it down.

"Just walk east on Winchester past the lights and it's on the south side. Either the first street or the second street past the lights."

"Thanks. I'll start there. Thank you very much for your help."

"No problem," she said, guiding me out. "Good luck with your search."

"Bye-bye," I said, waving to the baby. "Have a happy birthday."

"We will," said the woman.

Then the pretty white door closed in my face.

I walked east on Winchester, past the lights, on the south side. The neighborhood had changed over the years, but there were still signs of the bad old days. Like the dirty U-Bag grocery store still hanging in there between the organic butcher shop and the gourmet coffee roastery. Like the trashy rooming house at 79 Purvis Street, a monstrous Victorian with peeling red paint and, as near as I could tell from the sidewalk opposite, at least eight doorbells. There was a stack of ancient beer cases and a decrepit sagging sofa on the front porch. And on the decrepit sagging sofa was a decrepit sagging woman, who, astonishingly, looked quite a bit like me. The old me, that is.

I crossed the street to get a better view. The woman flicked her cigarette on the lawn, cleared her disastrously phlegmy throat, and lit another one right away. She was wearing stained sweatpants and a threadbare Speedy Muffler T-shirt. She was fat and ugly, and looked like me. Except the face was harder. Meaner.

"Take a picture," she said. "It lasts longer."

"Jeannie Coombes?" I asked softly.

"Who wants to know?" she sniped.

I stood immobile. Mute. This was not what I had expected. This wasn't anything remotely like Fantasies 1 through 12.

"Hell-*o-o*!?" She said it harsh. Sarcastic. "Can I help you?!"

No, I thought as I took off down the street. No, I guess you probably can't.

Somebody was waiting on my front porch. A pimply teenager clutching the coffee-stained copy of Nathan's screenplay, and five white tulips held together with a dirty elastic band.

"Allison Penny?" he said.

"Yes." I was getting used to this now.

Not waiting for giddy expressions of delight, he thrust the script and bouquet at me, then dashed to a smashed-up BMX and pedaled away. For the first time in hours, I wasn't thinking about Jeannie Coombes or Simon Penny. I was thinking about Nathan, about how he was the only person to listen to a passing remark and actually hear it and get it right (white tulips), and how I really wanted to see him, but really, really didn't want to tell him that I wouldn't be able to make it to his apartment for the special lasagna on Saturday night. . . .

"No problem," he said, going a little pale and drawing back from me. "We can do it another time."

"Can we, please?"

"Sure. No probs." He didn't sound very convincing. He was grinning grim. A heavy silence, and then: "I guess I should get that screenplay back at some point."

"What? I just got it, like, four hours ago." I laughed. "Give me a chance to speed-read it at least."

"Oh, I thought maybe you'd read it or something." He looked down at his feet. As if my reading his script was the reason I had canceled our date.

"You're crazy," I said, reaching for his hand. No response. The mitt lay limp. "How about one night next week?" I said. "How about Tuesday? You don't work Tuesday nights, right?"

"You're not working next week?"

"No. I was just filling in. I've actually asked the DeSouzas to find a replacement for me."

"Oh," he said, withdrawing his hand and folding his arms across his chest. He cleared his throat. "So how is Allison? Have you heard anything?"

"Nothing has really changed."

"Hmm."

"So, how about Tuesday night?" I said. "Do you want me to come over on Tuesday?"

"If you want."

"Of course I want." I moved in for a kiss. His jaw was rigid and motionless. Tough-guy stiff. I persisted, working my way in. The mouth relaxed a little, opened. The arms uncrossed as he began to melt into it and respond. Then we were embracing and everything felt good and okay again, and I imagined the flowers on the patio swelling sweet and vibrating in the dark, and we were smiling between kisses.

"So tell me why you can't come eat lasagna tomorrow?" He said it soft and playful.

Why indeed? Something about Heaven & Earth and Direct Access. Something about three thousand dollars and a hot tub overlooking the lake. I stepped back. "I'm sorry. I just—I have to go out of town for a couple days. There's something I have to see to." I couldn't easily explain it, and I didn't want to get into it. Even though I could tell he really wanted to know, and there was nothing soft and playful about the wanting to know.

He nodded, processing the lack of information.

"I'm really sorry," I said. "I'll call you Monday when I get back. And I'll come over Tuesday night, okay?"

"Okay."

After I left Nathan on the patio, I continued with the final leg of my cleaning route. I remember thinking, as I rolled my cart into IZ Talent Management: Well, this is it, the last office I'll ever have to clean, and the last time I'll have to contend with Peter Igel. I could hear the music playing, the faint jazz music coming from Igel's office. Friday night. As usual he was trying to de-thong some Cindy Crawford wanna-be.

I was pleased to discover, when I'd cleaned my way back there, that the bratwurst-containing filing cabinet had been removed. The entire cabinet gone. And still I could detect the faintest trace of rotting meat under the aerosol pine that had been liberally spritzed. "Excuse me," I said as I entered and made my way around the desk. The lady of the day was a beautiful black woman. Long and lean with a 1970s-style Afro dyed golden brown. She was seated close to Igel on the sofa, a binder of photos—her makeshift portfolio—spread open on her lap.

"It's the nose that's holding you back," he said casually, barely glancing at the binder.

"You think?" said the woman, studying her face in a photo.

Igel scoped me as I did my thing. "Excuse me," he said. "Have I seen you before?"

"I don't think so."

"You've modeled before?"

"Nope." I carried his trash can to the cart and emptied it. I could feel his eyes on me. He stood up and stared hard as I passed by to put the trash can back under the desk.

"Just a second," he said. "Would you like to model?"

"Um . . . I don't know," I said. "Maybe."

"Because you could probably make a great deal of money if you cared to."

The woman on the love seat smile-scowled and closed her binder. Igel rummaged through some things on his desk and picked up a strange metal instrument. "Come here for a moment," he said, gesturing for me to come close. "Just for a moment, I promise." He held the device up to my face. It reminded me of some sort of high-school math tool. Three hinged pieces of flat, pointed metal that accordioned in and out. "I knew it," he said, moving the instrument over different parts of my face, taking measurements of some kind. "What an eye," he said, laughing.

"What is that?" asked the woman on the love seat.

"This is a Golden Mean Gauge," said Igel. "It measures the golden ratio—one to point six-one-eight. Phi. What humans universally perceive as ideal beauty. Proportional perfection. You see," he said, moving the device around my face, "no matter how much the gauge opens or closes, the proportion remains the same. If I extend the gauge from the chin to the nose, the distance from her chin to lower lip is one, while the distance from the lower lip to the nose is point six-one-eight. Perfect. From the inside corner of the left eye to the inside corner of the right eye is one; from the inside corner of the right eye to the outside corner of the right eye: point six-one-eight. Smile," he said. I did. "Even her teeth. You see, the front tooth is one, and the one next to it: point six-one-eight. Beauty is essentially mathematics. And this golden ratio is present in all beautiful things. It isn't subjective, it's universal."

He continued measuring, and I thought, If that's true, if beauty isn't subjective, how do you explain the appeal of brutalism, the Pontiac Aztek, leisure suits, Fran Drescher. . . ?

"Yup," said Igel, tossing the instrument on the desk. "This young lady possesses a mathematically perfect face."

"Try it on me," said the woman on the love seat.

"Later," said Igel. "What's your name, then?"

"Allison Penny."

"Well, Allison Penny, shall we pop into the boardroom for a minute to talk it over?"

"I don't think so," I said, moving to my cart. "The thing is, I've already been talking to the people downstairs. At the Malcolm Anders Agency."

He laughed. "Sweetheart, that place is for catalog models. You can do better than that. Especially if you drop ten or fifteen pounds."

Huh?! "But I've already had photos taken. *At this weight,*" I said archly. "And they paid for it."

"Have you signed a contract with them?"

"Not yet, no."

"You're fine," he said with a wave of the hand. "Their mistake for not signing you first. They'll just have to eat the cost."

It angered me that he was so willing to rip off Fiona and the agency, until I remembered that's what I had been planning to do.

"Listen," said Igel. "IZ Talent is one of the top players in town. Why start at the bottom when you can start at the top? Do you know how difficult it is to get a spot on the roster here? Particularly, my roster."

"You should do it," said the woman on the love seat, urging me with a bulge of the eyes.

I thought it over for a minute. "Okay," I said. "I'll make you a deal. I'll sign with IZ Talent Management under one condition."

"What's that?" he said.

"That you personally and immediately undergo the following surgical procedures: nose job, lip augmentation, chin and pectoral implants."

He looked at me as if I were a dog wearing a funny hat, taking a piss on his desk. Half amused, half annoyed. "What are you talking about? Why on earth would I do that?"

"You see," I said to the beautiful woman with the non-phi nose, lounging leggy on the love seat. "That is the correct answer."

Then I rolled out of there for the very last time.

It was a satisfying moment. It would have been a fine capper to my final night at 505 Richmond. Unfortunately, it wasn't the capper, because when I took my cart back and collected my bags and went outside to wait for George, Nathan was out there, waiting for me. His presence registered like a punch in the gut. Panic filled me up and made me stupid.

"Hey," he said.

"What are you still doing here?"

"Oh, well, I had to re-pot a root-bound ficus." He laughed. "But really I just wanted to say good night."

"Oh. Thanks." I laughed like a demented person. I was thinking, Please, God, do not let George pull up until Nathan has skedaddled. "Well, good night," I said, willing him to leave. "Call you Monday when I get back."

"Are you taking a taxi?" he said, gesturing to the duffel bag slung heavy over my shoulder.

"Um, no. No . . ."

And then George pulled up. In the baby-blue Vanquish with the top down. He tapped on the horn and waved. Guilt grabbed my belly with hooked hands as I half-waved back. I looked at Nathan, who was looking at George. I didn't know what to say. I blushed hot, laughed apologetically.

"Well, I guess I was wrong about the ugly-man fetish."

Nathan smiled. "Have a great weekend," he said. Then he walked away.

He walked quickly away.

George interrupted my guilt-soaked reverie, stepping onto the boathouse sundeck with Don and Dawn in tow. "Who's ready for a hot tub?" he said, clapping his hands together.

"I think I'm ready for a nap after that lunch!" said Dawn. She sat on the lounge chair next to mine, gave me a condescending be-nice-to-the-bauble smile, and stretched out. Lunch had included two bottles of Chardonnay, much of which was consumed by me in an effort to drown the image of Nathan's backpack bobbing off into the night.

"I could use a nap," said Don, patting his belly.

"Shall we have a little lie-down, then?" said George.

"Sure," I said, standing up. Don and Dawn were getting on my nerves. The whole couples dynamic was scraping at my sensibilities. I was happy to get away for an hour or so, even if it meant a sexual encounter with George, something I'd been able to avoid to that point in the weekend. Shortly after we'd arrived on Friday I'd gone to bed with a horrible headache. George had stayed up to watch satellite TV. When I awoke on Saturday, he was already up and about, preparing for Don and Dawn's ten A.M. arrival. Breakfast had included a pitcher of champagne and orange juice.

"So you guys are gonna sleep down here?" said George.

"I think so," said Dawn, glancing at Don, deferring to him. He nodded: yes. "Yes," said Dawn.

"Okay. Come get us when you're ready. We'll do a hot tub and swim after siesta."

"Sounds like a plan," said Don.

I followed George up the cedar staircase to the cottage. It was the first time we'd been alone together since Don and Dawn had turned up.

"They're great, aren't they?" said George when we were inside.

"Yeah," I lied. I didn't think they were great, or even good. I thought they were interminably boring and insufferably stuck up. I couldn't help but notice over the course of two meals how often either Don or Dawn would refer to someone as a "character." Their dry cleaner, an "Egyptian fellow," was a "character." Their new neighbors, "an old Jewish couple," were "characters." Their Filipino cleaning lady was a "character." Dawn's Pilates instructor, a "crazy Serb," was a "real character." It became apparent that anyone who wasn't a WASP qualified as a "character" in the world of Don and Dawn.

"But I can't believe how big Dawn's got. The last time I saw her she was a rake. Amazing what a couple years of married life will do to you."

"She's not that big," I said. She was a little chunky, yes, but quite pretty—black hair cut in a 1920s-style bob, pale skin with pink cheeks, and wide-set blue eyes. Round, stupid eyes. "She's pretty."

"She used to be. Before she got 'broad in the beam,' as Mother says." He laughed and grabbed my ass. "I bet married life wouldn't ruin this one." He gave me what I construed to be a meaningful look, then leaned in and kissed my ear. "I think I'm ready for a lie-down," he said. "How about you?"

"I wouldn't mind a nap."

"You're not still sleepy?"

"A little," I lied.

"Why don't you go have a snooze. I'll take a shower and then join you."

"All right."

I got undressed and slipped under the quilt. I wasn't planning to fall asleep, but the fresh air mixed with the smell of cedar, and the sound of the shower going in the en suite bathroom, sent me drifting off.

"Psst . . ."

I opened my eyes and saw George standing beside the bed, half hovering over me. His hard cock was pitching a tent in the terry cloth around his hips. "Hi, there," he whispered, dropping the towel. I caught a whiff of Ivory soap coming off his moist pubic hair.

"Hi." He looked pretty sexy, to tell you the truth. I felt a jolt of desire for his damp, perfect body.

George took his cock in his right hand and slowly peeled back the quilt with his left. "Oh," he said. "What the hell happened to you?" He was staring at the bruises on my hip and thigh.

"Oh, um, I fell and crashed into a table at work the other day." I ran my fingers over the cumulus cloud of purple, yellow, and black.

"Jeez. That's too bad. Wow. It's really bad, huh?"

"Well, it doesn't hurt anymore." I watched his penis shrink and drop soft from his hand. *Plop.*

"Oh, good. Good. I'm glad it doesn't hurt." He pulled the cover back over me. "So you want to keep napping for a while?"

"No. I'm up now."

He picked the towel off the floor and carried it to the bathroom.

"Maybe I'll go for a swim," I said. I hadn't gone swimming since I was a kid. I adored swimming.

"Um, shouldn't we wait for the Dons?"

"Why?"

"To be sociable," he said. He came out of the bathroom and started dressing. His bureau was full of clean summer clothes, all folded and pressed. "I'm sure they won't be long. Hey, why don't we play a game?" he said. "How about a game of Trivial Pursuit?"

I had just about trounced George when Don and Dawn appeared at the sliding glass door of the screened-in porch.

They were both wearing flip-flops and white robes with *Idlewild*—the name of the cottage—embroidered in black on the tit. They had beach towels slung over their arms.

"Hey, guys, feeling rested and refreshed?"

"You bet," said Don.

"I just love these robes. It's such a good idea!" said Dawn, coming closer to observe the game. "Ooh, someone has all their pies." She put her hand on George's shoulder and squeezed.

"That would be me," I said. George had two pies, a sports pie and an entertainment pie.

"Oh!" Up went the eyebrows. "Good for you!"

"This lovely young lady is kicking your ass," said Don with a laugh. Everyone seemed amused and surprised by it. George had certainly looked astonished every time I'd answered a question correctly.

"I know it," he said, wiping the board clean. "Let's go for a swim."

George put on a pair of navy trunks, crisp and trimmed with white. He sat on the bed and surveyed my fluorescent pink bathing suit. It was hideous, too small in the tits and too big in the butt. It had cutaway sides that showed my bruises prominently, and the seat was covered with tiny balls of frayed material where the Rude Woman had sat on cement or some other rough surface. Still, I looked good in it. Downright *Sports Illustrated*. As Old Allison I didn't even own a bathing suit. I refused to appear in public with my exposed flesh bulging. Man, I was looking forward to a swim!

"You know, that suit doesn't really fit," George said.

"I know. I'll have to get a new one eventually."

"We have spares, if you'd like to borrow one."

"Don't worry about it. It's going to get wrecked in the hot tub anyway."

"I'm sure we have one that will fit better." He left the room and returned moments later with a navy one-piece trimmed with white piping. "Here," he said, tossing the suit to me. "Now we'll match."

Swimming felt gloriously good. Dear God, it felt good. The lake was frigid—sixty-nine degrees, according to the thermometer dangling slimy from a submerged lower rung of the dock ladder. But I loved the coldness all over my body, especially on my hot skull. I loved the strong strokes my new arms could make, moving me fast through fresh water, and when finally I couldn't take the chill for one more moment, when my teeth were chattering happy, I would climb, confident and carefree, up the ladder and onto the dock, with everyone's eyes on my goose-pimpled flesh. It was freedom I felt. Pure, exhilarating, yellow-day joy. If the sun wasn't behind a cloud when I emerged from the lake, I would flop down on my stomach on the dock and feel the warm starting between my shoulder blades. I would listen to my heart beating hard, inhale the good wood smell, and peer through the slats to the lake below, at my blue eyes reflected in the dark water. If a cloud was hanging in front of the sun, I would dash up the hill to the hot tub, sink into the churning, pleasantly scented chemical bath, and listen to the whir of the jets, feel them working on my glad muscles, and the bottom of my feet if I stretched my legs long across the expanse of tub. When my face was shiny with sweat and I couldn't take the boil for one more moment, I would dash down the hill and dive into the lake again.

Heaven.

"My gosh, you're like a fish," said Dawn as I emerged from yet another swim. I smiled and wrung out my hair, much water falling from locks onto the dock.

"Like a mermaid," said Don. And Dawn shot him a frown.

I found a dry spot and stretched out on the wood in the late-afternoon sun.

"Why don't you lie on a lounge chair?" said George.

He had asked me this earlier. "I'm okay," I said.

"You'd be more comfortable on a chair."

"I'm all right."

"Indulge me and try it for a sec."

I got up and lay down on a chair next to Dawn.

"I just don't know how you can stand it," she said, referring, presumably, to the sixty-nine-degree water. Her voice was edged with quiet hysteria. Her husband had been eyeballing me all day from behind insufficiently opaque sunglasses. This seemed to please George a hell of a lot more than it pleased Dawn.

"I find it invigorating," I said, watching three kids at the neighboring cottage take turns swinging into the lake from a rope tied to a big tree.

"Ugh!" Dawn shuddered and let out a peal of high-pitched laughter. She did not brave the icy lake. At one point, she had tried entering gradually from the beach area. I saw her standing for at least ten minutes, submerged to mid-calf, dipping her hands in the water and patting her upper arms with it. But no go. Eventually she lumbered back to the dock, applied a thick coating of SPF 45 sunscreen, and donned a colossal straw hat (a wide-brimmed affair that looked as if it could pick up several hundred channels). Don jumped in once, cannonball style, treaded water for twenty seconds, and then got out. George dived in twice, once before a hot tub and once after. A cooling in/out. I was the only one who swam.

At five o'clock, George announced that it was "cocktail time." I slipped away to take a long, hot shower. The shampoo smelled like mango. The moisturizing body lotion smelled like cucumber and avocado. I pilfered some soft cottage clothes from George's dresser—a baggy black T-shirt and a pair of khaki army shorts. I combed out my hair and plaited it in one heavy braid down my back. I felt fresh and slightly buzzed from too much sun. And I was famished. In a good way.

Off I went to the kitchen in search of something to eat.

There was a glass pan on the counter, full of thick steaks marinating in soy sauce and fresh garlic. The smell drove me wild. I swung the fridge door open. Another glass pan, this one full of gigantic scallops in a citrus marinade. There were peaches plump, blue plums, green grapes, cheeses of all kinds, pâté and dips: humus, Baba Ganoush, roasted red pepper . . . but I needed grease. I required crunch. I rooted around in the pantry until I stumbled across a snack bonanza: giant jars of honey-roasted peanuts, tinned cashews, and an embarrassment of cookies, crackers, and chips. I grabbed a bag of Barbecue Kettle Chips, ripped it open, and shoved a handful of delicious into my gape. After several fistfuls I calmed down, licked the orange residue off my fingers, dumped the remaining contents into a bowl, and carried it onto the deck, where the others had assembled for drinks.

"There she is," said George. He stood up and stirred a tall glass pitcher of martinis with a glass swizzle stick. "Cocktail?"

"Yes, please. Anyone want a chip?" I held out the bowl.

"No, thanks," said Dawn, putting up a halt hand, then patting her belly—international sign for "I feel I am too fat to enjoy chips."

"Not for me," said Don, chewing on a cigar. The smoke smelled wonderful.

I took a seat and placed the bowl in front of me. George handed me an elegant long-stemmed martini glass. "There you go."

"Thanks." There were fine ice crystals floating on top of the gin, and a curlicue of lemon rind at the bottom of the glass. I said, "Isn't it funny how beverages that make you clumsy are served in the most tippy glasses, while beverages that make you alert are served in heavy ceramic mugs?"

"That's true," said George with a tolerant smile.

"What a cute observation," said Dawn, as if I were a five-year-old who had just tied my shoes successfully for the first time.

"Cheers." I raised the glass and took a sip. My God, it

tasted good! Clean and sharp and impossibly bracing. I alternated swallows of martini with handfuls of greasy chips. I smiled and nodded at the conversation bouncing across the table, but I was focused on the truly amazing deliciousness of the martini and chips, the pleasant sun-kissed feeling of my flesh, and the tantalizing smells all around me: the sweet cigar smoke in the piney air, the mango coming off my damp braid, the hint of avocado and cucumber when I brought my hand close to my face. It occurred to me that all I'd have to do is smile and nod politely, all I'd have to do is be unbruised and a willing backsplash for semen, all I'd have to do is wear the navy suit with the white piping, and all this could be mine. It really could. I could marry George. I could marry him and move into his penthouse loft and soak in his claw-footed tub. In the winter I could frolic at his condo in the Caymans and accompany him on his business trips to the Bahamas. In the summer I could head up to the cottage and stay for an entire season while George helped his father with real-estate developments or played movie producer in the city. I could go from hot tub to lake all summer long, smiling and nodding on weekends if necessary. It would be endless luxury, but more important, it would be the end of drudgery. No more scrambling to make the rent, no more crappy low-paying jobs, no more peeling-ceiling apartments (I shuddered as a flash of Jeannie Coombes on her porch flitted through my head), no more Laundromats with washed Kotex pads and mucus-encrusted children, no more Sunny Delight orange drink. I sipped my martini and watched a bird fly across the low sun. I imagined a life of perfect cocktails and crunchy Kettle Chips and banana-leaf body wraps and all the time in the world to do whatever the hell I wanted. I could read *Remembrance of Things Past*. Or take up fencing.

"Sounds like a plan," said Doug when George suggested firing up the barbecue.

"Shall us girls make the salad?" said Dawn.

"Yes, let's," I said, and the perkiness of my voice surprised me. I downed my drink and followed Dawn into the huge kitchen, where I tipsily chopped up the reddest tomatoes with the sharpest knife on the biggest butcher block I'd ever seen.

After dinner, George and Don went out to the deck to smoke cigars, while Dawn and I cleared the table and loaded the dishes into the dishwasher. Dawn castigated herself for having consumed too much food, and complained about a recent dental whitening procedure that had left her teeth inordinately sensitive to hot and cold. She asked me if I had had mine done. I said no, I hadn't. She asked me if I thought Matthew Broderick would be at Heaven & Earth later. I said I didn't know. She asked me what I was going to wear. I said a red shift.

Eventually we all reconvened in the main room, in front of the impressive quartz fireplace, to sip wine and have dessert, wild-blueberry pavlova with fresh whipped cream, whipped up fresh by me, don't you know. *Shall us gals prepare dessert? Yes, let's!* Don and Dawn were going on about how much fun we were all having and how they should purchase a cottage in the area. George was telling them about a property that was for sale. But it wasn't on the same lake, and Dawn and Don wanted one on the same lake so they could boat over. I wasn't really paying attention or participating in the conversation. Earlier, Dawn had asked me what I did for a living. I was about to answer, when George interjected, "Allison's between jobs at the moment."

"Oh," said Dawn, smiling. "Me, too. Although I do a lot of volunteer work and fund-raising activities."

I smiled back. I didn't say anything. I didn't say very much at all after that. For example, I didn't say a thing when Don started ranting about a high-profile artist who had received government funding for a painting that Don felt he himself could have done with his eyes closed. I didn't make a peep when Dawn said that her book club read all the titles recommended by Kelly Ripa. I was quiet as a mouse when George admitted he rarely read anything besides the sports and financial pages. I just sipped my wine and smiled politely and stared into the impressive quartz fireplace.

"I like the looks of that place next door," said Don.

"What, the Parker place?"

"The big stone one."

"Yeah. It's prime. Awesome boathouse. But they'll never sell. It's been in the family forever. The Parker kids will get it next."

"Too bad," said Don.

"No, honey, it's good to keep these things in the family," said Dawn. "That way you can retain the integrity of the lake."

"That's true," said Don. They exchanged a knowing glance. Dawn rolled her eyes and laughed.

George said, "The Dons had to sell their last cottage."

"These *awful* people moved in next door," confided Dawn.

"Nah," said Don, "they were nice enough, there was just too damned many of them."

"We tried to count once, and we couldn't even tell how many were in there!" laughed Dawn.

"It was like they imported an entire village every weekend. There'd be tents set up on the lawn—"

"No way," said George, laughing.

"I'm telling ya, frickin' pup tents all over the lawn to hold the spillover." Don laughed. "And they roasted a goat out there. Remember, honey? At least we thought it was goat."

"They were *characters*," said Dawn. "That's for sure."

"Are you okay?" said George.

I had stood up and stumbled over to a table. I was leaning on the table with both arms. My heart seemed to think I had just run the Boston Marathon.

"What's wrong?" George stood and came toward me.

"I don't know. I think I just need some air."

"You sure?"

"Yeah," I started to move toward the sliding glass doors. That's when the first bizarre thing happened. All of a sudden, with no warning, the contents of my stomach erupted out of my mouth. It was incredible, as if the stomach collapsed violently into itself, forcing everything out in one hot shot. Like a sledgehammer coming down on a burrito. Insides out. An entire evening's worth of intake: martini and Kettle Chips and mesclun salad and New York steak and giant scallops and corn on the cob and wild-blueberry pavlova and several glasses of Burgundy wine spewed out in one fast blast onto off-white carpeting.

"OH MY GOD!" shrieked Dawn, jumping up off the sofa and clawing at herself.

"Holy shit!" said George. "I'll call Phil Hanson; he's two cottages down!"

"Is he a doctor?" shouted Don. And I wasn't too sick to think: No, brainiac, he's a fucking fan dancer. He's the guy who irons the little creases into the paper cupcake holders.

"Yes," said George, dashing into the kitchen.

Now, here's the next bizarre thing that happened. George ran back from the kitchen—not having called Phil Hanson—and like a gunslinger, aimed an aerosol can at the pile of stinking vomit. He pressed the trigger. A long squiggle of white shot out of the nozzle like Silly String. George kept spraying until the pile was completely covered in expanding white foam. *Then* he ran back to the kitchen and called Phil Hanson.

I described my symptoms—palpitations, dizziness, nausea—to George, who relayed them via phone to the doctor. Then I barricaded myself in the bedroom's en suite bathroom, and brushed my teeth and washed my face. I lay down in the cool bathtub and listened to the hushed voices murmuring outside the door. *Probably too much rich food. Think we'll be able to go? Well, you guys can go. But what about you?*

Silence then, until Phil Hanson tapped on the door. I got out of the tub and admitted him to the room. He interviewed me and took my pulse—which had slowed considerably but was still going at a mad gallop—before making his diagnosis:

anxiety attack exacerbated by alcohol consumption. "Alcohol is a stimulant, you know? Did you know that?" he asked. "I didn't know that," I said, trying not to look at his spider-veined nose. He gave me an Ativan to take right away. It was from his wife's stash; I saw the name on the prescription bottle: Sharon Hanson. He left another one for me to swallow in the morning if I needed it, and told me to see my GP if I ever felt this way again. When he went into the bedroom to speak to George, I eavesdropped on their lowered voices. "Is there anything I should do?" said George. "Just keep her calm, you know . . . rub her back, watch a funny movie. That sometimes works for Shari. Try to make her laugh."

"We're supposed to go to a club opening later."

"What, that Heaven thing?"

"Yeah."

"You have invites?"

"Father is buddies with the guy who owns it."

"Sweet. Well, let her rest awhile. Then if she feels up to going, there's no reason why she shouldn't."

"Okay. Thanks, Phil."

The doctor said, "But if you're not going to use those invitations, give me a call."

When I heard them leave the room, I went in and lay down on the bed and thought about Sharon Hanson, eating Ativans and watching funny movies while the world swirled around her. Then I had a vision of all the pretty wives in all the pretty cottages doing the same thing.

A couple of minutes later George returned.

"How are you feeling?" he said.

"A bit dizzy."

"You're not still nauseous, are you?"

"A little."

"Um . . . would you mind if I asked you to lie down in another bedroom? It's just, this bed is brand new and Father will—"

"No problem." I got up.

"Here, it's just across the hall. . . . Unless, do you feel like watching a movie or something? We have that new Danny DeVito comedy—"

"No, thanks."

"The Dons went back to the boathouse."

"I don't feel like watching a movie." I lay down on one of two twin beds in the small white room. There was a decorative washbowl and pitcher on a pine stand. George carried the washbowl over and set it on the floor beside the bed.

"In case you need it," he said.

"Thanks."

"So, you want a backrub or something?"

"No, thanks."

He sat on the end of the bed and I could see him trying to think of something funny to say, something that would relax me as per doctor's orders. "Hey," he said, laughing. "Did you see those kids today?"

"What, swinging on the rope?"

"Yeah. The Parkers. Gross, eh? We call them the Porkers, or the Three Little Pigs, or"—he assumed a heavy Scottish brogue—"*the fat bastards.*" He laughed.

I did not laugh. I said, "I think I'd better close my eyes for a while." The Ativan, thank goodness, had started to kick in.

Total blackness. Complete silence.

I was alone. I knew it even before I found the lamp, and the note: *Allison, thought it best to let you sleep. We've gone to check out the club. Shouldn't be too late—G.*

Right. Nice. Who cares if Allison is puking/panicking alone in the cottage? Gotta catch a glimpse of Kurt and Goldie, or Matthew Broderick, who's filming a movie in the area. Best to let her sleep. Yes. Because if I wake her, she might not want to go to the exclusive club, she might ask me to stay with her at the cottage, which would impede my ogling of Goldie and Kurt. Grrrr!

I went to the main room to find a clock. Two forty-seven

A.M. I thought about calling a taxi, but I had no idea where to call it to: *Um, the big cottage by the lake?* I thought about hoofing it—it wasn't far to town—but it was dark and scary, and I was reluctant to become an all-you-can-eat blood buffet for bugs. I thought about going back to bed, but I was far too awake now for that. I cupped my hands on the window and peered outside. Don and Dawn's SUV was not in the driveway. Was the Vanquish still in the garage? I put on a bug jacket and crunched across the gravel drive, dodging rioting moths in the exterior light.

I hoisted the door.

It was well after three A.M. when I arrived at the club. Still, there was a cluster of dolled-up twenty-somethings hovering around the entrance, trying to get in. Great, I thought, eyeing the beefy bouncers as I high-heeled my way to the door. Here we go again. I had visions of my ex-roommate, Elda, stomping, rebuffed and irate, down Richmond Street. But as I got closer, as I mentally rehearsed the pretext about George being inside and having my invitation, the biggest and beefiest bouncer simply unhooked a velvet rope and took a beefy step aside. And I can assume only that I looked like I belonged, because I didn't need George Thomas in order to gain entry to Heaven & Earth. All I needed was to be gorgeous in a gossamer slip dress, and they just smiled and let me in.

Yes, they did.

And it was music, bodies, lights, smoke, and several minutes before I adjusted to the atmosphere inside, to the mad percussive motion and the flash of strobe, to the heads thrown back in laughter and the trays of drinks floating by, and I was seeing without comprehending for at least five minutes until it all began to settle into some kind of focus.

The room was huge with a high ceiling. Everything white and illuminated. The floor, lit from below, glowed white. As did the bar-stool stems at the curvy white bars, which were hung from the ceiling. White clouds—suspended by barely visible wires—floated above the massive dance floor at different levels. On each cloud was a nearly naked go-go dancer dressed as an angel. Half were males (in white thongs and wings), half were females (G-strings, pasties, and wings). The slutty angels gyrated to the music and sprinkled handfuls of glitter onto the dancers below. I grabbed a cocktail from a passing tray and sipped quickly, moving through the crowd looking for George or Simon Penny.

When I had done a full pass of the main floor, I descended to the basement, where the design concept of the club fully registered. Downstairs was a dark, comparatively quiet area, the Earth part of Heaven & Earth. Throughout the room were giant papier-mâché tree trunks that stretched from floor to ceiling. The ceilings were low and had been done up to look like a thick canopy of leaves—gazillions of tiny paper leaves hung from branches that extended out from the papier-mâché tree trunks. Also suspended from the branches were hundreds of dimly lit patio lanterns that glowed red and barely illuminated the veiny detail of the paper leaves. Love seats and tables were scattered here and there in the intimate faux-forest. Obviously, Earth is where you went to have a conversation. Heaven was where you went to dance.

I downed another drink while I strolled around, looking for familiar faces. No go. I went back upstairs to the chaotic swirl of Heaven, where I foolishly plucked yet another cocktail from a passing tray. Oddly enough, even though the club was thick with smoke, it didn't seem to bother me. Apparently, my new body wasn't allergic. Another extremely welcome improvement.

I positioned myself on the sidelines of the dance floor and watched the hypnotic pulse of humans moving to the music. As I declined offers from men of all ages to go shake my groove thing, it occurred to me that I had never danced in public. Never. Only alone in my bedroom had I danced, and the booze and the beat were making me bold. After finishing my drink and starting another, I thought, This isn't eighth grade, I don't have to stand snarky on the sidelines. Then a "Disco Inferno" remix came on, and the next thing I knew, I was putting my glass on the floor and shimmying shy into the throng.

And it swallowed me up. Swallowed me whole. And everywhere I looked there were beautiful bodies and beautiful clothes and beautiful hair and beautiful teeth. The strobe light flashed and the glitter fell shiny from the angels onto the beautiful throbbing throng, and I was in the belly of the beautiful glittering beast—in sync with it, a part of it, moving with the mob, my eyes half-closed. Then men started bumping one another out of the way so they could dance directly in front of me, shaking their gym bodies manic in front of me, bumping one another out of the way. It struck me as some kind of ludicrous display, some kind of mating ritual that I might see on *Mutual of Omaha's Wild Kingdom.* And I began to laugh. I laughed again when I caught a glimpse of Dawn and Don, herky-jerking around the floor, spastically trying to find the beat, and failing tragically. Eventually, I returned to the sidelines to stand snarky where I belonged (a fat woman trapped in a supermodel's body) to sip my drink and mock the dancers (my specialty). I noticed an emaciated woman— skinny skinny in a striped vinyl dress, with a peroxide buzz cut and improbably giant jugs. She reminded me of a doll. Concentration Camp Barbie. I wished I had someone to tell it to. But I didn't. I really didn't.

So I just stood there on the sidelines, feeling more alone than I'd ever felt before, drinking and drinking, until the crowd thinned out, and the waitstaff began collecting glasses and ashtrays, until I felt something ping me on the top of the head. I looked up, just in time to get hit squarely on the forehead by a cocktail onion (after it ricocheted off my face, I saw it roll across the floor). Then I noticed, beyond the clouds, where the go-go angels no longer gyrated, an iron catwalk, and leaning over the railing were two men, both of whom I recognized. One was a movie star whose career had been derailed by drug addiction. The other was an aging rock star—lead singer in one of the big heavy-metal bands, Tiger's Eye or Bubonic—who was now also an actor. I had seen him featured recently in *TV Guide,* for doing a guest spot on an episode of *The Trouble with Angie.*

Of course, I thought, the upper levels of Heaven were naturally reserved for the gods, the gods of movies, music, fashion, and finance (no wonder I hadn't seen George or my father all night). And one of those gods—the rock star/actor—was waving and gesturing for me to come up and join them. I gave him the I-don't-know-how-to-get-there shrug. He pointed to the far right corner of the room.

I weaved my way to an iron stairway that was being blocked by a bouncer wearing a wireless headset. The rock star/actor shouted something down, and the bouncer allowed me to ascend to the upper stratum, where I was greeted with an effusive hug. "Hey, angel, what's your moniker?" The rock star/actor introduced me to the drug-addicted movie star, who gave me a bleary-eyed sluts-like-you-just-make-me-tired smile, then the lead singer of Tiger's Eye or Bubonic pulled me aside and informed me that he would really like to bang me if I was into it. I was not into it. I excused myself to go find a bathroom.

At the end of the catwalk was a pair of white vinyl doors. Through the swinging doors was a small VIP lounge. No George. No Simon. Just three strung-out girls, obviously models, on a white vinyl couch. One was sprawled back, her arms and legs spread wide, her rib cage jutting. The other two were hunched forward over a table, snorting what I assumed to be cocaine. I went to the bar and fixed myself a gin and tonic. Then I carried it into a corridor that led off from the lounge, in search of a bathroom.

I found one. Inside was a smudged-mascara woman, who I realized, as I ducked into a stall, was Tracy Benson, the formerly cherubic child star of *Mother Knows Better.* Tracy Benson, all grown up with a pierced navel and a piercing nasal voice, scrubbing something off her cleavage-hugging halter top and slurring loud into a cell phone. . . . *I don't know, some fuckin' club. Fuck, I am wasted . . . What? No. Some fuckin' guy. I don't know. Thomas something, some film guy. Yeah. I think so, he was talking about something . . . I can't remember, but it sounded, you know, real and everything. I don't know, Mimi Rogers . . . Anyway, he better be 'cause he just cranked all over my new Gauthier. No, I'm not fuckin' kidding . . . I don't know, there's all these fuckin' rooms up here. Anyways, fuck it. Who cares. I am, like, totally fuckin' wasted.*

I was feeling rather wasted myself as I downed my drink and lurched out of there. I moved down the corridor, checking each room, trying to locate George, which is how I finally found my father. He was with a group of people in a large office. He was sitting on a sofa, with his feet up on a glass coffee table. He was wearing white pants and a white shirt open to the navel. A male go-go angel was curled up fetal beside him, passed out with his head in my father's linen lap. The angel's hands were tucked between his glittered thighs, and his mouth hung open. His wings had been removed and were lying on the floor beside an overturned champagne bottle.

"Oh, here's my chancey-chance-chance to get some money back," said a man who had spotted me peering in from the corridor. "Step in here for a moment, young lady!"

The man was at least forty, but he was dressed like a teenager. I recognized him. A comedian, one of the lesser cast members on *Saturday Night Live* several seasons ago. He was starring in a lousy sitcom now, playing a divorced stay-at-home dad who is hopelessly in love with his jet-setting ex-wife. He sat on a sofa opposite my father, stroking the thigh of another male go-go angel. This one was awake, leaning languidly against the comedian, a dozy expression on his angel face.

"Come in, come in," said Simon Penny, checking me out as I entered the room. "Care for some champagne?"

"No, thanks." I was shocked at how much younger he looked than my mom, and how attractive he was. There was nothing fatherish about him. He was a tanned Rupert Everett with sky-blue eyes and a waxed chest.

"How about a line?" he said. "OxyContin?"

"No."

He seemed surprised that I'd refused the drugs. I noticed then that the comedian was staring at my tits. Not in a lascivious fashion. He had cocked his head to one side and was rubbing his chin in an exaggerated ironic I'm-trying-to-decide-something pantomime. "Hmmm . . ." he said. And his angel giggled. "Fake!" said the comedian, as if he were a jury member boldly pronouncing a verdict. Then in a soft and slow voice: "But not saline, no . . . silicone."

"Don't be absurd," said my father. "Those are obviously genuine. You owe me another hundred, fool."

"Dream on, bubba," shouted the comedian, with a Southern accent. Then, evenly, with a British accent: "Young lady, would you be so good as to clear up the matter and set this poor boy straight— Oops! Unfortunate choice of words that. We don't want to confuse him any more than he already is!"

"I'm not confused. I'm omnivorous."

"Oh pul-ease!" said the comedian. "Pick a fuckin' team, asshole."

"Yeah, yeah," said my father. "Why don't you pay up and shut up."

"They're fake! Tell him, sweetheart."

I said, "Your little game is almost as pathetic as that sitcom you're on."

"Ooh, feisty!" said my father.

"Feisty and *fake*," said the comedian. "So hump you, Jack." He bent forward to inhale a pile of white powder off the table.

"You'll have to forgive my friend. . . ." My father pushed the unconscious angel off his lap and stood up. He moved toward me. "He thinks he knows everything, but clearly he doesn't know anything about beautiful young women." He pushed a strand of hair off my face and smiled crocodile. "What's your name?"

"Oh, vomity-vomit!" said the comedian, pinching his powdered nose and snuffling with his head back. Then, as if he were Mr. Rogers patiently explaining something to a retarded child, he added, "You're right, I don't know anything about beautiful young women. That's because I am a fag, and fags don't give a hoot about beautiful young women and their beautiful fake boobies, *remember*?"

"Shut your jizz-hole," said my father, smirking at the comedian. Then he leaned in, dropped the grin, and fixed me with a penetrating blue-eyed gaze. "You sure I can't offer you anything?" he said softly. "A toke? Or a drink? We could go to the lounge." He moved closer, brushed his hand across my bare thigh. "I'm sure there must be something you want. . . ."

Yes. Something. But what?

Initially, I wanted connection. Access. His side of the story. I suppose what I wanted was a parent, someone who would give a shit, maybe even love. Recently, I wanted confrontation. Attack. Words that would wound. Perhaps somewhere in the worm holes of the unconscious I may have even wanted approval. And regret. *Hey, look: picture perfect after all, but you blew it, asshole!* In the past I wanted all of those things. But now that it was real, now that this obnoxious zero was standing in front of me with his waxed chest and his powdered nostrils and his phony blue gaze right in my face, I was almost entirely free of want. Now all I wanted was to leave the club.

"I have to go," I said finally.

He looked at his watch. "It is late. Maybe you'd like me to give you a ride somewhere?" Again with the hand on the thigh.

"No, thanks." *Thing doesn't want to go play in traffic.*

"Well, maybe I'll see you here another time. What's your name?"

"Allison Penny."

He didn't even blink. "You're on the list?"

"No," I said. "I'm not on the list."

"Would you like to be?" He reached out and squeezed my right breast. Hard.

I knocked his hand away. "No, I wouldn't!" Much laughter as I stumbled out of the office, as I heard my father say to the howling comedian, "Yeah, well, you owe me a C-note, dumb-ass!"

Down the corridor I went, through the VIP lounge, past the wasted Tracy Benson in her George-soaked Gauthier, across the catwalk and down the stairs that were no longer being guarded, through the beautiful empty club, toward the front exit. But just before making my escape, something popped into my head, and I didn't leave the club. No, I didn't. I headed back down to Earth, hid behind a sofa, and didn't leave the club until I was certain everyone else had. Until just before dawn.

And if you want to know what it was that popped into my head, it was this: Thing doesn't want to go play in traffic, no. And Thing doesn't want to be on the list. But maybe Thing would like to take you up on one of your other charming suggestions.

Maybe Thing would like to go down to the basement and play with matches.

12

Burning down Heaven & Earth was my last ugly act.

I was furious when I lit the first papier-mâché tree trunk on fire. I was thrilled and delighted when I saw how quickly the blaze leaped and licked across the thousands of paper leaves on the ceiling,* but when I dashed to the exit and caught a glimpse of myself in the long mirror behind the bar,

*Not such a brilliant design after all, Simon Penny.

I was stopped in my tracks by fright. This is what I saw in the reflection: a warped smile, blond hair streaming, flames dancing around a red dress . . . I looked satanic, like a beautiful demon. A false Eve in a fiery faux-garden. I thought: Who in the hell is that?

Then I ran.

As I sped from the conflagration in George's baby-blue Vanquish, I tried to make sense of the past week, my first week of beauty—all the astonishing new experiences, all the uncharacteristically ugly acts: breaking up Virginie and Fraser, kicking my mom off the wagon, exposing Andrew McKay, sabotaging Igel, scamming photos from Fiona, shamelessly using George . . . and worst of all, most excruciating of all, betraying the one human I truly cared about, the only human who cared a little about me.

And now this. It didn't have to come to this. I didn't have to be that girl in the mirror. I didn't have to burn down the beautiful exclusive club. I could have just stayed where I belonged and longed to be: at home with Nathan, eating deathbed lasagna on a lumpy mattress.

13

The sun was coming up warm and yellow as I got the Vanquish back in the garage and slipped quietly into the cottage. George was passed out in the big bed, snoring. I collected my things and carried them across the hall to the small room in which I was ostensibly sleeping. I changed, packed, and wrote out a note for him to find when he awoke (including an IOU for three thousand dollars and one bug jacket). I had just opened the front door when I heard, "What's going on?" George was standing nude in the hallway behind me, rubbing one eye. "Where are you going?"

"I'm gonna walk to town and grab the bus home."

"Home? Why, are you still sick?"

"No. I feel much better, actually."

"Then why are you leaving?"

"Well . . ." I could have told him that it was because he'd abandoned me, left me alone and panicky in the cottage, or because he'd gone off and shot his load on the formerly cherubic child star Tracy Benson. I could have said that it was because he cared more about his lousy carpet than calling Phil Hanson, or because he lost his erection when he saw a few bruises on my hip. I could have told him that it was because his obsession with celebrities sickened me, or because I detested his smug, racist friends, or because he was so damned easy to beat at Trivial Pursuit. I could have told him that it was because he had made fun of those kids swinging lovely into the lake, or because I couldn't endure one more day in his presence, not for all the swimming and banana-leaf wraps and martinis in the world.

But I didn't.

I said, "Because I came up here for the wrong reasons. I've been seeing you for the wrong reasons, and I'm sorry about that. To be honest, I'm interested in someone else. Well, more than just interested."

"What are you talking about? Who?"

"Someone I met at work."

"What, cleaning that building?"

"Yeah."

"Some janitor guy?"

"He waters the plants."

George looked incredulous. "Is this that guy I saw you talking to when I picked you up?"

I nodded yes.

"That bald guy in the bad Dockers?"

"Bald*ing*," I said.

George laughed. "You're shitting me, right?"

I smiled and stepped out onto the porch.

"Some balding geek who waters plants and wears bad Dockers . . . You're telling me that's what you want?"

"Yup," I said, closing the cottage door behind me. "That's what I want."

14

Unfortunately, what Nathan wanted, seemingly, was for me to leave him alone. I had called him at the video store as soon as I got back to the city. Another clerk answered, told me to hold while he got Nathan, then came back on the line to inform me that he had left for the day. Right. At 11:55 A.M.? Perhaps Nathan didn't want to get into things while he was at work. I left a message at his apartment, asking him to please call me when he got home. Then, since Virginie had buggered off with her answering machine, I arranged for voice-mail service with the phone company.

It felt good to be back in my peeling-ceiling room. No smiling and nodding required. My ugly old futon welcomed me in. I found the sweet spot, an Allison-shaped indentation between lumps, and snuggled down with Nathan's screenplay—*An Honest Man.* It was a dark comedy about a bored billionaire who sets up an elaborate game to test the mettle of those around him and see if he can find a truly incorruptible man. It was clever, funny, and even poignant in spots. It had lots of ingenious plot twists and a nifty surprise ending. I read the whole thing in one sitting. Later, after dinner, I reread it. I was hoping Nathan would call me back so I could tell him how much I liked it. But he didn't call me back. No, he didn't.

All night I waited for the phone to do what it was supposed to, but at midnight, when I could no longer stave off slumber, it was still sitting there, as mute and mocking as a mime.

The following morning I had to go to 505 Richmond to meet with Fiona and see my model photos.

"Aren't they something?" she said.

"They're incredible."

"Do you like the ones I picked?" She had selected four to be blown up. Two full-body shots and two head shots—one smiling, one serious. I looked eerily model-like. Flawless.

"They're amazing. But the thing is . . ."

"What?"

"Well . . . I know this is terrible timing, and I'm sorry, but I've decided that I don't want to be a model."

"What? Why on earth not?!"

"Because it's just—it's not me."

"Of course it's you. Look."

"No, I know . . . but it's not. It's not what I want to do."

"I see." Fiona laughed mirthlessly. "Well, I wish I'd known that earlier, Allison. I submitted you for a job this morning."

"I'm really sorry," I said.

"Well, they'll probably want someone with experience anyway. But if it had been a local thing, and they wanted to hire you, it would've been very awkward for me."

"I'm sorry. Honestly. And I'm going to pay you back for the pictures."

"Fine."

"Um, how much . . . ?"

"Nine hundred."

Gulp. "Well, I'll pay you as soon as I can."

Fiona smiled wryly as she gathered up the photos.

"I will," I said. "As soon as I get a job."

"I thought you had a job."

"No, I quit the cleaning thing." *And I'm living off a loan from George, and my roommate bugged out on me, and my credit card is maxed. . . .*

"Well, best of luck to you, Allison." Fiona stood up and extended her big man hand for a shake. She said it kindly, without bitterness.

"Look," I said, "if that job you submitted me for comes through, I guess I could do it."

"It's a long shot, trust me, but I appreciate the offer." Fiona withdrew the warm hand and showed me out of the office.

"Art & Trash."

"Nathan?"

Silence.

"It's Allison."

"Hey."

"Can you talk for a sec?"

"Um, I'm sort of busy right now. With a customer."

"Oh. Well, I'm in a phone booth. Can I hold or do you want me to call you back?"

"Actually, it's kind of busy in here."

"I need to talk to you. Should I call you at home later?"

"I'm working tonight."

"Oh, right." I waited for him to tell me when it would be convenient to call, but all I got was silence. "Okay," I said, "I guess you have my number."

"Yes, I do," he said.

And I knew he meant something else by it, and that I would never hear from him again. "Listen," I blurted, "the guy who picked me up that night, George, we're not involved, okay?"

"Whatever."

"I mean, we dated briefly, but it's over. Totally over."

"You know, it's really none of my business."

"But it is your business. If we're going to be seeing each other."

"Well, that's the thing. I don't think we should. I don't think that's such a good idea."

"Why not?"

He laughed. "I don't know, it just—it doesn't make any sense; it wouldn't work. And to be honest, I'd prefer to spare myself the misery."

"Thanks a lot."

"You know what I mean. Or maybe you don't. Maybe it would be hard for someone like you to understand. It's just— I don't want to get embroiled. The weekend was bad enough."

"I'm sorry. I shouldn't have canceled and I shouldn't have gone. But there are reasons why I went, complicated reasons, which I can explain. And I swear to you, I'm not interested in George!"

"Okay, maybe not George, but you probably get hit on a thousand times a day, you know, by studs in sports cars with glam jobs and full heads of hair. I can't compete with that."

"Yes, you can, actually."

"No. Not a chance. And anyway, I don't want to have to try. I don't want to be obsessing about it all the time. And I would be. I know I would." He laughed. "I don't even know why you're interested in me in the first place."

"I just am, okay?" Stupid answer. "I loved your screenplay, by the way."

"Uch, the second act is a mess."

"Well, I thought it was good."

"I should probably get that back."

"Yeah, you should probably come over tomorrow night and get it," I said.

Silence followed by a sigh. "Do me a favor, okay?"

"What?"

"Just mail it to me when you have a chance."

"But—"

"I gotta go." Click. Dial tone.

I stood in the booth feeling hollow and small, staring mutely at the street and the people passing by. Clearly, Nathan had no interest in hearing my complicated reasons for driving away with the man in the Vanquish. I had been written off. He would spare himself the misery. And it wasn't hard for "someone like me" to understand, because I wasn't someone like me. I understood perfectly. Old Allison was too unattractive for Nathan to date, and New Allison was too beautiful. Oh, God, I thought, at least when I was ugly I could depend on a warm conversation three times a week. Now . . . now I was alone in the booth with the people passing by, and the phone beeping its ugly message about the severed connection, and I couldn't hang up and try my call again. No. He would spare himself the misery. I stood in the booth with tears in my eyes and the phone in my hand, and I wanted to call someone. I wanted very much to talk to someone. . . . But there was no one no one no one for me to talk to.

Or was there?

Maybe there was someone, someone who didn't fit my idea of the picture-perfect mother, just like I hadn't fit Simon's ideal of the picture-perfect daughter.

She was sitting on the porch when I arrived. Same sweatpants. Different T-shirt. This one said: I ♥ New York.

"You again," she said, flicking her cigarette on the lawn.

An attosecond impulse to bolt, but I resisted. I strode to the porch stairs, then stalwart, chin out, I gravely and bravely pronounced: "My name is Allison Penny. I'm the daughter you gave up for adoption twenty-two years ago."

The woman stared for a moment, then erupted into a wheezy cackle. She was missing teeth, three or four on the left side of the upper plate. "I'm not Jeannie," she said. "I'm Maureen. Her sister."

"Oh! Oh. Is she—would it be possible for you to tell me how I can get in touch with her?"

She cocked her head. Shifty. Suspicious. "Why don't you come in for some tea."

"All right."

She wheezed her way up to the second floor and unlocked a door that had 2B written on it in ballpoint pen. I followed her into a filthy apartment that smelled like cat shit and cigarettes. There was a small bedroom with a wide doorway, and a larger room that served as a second bedroom/living room/kitchen—if you could call it a kitchen. In one corner was an arborite table, a food-encrusted hot plate, a Stone Age microwave, a bar fridge, and the world's smallest sink. No counter, just a tiny ceramic sink sticking out of the wall. Underneath was a litter box that could have benefited from nuclear strike, likely the only way to refresh it at that point. No bathroom for humans in sight. Presumably, somewhere in the house there was a shared facility.

"You want tea or somethin' else?"

It was stifling in the room. "Um, something cold would be good. Water?"

"I got soda."

"Thanks."

She opened the fridge and pulled out two jumbo bottles of dubiously hued no-name pop. "Grape or Cherry?"

"Um, grape, I guess." I found a wooden chair that wasn't covered in cat hair and waited while she poured the drinks into Styrofoam cups. I lost a staring contest with a rheumy-eyed feline—a cat so fat it apparently couldn't reach all the way around to groom itself. It had a patch of oily black back fur flecked with dandruff.

"Cheers."

"Thank you." I sipped to be polite. Worse than I expected. Ninety-nine percent syrup and dye, one percent H_2O. It was flat, too, like a tumbler of melted Popsicle.

"So," she said, settling on the edge of an unmade sofa bed, "what do you want with Jeannie?"

"Want? Um, I just want to meet her."

" 'Cause if yer lookin' to get somethin' . . ." The woman was giving me an I'm-onto-you smile, as if I were a con woman who had come to shake her down. For what? For the jumbo jar of Skippy peanut butter on top of the microwave? For the macraméd Phentex plant holder dangling, empty, from the ceiling?

"I don't want anything from her. I just want to see her. I just want to know who she is."

The woman looked suspicious. Also wily.

"Are you her?" I said.

"I told you, I'm *Maureen*. Her sister. I wish I was her. Then I wouldn't have to do nothin'. Then I could sit around all day paintin' pictures."

"Jeannie's an artist?" I felt a swell of hope and happy. I saw her in a smock, in a well-lit studio space, her long hair swept into a Katharine Hepburn—style bun.

Maureen snorted. "She isn't no artist. She isn't anything." She lit a cigarette and launched into a terrible tirade about how she, Maureen, had to do everything. Everything. How she had to do all the cooking and cleaning (?), shopping and bill-paying. How she had to have knee surgery—she rolled up her sweatpants to show me the gnarled knee—and how much her knee hurt all the time, and how she couldn't stand on it for more than an hour, which is why she had to quit the job at the restaurant and why she couldn't work anymore. She told me how she had been burdened with Jeannie since their mother passed away, when Jeannie was fourteen years old, and how it had interfered with her marriage and was the main reason her husband took a powder. She told me how tired she was of doing *everything,* and how she didn't get any thanks for it, no thanks from anyone, not from Jeannie or anyone else, and how she could sure use some help if I really was who I said I was.

"Jeannie lives here? With you?"

"I just told ya! I've been takin' care of her my whole life! And nobody's been takin' care of me, I'll tell you that much. And that one's got a temper on her, believe you me. No one else knows how to handle them tantrums she throws. But I know how to handle her all right."

I got a chill when she said that. I pictured some kind of *What Ever Happened to Baby Jeannie?* thing going on (perhaps involving the dangling plant holder).

"She's lucky. Darned lucky to have me. If it wasn't for me, she'd be out on the streets. She'd be dead or something."

"So . . . where is she now?"

"She's over at that Healing Art Center. She's there most days, thank God, 'cause I can't watch her every minute of the day. I gotta have time to do everything. I can't watch her every minute of the day."

"Is it close to here? Can I go talk to her?"

She laughed. "Yeah, you can go talk to her, you can talk all you want, but she won't talk back."

"She doesn't talk?"

"Not since we was kids." She laughed. "When we was little I couldn't shut her up. Now she don't say a word. Except in her sleep. She wakes me up, and I can't get back to sleep. I don't know how I'm supposed to do everything if I don't get proper sleep. I need a door for that room. I asked the landlord for a door, I asked him ten times for a goddamned door for that room! But he won't do it. He don't do nothin' around here. 'Cause he's lazy," she hissed, "a *you-know-what.*"

I did not know what, and I didn't want to know. I stood up. "I think I'll go over to that art center. Could you tell me where it is?" It felt like a hundred degrees in the room. And no air to breathe. Just cat exhalation and bitter smoke.

"Yeah, I can tell you."

I waited.

"So, you look like you did all right," she said.

"I guess."

"Rich parents?"

"I take care of myself."

" 'Cause it was my decision, you know. You can thank *me* for that one."

I carried my drink to the sink.

"Still sayin' you're Jeannie's daughter?" she asked with a snide smile.

"I am her daughter."

"Well, I don't mind, but you sure don't look nothin' like her."

"I guess I look like my father, then." I said it as a question. I was curious about that, too.

Maureen laughed. "I guess. I guess she musta got attacked by Mr. America if you're really who you say you are."

Air. I needed air. I stumbled out of the house and inhaled a lungful. Even with the exhaust from the traffic, it felt cool and sweet. Water was next. I was sweat-drenched and frenzied by thirst. I lurched into the first variety store I could find, grabbed a jumbo bottle of club soda, and drank most of it. I paid for it, then drank the rest.

The Healing Art Center was a short walk away on Berkshire. I was expecting some kind of stand-alone building, but the center turned out to be a large storefront between a used-clothing store and a Home Hardware. The window was full of paintings, soapstone sculptures, macramé plant holders, clay ashtrays, and a few clumsily constructed birdhouses. There were price tags on most of the items, ranging from five to fifty dollars. Written in paint along the bottom of the window: *Please Support Emotional Expression and Healing Through Art.*

A bell rang when I walked in. One woman looked up and smiled. No one else looked up. Everyone else kept doing what they were doing, which was sitting on benches at long plastic-covered tables, painting or drawing or mucking around with lumps of clay or chunks of soapstone. "Love Shack" by the B-52s was playing tinny on the radio. The smiling woman approached me.

"Hello," she said. "Welcome." She was about fifty years old. Pudgy. She was wearing a T-shirt that had a cat's face depicted on it in fabric paint and sequins. The eyes were googly. Sewn on. The woman smelled like Elmer's white glue. "Can I help you?" she said. Something about her made me want to explain the situation. So I did. "Well, I'm thrilled to be the one to introduce you, but don't expect too much, okay? Jeannie is nonverbal, and a wee bit . . . antisocial. She doesn't really care for new people—that is, it takes quite a while before she'll respond to someone she doesn't know."

"That's all right."

"And even then sometimes . . ."

"I understand."

The woman took me by the hand and led me through the labyrinth of tables in the surprisingly deep room. Some of the paintings I glimpsed as I walked by: a giant eyeball leaking fat blue tears; a house falling down; an angry red man with sharp fang teeth and black paint exploding from his mouth. She steered me to the back of the store where a woman was working alone at a card table. She was painting on paper, the right hand a blur of brush strokes. And I recognized her! Yes, I did. A cold shiver wowed through me, vibrated all through me as I realized that this was the hideous-looking woman with the layered sweaters and the rubber boots and the kohl-lined lemur eyes who had been hovering over me in the park that day when I fell asleep after meeting Fiona at McDonald's.

"This is Jeannie," said the woman in a cheerful voice.

Jeannie looked up from her painting. Wary. Today she didn't have greasepaint flowers big on her cheeks, and I could detect the resemblance between us. Not the eyes. No. The huge eyes were foreign. But the mouth, the shape of the face, the stringy hair, the squat, bloated body . . .

"Jeannie, this is Allison. She came to meet you!"

The kohl-lined lemur eyes fixed on my face, and I was being scrutinized in a most unusual way, as if those animal eyes were taking the full measure of my soul. I took one cautious step closer. I smiled. I wanted to say something, at least hello, but it was all I could do to keep my mouth from trembling, to keep my breath relatively steady, to keep from falling apart and sobbing crazy. I had imagined this happy moment so many times over the years. Now it had arrived, and I couldn't find the words, words I had rehearsed over and over, again and again. I could feel an escaped tear trickling down my face into the corner of my mouth, and those kohl-lined lemur eyes took it all in, wide and watchful.

Then finally, after who knows how long, she did something.

And it was nothing like I had imagined or hoped it would be. My mother didn't open her arms and fold me warm into her bosom and say: *Daughter, how I've wondered and missed. Daughter, how I love love love.*

No. It was better than that. More tender.

My mother reached for my right arm, took me lightly by the wrist, and pressed the paintbrush gentle into my hand.

15

I spent the next three days at the Healing Art Center. I really should have been out looking for work, but I was enjoying my time with Jeannie. We would paint together at the card table at the back. I would bring good things for lunch, and if it wasn't raining, we'd go to the park to eat. Olga, the woman who ran the center, said it was amazing how Jeannie had responded to me, how she'd never seen anything like it, and how wonderful it was. It *was* wonderful. Apart from Nathan, I had never experienced such a strong undercurrent of connection with another human. Jeannie and I clicked. I felt strangely peaceful in her presence, painting away at the card table at the back. At night, I was restless, depressed, and had trouble falling asleep, my brain feverishly trying to formulate the speech that would make Nathan change his mind. But while I was painting with Jeannie at that card table at the back, I felt calm. Even good. I decided to support emotional healing through art. I bought one of Jeannie's canvases to hang in my bedroom. All of her work was Matissely colored, garish and naive, but oddly powerful. Or maybe I was just projecting. Olga said Jeannie's paintings were popular and sold regularly (and that the money was turned over to Maureen, Jeannie's guardian). The one I bought was a rectangle divided into sixteen squares. Each square had a different-colored background, and on each background was a different-colored heart with something in it. A blue heart with a green tree on a yellow background; a green heart with a red flower on a pink background; a yellow heart with an orange cat on a blue background. Then there was the square in the lower left-hand corner, the one that made me wonder and worry about Maureen: a black heart with a white cigarette on a gray background.

By Wednesday, I had started to cultivate a sort of *Movie of the Week* fantasy about Jeannie starting to speak again. To me, of course. Only to me. It didn't happen. I would talk to her, or sing along to the songs on the radio, which she seemed to like, but she didn't utter a word. Still, I nursed the fantasy.

On Thursday, Olga introduced me to a young woman who had come to the center to volunteer. Olga told the teenager that I was Jeannie's daughter, a "wonderful daughter." I experienced a warm glow that rapidly dissipated. On Friday, I didn't go straight to the center in the morning. Instead I went to check on my adoptive mother.

I found her passed out in the just-for-show living room, lying under the white piano in her Brazilian Ball gown (I peeked through the window after she didn't answer the bell). It scared me at first, until I noticed the framed pageant photo on her stomach, rising and falling with her breath. I fished out the spare key, the one she didn't know I knew about, from the barbecue, called her usual caregiver at the Bellwether Rehab Center, and packed a bag. As I maneuvered her out of the house and into the yellow Audi, she slurred and cursed in a voice too loud. *What the heller y'doin? / How th' fuck joo get in here anyway? / Where we goin?! / I want my goddamned car keys, missy, d'ya hear me? / Where th' fuck is Allison? / She's 'posed to take me shopping. . . .* I told her that Allison had found her birth parents and had gone to live with them in Vancouver. I told her that from now on she'd have to find someone else to chauffeur her around. "That bitch," she moaned. "That selfish little cow!"

After that I looked forward to Jeannie's silent communication.

After that I thought: Who needs words?

16

I made a lasagna.

I couldn't find a recipe that involved fresh artichokes, but I found one that called for five kinds of cheese and much Italian sausage. On Saturday, I shopped and prepared the sauce. On Sunday, an absurdly hot day, I tackled the construction. It turned out to be an arduous, steamy task, and I kind of screwed it up. I had laid out the noodles on paper towels to dry (as per instructions), but the decorative towels adhered to the pasta, and I had to peel and scrape each noodle—some less successfully than others—before layering them into the massive pan. Then, somehow, even though I checked the baking lasagna every ten to fifteen minutes, I still managed to char the surface brown with black edges.

Oops.

The thing weighed about seventy-five pounds when it was done—*Yield: serves six . . . thousand*—and took several hours before it was cooled down enough to wrestle into a taxi. I arbitrarily punched in the door code for someone named J. Luscombe when I got to Nathan's building. "It's me," I said. And J. Luscombe buzzed me in. So far so good, I thought as I lugged the lasagna to the elevator and pressed the button with my forehead. I waited. I waited some more. It was hot in the building, and the lasagna was making it hotter. I set the pan on the floor and hammered on the elevator button. I stretched my arms.

"Is broke," said a man in a Tyrolean hat who'd emerged from his apartment with a cane in one hand and a small bag of garbage in the other.

"What? No! You can't be serious."

"What floor you go?"

"Twenty-two."

"Is bad," said the old man, shaking his head and shuffling slowly down the hallway. "Is very bad."

And it was. Very, *very* bad. Like hauling anvils up Everest in the middle of hot August. I needed a Sherpa, and by the time I got to the twenty-second floor, a shower. I was literally drenched in perspiration, and there was a band of tomato sauce across the bottom of my shirt where the pan had rubbed. I lowered the thing onto the mat outside of Nathan's apartment and collapsed into a rasping heap beside it. My plan was to leave the lasagna at the door—a wordless, somewhat burnt offering—but Nathan must have heard something (my head hitting the wall as I collapsed, my gasping for breath, my quadriceps screaming in pain?) because he opened the door and looked down at me.

". . . elevator . . . broken," was all I managed to pant out.

Nathan crouched down and lifted the foil wrap off the pan. He stared at the charred lasagna. Then he leaned in and scrutinized one of the brown noodles. "What is that?" he said, pointing to the copper-kettle pattern that had been baked onto the surface. "Is that paper towel?"

I nodded yes, shrugged sorry. "I can explain. . . ." I wheezed.

"No, I know, it's when you leave the noodles there for too long."

"No, I mean about other things." I wiped sweat off my face and noticed that it was streaked with tomato sauce. I felt like an idiot, a loser, but in retrospect I think the paper towel / tomato sauce helped me out.

Nathan stood up and gestured for me to enter.

We sat at opposite ends of the hideous velveteen sofa. Far away in a small room. Nathan stared at the floor while I explained as best I could about George, my adoptive dad, and why I had gone to the cottage. It was tempting to tell about torching the club; I even considered divulging the Morph, which would've gone a long way in justifying my dodgy behavior, but I held my tongue. Maybe someday in the future when things were solid, when Nathan could be reasonably assured that I wasn't a raging pyro or any other brand of maniac, I could spill secrets. Now was not the time. I was there to patch things up, not tear them further asunder, so I merely stated my case, apologized for my actions, and asked for his forgiveness. I told him that I would absolutely earn his trust if he could see around to giving me another chance.

Nathan didn't respond when I was done. He stared at the floor. He chewed on a hangnail. Finally he said, "It's just too odd."

"What?"

"You going to all this trouble to see me again. I mean, why? Why me?"

"Why not you?"

"Oh, come on," he said. "Look at you. You have to admit it doesn't make sense."

"It may not be typical, but it does make sense." I inched closer to him on the sofa. "You're smart, funny, talented, kind—"

"Stop, please."

"Honestly, Nathan, it wouldn't make sense for me to not want to see you again."

He sighed, wiped sweat from his curiously shaped forehead, and continued to stare at the hardwood.

"Listen, do you want to try some lasagna? I think if we cut away the surface burns, it'll probably be really good."

"I'm sorry," he said, "I can't."

"Oh." A storm cloud settled in the center of my chest.

"Yeah, actually, I have to, um . . . I have to be at my parents' place for dinner in, like, half an hour."

"Oh. Okay. No problem."

Nathan stood up.

I didn't want to, but I stood up, too. "Well, I guess that's it, then." I picked up my purse and swung it over my shoulder.

"Not quite," said Nathan, going into the bathroom and returning with a towel. "You're covered in sauce," he said, smiling. "You should probably clean yourself up a bit if you're going to meet my folks."

"Smoke on the Water." That's what Nathan's dad played on the Majestic Monster Tuba ten minutes after we arrived for dinner. It was horrendously off-key and Nathan looked mortified, especially after his mom came in, brandishing a bottle of Danzy Jones Whiskey Liqueur, and demanding that he stop, lest he "scare Nathan's new friend away." But I thought it sounded good.

I liked it very much indeed.

17

We slept at my place that night, due to the broken elevator and twenty-two floors. It was lovely. Humid and sticky and great. In the morning Nathan went bleary-eyed to work, and I didn't. I lounged for hours on the futon, perusing the want ads, drinking coffee, and waiting for Nathan to call me and let me know if he could zip out for a late lunch. He had to work that night at 505 Richmond, and the thought of not seeing him until eleven P.M. was too terrible. Of course, I was on the john when the phone finally rang. I clamped my bladder shut and lurched out of the bathroom.

"Hello."

"Allison?"

"Yes."

"It's Fiona. Are you okay? You sound out of breath."

"No, I'm—" Leaking urine down my thigh. "I'm fine."

"Listen," she said. "Can you do me a favor?"

"Um, sure."

"You know that job I submitted you for?"

"Oh—"

"Don't panic," she interrupted. "You didn't get it."

"Okay."

"But they're holding go-sees in town tomorrow afternoon, and they'd like to have a look at you."

"Okay."

"Now, it's highly unlikely they'd consider you for the job; it's a huge campaign. But they liked your look and probably want to check out a new face for future reference. Anyway, it'll be less complicated for me if you could just go and let them see you. I don't want to piss them off."

"No problem. So, what's it for, anyway?"

"Calet," she said. "They're looking for the new face of Calet #7. And it's too bloody bad you don't want to do this, Allison, because you're the only girl from the agency they'd even deign to look at."

Well, of course, I thought as I crawled across the floor, mopping up the trickle of piss that led from toilet to telephone: Who could be more Feminine, Timeless, or Sophisticated than I?

So I went. And they looked. They looked at a lot of girls. I had never seen so many genetically blessed individuals in one location. I felt very alien when I took my place in the waiting room, a holding pen populated by a bevy of pouty-lipped beauties with a combined body-mass index of about eleven. An edgy energy permeated the room as the girls came and went or waited their turn to be ogled (short intervals behind a not entirely soundproof door that lasted anywhere from thirty seconds to three minutes). There was a surface camaraderie, pretty smiles, giggly chitchat—a lot of the girls seemed to know one another—floating atop a heavy bottom-note of competitiveness as the females ferociously sized one another up, feature by feature, and strained to hear what was going on in the next room, then checked their watches to see precisely how long each one had been granted with the powerful Calet people.

I thought: I'm really glad I decided not to be a part of this racket; I'd rather empty trash cans for the rest of my life than have anything to do with this. But three days later, when Fiona called to breathlessly and frenetically inform me that I had somehow blown them away with my "personality," and the gig was mine if I wanted it, I told her yes, absolutely, I would do it.

It was Maureen who changed my mind.

Here's what happened. On Friday morning, when I went to the Healing Art Center to visit Jeannie, I found her at the card table at the back, with her left arm in a cast almost to the elbow. Olga pulled me aside and told me that she had broken her wrist.

"How?" I asked.

"According to her sister, she fell." Then she showed me the painting that Jeannie had done on the previous afternoon. It was a face mangled by rage. A woman's face. Maureen's face. "I've seen bruises on her arms before," whispered Olga. "I don't believe she fell."

18

Shortly thereafter Allison Penny became the new face of Calet #7. I was flown to Los Angeles and put up in a pleasant hotel for just over a month while the TV commercials were filmed and I was launched, so to speak. During this time, I spoke daily to Nathan, who checked in weekly with Jeannie and Olga.

On the whole, I found the Calet/L.A. experience to be bizarre and unappealing. The directors were fascinating creatures, but the work itself was frequently boring and often mortifying. In one commercial, I had to swing back and forth on a perch in a giant golden birdcage. In another, I had to be chased and carried off by a "Statue of David" that had come alive. In the third, I had to waltz endlessly around in a velvet-and-taffeta number that weighed about three hundred pounds. The days started early and went late, and there were always dozens of people buzzing around: producers, publicists, directors, photographers, hairdressers, makeup artists, set designers, stylists, managers, assistants, actors, models, journalists, aestheticians, cinematographers, agents, writers, moguls, groupies, gaffers, and grips. Of course, everybody was pleased to meet me. Allison Penny suddenly had a million friends. And Nathan was right: I was hit on repeatedly by studs with glam jobs and sports cars and full heads of hair. "Model whores" is what they're called, apparently—a sorry subgroup of males whose raison d'être is to date propitious genetic anomalies. It was an ordeal. Exhausting. Nevertheless, I was well compensated for my four weeks of pretty service. Fiona negotiated a contract that covered worldwide rights for television, print, POP, magazine and newspaper. For this I received a shocking $2.3 million (I like to think of it as $230,000 commission I took out of Peter Igel's pocket).

Here's the first thing I did when I got home: I arranged to pay off Maureen and take over guardianship of Jeannie. Then

I sent three thousand dollars to George. I made a generous donation to the Healing Art Center and bought a house in which Jeannie, Nathan, and I could live. A good thing for all involved. Another good thing I did was slip copies of Nathan's screenplay to the celebrity directors who filmed the Calet ads. One of them, Jason Soderman, read it and liked it. Not enough to want to shoot the thing, but enough to want to read the next screenplay Nathan comes up with. He also promised to pass the script on to an agent pal at William Morris, and Nathan and I are on tenterhooks, waiting to hear back. In the meantime, I've convinced him to quit his job at 505 Richmond and try writing in the evenings.

So now it's the three of us in my slightly wonky, one hundred-year-old Victorian house. It's not completely furnished yet, but it has a fireplace, and a claw-footed tub, and a cool blue swimming pool in the yard, which backs onto the Beltline Trail. I had an art room constructed for Jeannie in the third-floor loft, and a desktop recording studio for me to fool around with in the basement. Nathan's office is in the spare bedroom that looks out onto the garden. He likes admiring the plants while he types, knowing he no longer has to tend them. The three of us do our own thing and we get along well. We paint and write and sing. We eat deathbed lasagna and watch good movies and swim under the sun. Jeannie, like me, loves to swim. Ever since she had her cast removed, we've spent hours a day bobbing around in the pool. Jeannie still hasn't spoken, but I've noticed just recently that she's started to hum—there's a stereo in the art room; she's been listening a lot to my Chet Baker box set.

Of course, Fiona telephones regularly with "lucrative opportunities." As soon as the Calet campaign hit airwaves and magazines, she started to receive inquiries from everyone and their grandma. Fortunately, my Calet contract is exclusive and precludes me from modeling for anybody else for two years. I am, however, permitted to do movies, television, and rock videos, and the offers have poured in. If I wanted to, I could have played a spy in the new James Bond film; I could have minced around semi-clad in an upcoming Aerosmith video, or portrayed the coach's love interest in a movie about a soccer-playing kangaroo. But I didn't want to. All I've ever wanted to do is sing. So a couple weeks ago, I went to the Gladwell Hotel and got my old job back as KJ. Now that I'm no longer allergic to smoke, it's perfect. Eight bucks an hour, plus half-price draught. I was delighted to see that all the regulars were still hanging in, making microphone magic. I was especially gratified to find eighty-plus Edgar Whittle still crooning "Stand by Your Man" every Monday, Wednesday, and Friday nights.

Poor Fiona was apoplectic when she heard about my employment. "The Gladwell Hotel?! I know you're an odd duck, Allison, but why on earth would you want to be a maid in that dive?"

"I'm not a maid. I'm a karaoke host. I like it there. I like to sing."

"Sing? You can sing?"

"Sort of."

Three days later Fiona brought me an offer from EMI. So even though my voice is completely uninteresting now, it seems I can have that singing career after all if I want it.

Sheesh.

19

"I have an idea," I said. Nathan and I were dangling our feet in the pool on a warm Sunday night. "Why don't you write a movie about an ugly woman who wakes up beautiful one day?"

Nathan was feeling pressure to come up with an idea for his new script. He had already started two and abandoned them. "What do you mean, 'wakes up beautiful'?"

"Well, she goes to bed ugly and wakes up transformed for some reason."

"Like Gregor Samsa?"

"Right. But it's not symbolic; it's not a physical expression of what she's feeling. It's real. She's inexplicably beautiful. And you show how everything in her life changes because of it. Suddenly, everyone treats her differently. She can get sex and love and good jobs, access to all kinds of exclusive worlds—"

"And revenge on people who were dicks to her when she was ugly."

"I guess . . . if she's that kind of person. But, you know, you could just show how her life improves immeasurably in every area and in every way."

Nathan mulled it over. "So for a while she thinks it's just great being beautiful, but then the reversals start."

"Reversals?"

"Yeah. Bad stuff. Drawbacks."

"Like what?"

"I don't know . . . like people assume she's an airhead, and don't take her seriously anymore."

"But if she wasn't an airhead, all she would have to do is open her mouth to disprove them."

"That's true."

"It's not really a big drawback."

"Okay, well, maybe a jealous rival tries to sabotage her. Throws acid in her face or something."

"Too extreme," I said. "Too movieish."

"Or maybe she's really shy and introverted to begin with, right?"

"Yeah."

"Then she becomes beautiful, and it allows her to be more confident and extroverted. She makes friends, advances through the ranks at work, gets the guy of her dreams. . . ."

"Uh-huh."

"Then the beauty vanishes almost as suddenly as it

appeared—she's in a car accident or something, something that leaves her totally mangled and malformed. . . ."

"And?"

"And she discovers that the boyfriend still wants her, the friends still appreciate her for who she is, et cetera, et cetera, and that all the beauty had done was allow her to come out of her shell and take a chance on life."

"God, no," I said, laughing. "Definitely not!"

"Why?"

"Because it's bullshit. Totally unrealistic. For one thing, the boyfriend wouldn't want her in her ugly state."

"How do you know?"

"I just know."

"But maybe they're soul mates." Nathan nudged my foot underwater.

"Maybe they are, but it doesn't matter. He wouldn't want her." *No chemistry.* "If he stayed, it would be out of guilt, and as a friend."

"But if you're doing an ugly duckling tale, she has to somehow learn that it's what's inside that counts."

"No. That's the point. She learns the opposite. It's not what's inside that counts. It's what's outside. When she was ugly she had nothing. Nothing. Then she turns beautiful and gets everything. What she learns is that beauty is a tremendous power, and that its power is pervasive, more pervasive than even she realized. She learns that it's much, much better to be beautiful, no matter how many clichés about skin deep and eye of the beholder. Being beautiful enables her to get whatever she wants."

"But if she gets everything she wants, where's the story, where's the conflict?"

"I guess the conflict is in her figuring out what that is."

"Hmm . . . Okay. So in the end, what does the beautiful girl really want?" said Nathan, nudging my foot again.

"First of all," I said, nudging back, "she wants love from someone she admires and adores."

Nathan smiled. "What else?"

"Well . . . she wants strong familial bonds and affection, work that she truly enjoys doing, a pleasant and peaceful place to live. . . ."

"Is that all?"

"No. She wants the beauty to last, so that all those other things will last."

"And in this movie of yours, the girl gets everything she wants?"

"Yes."

"A happy ending?" he said.

"Hopefully."

"Well, it's an intriguing premise," said Nathan. "I just don't know if anyone would accept it.

"I know," I said, smiling to myself. "That's the thing."

Nathan withdrew his legs from the pool and stood up. "So, what do you say we doff our duds and go for a swim?"

"I say yes."

"After, we can get into bed and watch that Randall Cole movie."

"Sounds good."

"We still have ice cream, right?"

"Right." I took off my clothes and slipped into the water. I swam briskly to the shallow end.

"How is it?" said Nathan when I surfaced.

He was standing at the edge of the diving board, his palms propped on his love handles, his freckled body gleaming pale and shimmery from the illuminated water below. Moonlight reflected off his curiously shaped head.

"It's beautiful," I said.

Nathan dived in.

Thanks to the reading squad: Esmé, Randall,
Robyn, Ron, Stuart, Terry, and Daphne.
Thanks to Monika Shnarre. Thanks to Carl Theriault.
Thanks to Leigh, Claudia, Rachel, and everyone at
Three Rivers Press.

The author gratefully acknowledges the support
of the Canada Council for the Arts.